MARVEL LEGENDS OF ASGARD

The PRISONER of TARTARUS

RICHARD LEE BYERS

ACONYTE

FOR MARVEL PUBLISHING

VP Production & Special Projects: Jeff Youngquist
Associate Editors, Special Projects: Caitlin O'Connell & Sarah Singer
Manager, Licensed Publishing: Jeremy West
VP, Licensed Publishing: Sven Larsen
SVP Print, Sales & Marketing: David Gabriel
Editor in Chief: C B Cebulski

Special Thanks to Wil Moss

First published by Aconyte Books in 2022
ISBN 978 1 83908 157 6
Ebook ISBN 978 1 83908 158 3

Cover art by Grant Griffin

Distributed in North America by Simon & Schuster Inc, New York, USA
Printed in the United States of America
9 8 7 6 5 4 3 2 1

ACONYTE BOOKS

An imprint of Asmodee Entertainment Ltd

Mercury House, Shipstones Business Centre

North Gate, Nottingham NG7 7FN, UK

aconytebooks.com // twitter.com/aconytebooks

The Prisoner of Tartarus

A thunderous roar sounded behind them. The creature was so grotesque that Heimdall's first look at it nearly shocked him into paralysis. The greater portion of its body was that of some fearsome hunting cat. Midway down its back, however, sprouted the shaggy horned head of a goat, wisps of smoke leaking from its mouth and nostrils. At the rear, fur gave way to scales, and a thick neck with a wedge-shaped head, a flickering forked tongue, and long, pointed teeth oozing venom.

Reflex hurled Heimdall to one side, but even so, only the fact that the flames shot out in a relatively narrow flare saved him from incineration. As it was, the fierce heat seared and blistered his side.

Off balance and unable to arrest his forward momentum, frantic to stop the attack, Heimdall slashed wildly. Heimdall was all too aware that the other portions of this hodgepodge horror might be about to assail him while he was barely able to see what they were doing. He didn't dare take his eyes off the menacing snake head for a good look.

MORE LEGENDS OF ASGARD

The Head of Mimir by Richard Lee Byers
The Sword of Surtur by C L Werner
The Serpent and the Dead by Anna Stephens
The Rebels of Vanaheim by Richard Lee Byers
Three Swords by C L Werner

For Ken

PROLOGUE

Fandral the Dashing ran a comb through his blond hair and goatee, straightening his green ermine-trimmed tunic before opening the door to the training hall. The fussy adjustments to his appearance were unnecessary. He already looked fine, and it wasn't as if he was headed into a romantic liaison with some lovely lady of Asgard. The children who awaited him, warriors in training all, wouldn't notice minute imperfections or care if they did. Still, one didn't uphold a reputation for being the handsomest man in the Nine Realms without attention to detail.

Besides, today was a special occasion. Heretofore, the youthful warriors-to-be had learned to fight with broadsword, battle-axe and mace, with mail, shield, and helmet, and that was all very well. But Fandral had selected a dozen of the best students to master a different style of swordplay, the kind he himself practiced with his cut-and-thrust blade *Fimbuldraugr*, a system that relied on finesse and agility to vanquish opponents while preserving the practitioner from harm.

Upon entering the timbered hall, its rafters high to

accommodate the swing of two-handed swords and its walls hung with weapons and armor, and one area filled with wooden target dummies carved to represent one or another of the foes of the Realm Eternal, he found the boys and girls awaiting him. Eight looked as excited as expected. Four, however, had a tense, wary look about them. Plainly, Fandral thought, something unfortunate had happened.

When he turned to the table where he'd laid out the practice blades for the lessons, he began to understand what. He'd had the smiths make twenty, but only nineteen slender, blunted training weapons remained.

He turned back to the children lined up before him. "One of the new swords is missing," he said. "Does anyone know why?"

No one spoke up.

Fandral sighed. He was disappointed that none of the suspicious looking four had spoken up, but perhaps he too would have had difficulty finding the courage to confess to a teacher when he was their age. "Well, fortunately, we still have enough for everyone to train. Come forward and take one, then fall back in line."

His students spent most of the first session learning basic blade techniques and footwork with no one in front of them. Fandral knew better than to start them working with partners right away. That was a good way for a beginner to lose an eye. It was only at the end of the lesson that he paired them up to practice attacks and parries, as slowly and exact as directed.

The exercises, tame and rudimentary as they were, still engaged the students, and at the end, they exited the training hall in chattering high spirits. Perhaps in one case, that mood was due in part to relief. Fandral let the boy make it almost all the way to the door. Then he said, "Trygve. Bide a moment. I want to talk to you."

Trygve stiffened as though someone had struck him, then turned back around. He was a black-haired lad, lanky, all elbows and knees, but nimble and dexterous even so. "Should I help you straighten up?" he asked. He'd reached the age where his voice broke halfway through the question.

"No," Fandral said. "You know why I held you back. Because you know what happened to the missing sword."

For an instant, Trygve's long face twisted as if prepared to deny it. But he was no Loki, no dissembler through and through, and he left the lie unspoken. "How did you know?" he asked.

"A skilled swordsman learns to notice and interpret even the briefest flickers of expression." Fandral smiled. "The knack also comes in handy when you're wagering on certain games of chance. You and three others – Asger, Darby, and Hege – looked nervous when I came in this morning. When I asked about the sword, you lowered your eyes, and Darby's eyes shifted in your direction. Were the others involved with taking the blade?"

Trygve shook his head. "I swear they're not. It's just that they're my friends, and I told them what happened to the sword."

"What did happen to it?" Fandral asked.

"Well… I was eager to start the training. Yesterday I got into the hall after everyone had gone, picked up the blade, and began practicing. I thrust it at one of the training dummies, and it snapped in two."

Fandral nodded. "That can happen with a light blade if you

don't know what you're doing. It's one of the reasons you need instruction."

"Yes, sir. Afterward, I carried the pieces away and hoped you wouldn't notice one sword was missing. Are you going to expel me from the training? Or tell my parents?" From Trygve's dull tone and hangdog expression, it was plain he expected both punishments.

"No," Fandral said. "As I said before, it's not a calamity. We still have enough swords. Although others may break over time, and I'm not looking forward to the day when I have to go back to the smiths and ask for more. Apparently, these 'bodkins' don't fit a dwarf's notions of what a proper weapon should be. You'd think that as a thane of Asgard and the fellow accounted the finest swordsman in the Nine Realms, my judgment would suffice, but as it turns out, only after a fair amount of arguing."

Trygve smiled a small, tentative sort of smile. "Then… are we done? Can I go home?"

"Not just yet," Fandral answered. "The loss of one sword is no disaster, but I am disappointed in you, Trygve. Why didn't you tell me the truth when I first asked?"

Trygve hung his head. "I didn't want you to kick me out of the training. And… well… I didn't *exactly* lie. I just didn't speak up. Everybody's heard the tale of how *you* used trickery to defeat those fire giants!"

"So I did," Fandral said, "and deception is permissible in battle. But in other circumstances, we should tell the truth even when it's awkward or unpleasant. The truth *matters*." He thought for a moment on how best to illustrate the point. "You know Heimdall."

The lad shrugged. "Everybody does. He guards the Rainbow Bridge."

"Well, if he hadn't cared about the truth, neither you nor I nor anyone we know would be here today."

Trygve cocked his head. "Really?"

It was clear that Fandral had engaged his curiosity, which pleased Fandral because he liked telling tales even when he wasn't the hero. "Indeed. Sit down and I'll tell you the story. It happened long ago, before Bifrost even existed. Although, it was about to."

ONE

THE UNDERWORLD:
SIX DAYS UNTIL BIFROST

The prisoner knelt bare-legged on gravel with edges sharp as razors. His knees were raw, cut and bloody, and so were his fingertips, for it was his task to pick up every stone and drop it into the clay urn beside him.

He had the feeling that in better circumstances, if allowed to proceed carefully and rest periodically, he might succeed in picking up the gravel without hurting his hands, because even in the smoky, starless perpetual night that prevailed here, he saw the rocks with exceptional clarity. Unfortunately, though, his hearing was equally acute, so much so that every scream, groan, and grunt arising from his distant fellow captives jolted him and made him fumble.

Nor was rest a possibility with the guard standing over him ready to lay a whip across his back if he faltered. His own voice excruciatingly loud in his ears, the prisoner had at first pleaded for a respite, but to no avail. The sentry's only response was to lash him until he resumed his labor. The lack of mercy attested to the guard's inhuman nature: scarcely less than the gleam of crimson eyes inside his crested casque and the mottled ophidian scales on his limbs. Or the fact that he himself was evidently impervious to both fatigue and boredom.

For a time, the prisoner had dared to hope that once he picked up every last bit of gravel or filled the urn to the brim, the guard would unlock the fetter chaining him to a stake in the ground and permit him to go on his way. If that had happened, it would have filled him with happiness even though he had no idea where he might or should go. Eventually, though, he realized his task was never going to end. No matter how many stones he gathered, somehow there always seemed to be as many as before, and the tall clay vessel never grew full.

It was impossible to guess how long his torment had lasted. With his heightened senses, he could see and hear a fellow prisoner evidently condemned to roll a boulder up a slope only to have it roll back down again. For a while, he tried to gauge the passage of time by noting each rumbling descent. Eventually, though, his own misery distracted him, and he lost count.

Trembling with pain, fatigue, and fumbling at his task, he likewise couldn't have said how long the diminutive figure had been sneaking up behind the guard. He only knew that eventually he caught the scuffing sound of a light, stealthy step, glanced to the side, and glimpsed a small man with a short brown beard and dangling mustache, clad like the prisoner himself in tunic and sandals. The newcomer moved slowly, taking advantage of every bit of cover the barren, irregular ground and drifting veils of eye-stinging smoke provided. His caution served him well. He'd nearly closed the distance to the sentry without being spotted.

The prisoner had no idea whether the newcomer meant to help him. But it seemed certain he intended ill to the guard, and that was reason enough not to give away his approach.

The little man drew nearly close enough, then gathered himself to rush in. At that instant, something – pure instinct, perhaps – finally alerted the guard to the danger. Just as the newcomer charged, he pivoted, sprang backward, and raised the whip.

The lash cracked as it swept down. The other combatant dodged the strike, and the whip merely battered a puff of dust from the ground. Then, despite the guard's attempt to open up the distance, his onrushing foe was too close for the whip to be of any use. The creature dropped it and snatched for the sword sheathed at his side.

Stooping, the sentry jabbed with the weapon, and, shifting back and forth, the small man evaded the thrusts as he had the sweep of the whip. After the third one, he seized the creature by the forearm before he could withdraw the limb, tripped him, and having deprived him of his balance, yanked his adversary off his feet to slam him down on the ground.

The guard tried to scramble back up, but before he could, the newcomer flung himself onto his back, and the impact knocked him back down. The attacker jammed an arm between the bottom of his helmet and the top of his cuirass and applied a chokehold.

Had the creature sawed or stabbed at the arm cutting off his air, he might have relieved the strangling pressure. But he jabbed over his shoulder instead, and the little man avoided those attacks as well. Until, unconscious or dead, the sentry stopped struggling.

The newcomer turned to look at the prisoner. "You could have helped," he panted. "He came close enough for you to trip him."

That possibility had never occurred to the prisoner, but now he realized he could indeed have aided in the fight, and he felt a sense of shame. "I'm sorry," he mumbled.

"Well, I managed." The newcomer opened the leather pouch hanging on the guard's belt opposite the scabbard. "Aha! I bet this is the key to the shackle."

He was right. The key clicked as it turned in the lock, and the fetter sprang open. Afterward, he steadied the prisoner as he stood up. The captive's back gave him a pang when he straightened after bending forward for so long, but the pain was a small thing compared to the relief that came from no longer grinding his bare knees on the hard, sharp pebbles.

Once the rescuer was satisfied the prisoner could stand unaided, he took another look at the fallen guard. "I don't think you could squeeze into this armor. You're lanky, but this thing was skinny as a snake. Which makes sense, I suppose. Anyway, you should take the sword and sword belt. The blade's not one of those big two-handed cleavers you're used to, but it's better than nothing."

The prisoner's feeling of relief was giving way to bewilderment. Who was his rescuer, and why had he freed him? For that matter, who was he, the captive himself? What was this place, and why was he here? It was evidently a place of punishment, so had he done something to deserve this punishment?

He decided questions could wait until he and the newcomer vacated the immediate vicinity, before someone else came along and discovered the escape in progress. Even if he deserved punishment, the thought of returning to it was unbearable.

Accordingly, he collected the sword and sword belt as directed. Based on what his rescuer had just said, he hoped that gripping the wire-wrapped sword hilt would trigger a flash of memory, but it didn't. The weapon made a tiny rasping sound – loud as the hiss of some colossal serpent to his ears – as he slid it back into its scabbard.

"All right," said the newcomer, "now let's get away from here." He strode off, and the prisoner followed. The small man changed course periodically to avoid coming too close to the site of anyone else's torture, possibly to avoid the notice of any other guards.

At first, the prisoner hobbled, but once he was no longer kneeling on the gravel or picking it up, the cuts it had inflicted soon stopped hurting and bleeding. As did the whip welts striping his back. He inferred he must be able to recover from such injuries quickly.

He found no relief, however, from the way what should have been faint, if not inaudible, sounds bashed and staggered him, nor from the stunning barrage of countless minute details contained in every moment of sight. He could do nothing about the onslaught of noise but took to walking with his eyes closed as much as possible, squinting briefly every several steps.

This strategy made him trip repeatedly and slowed his progress in general. At length the small man looked around and said, "I know the torture hurt you, but can't you go any faster?"

"I'm sorry," the prisoner said. "It's just... I'm seeing and hearing too much. It's overwhelming."

His rescuer's brown eyes narrowed in puzzlement. "But you can control how much you see and hear."

"How?"

His rescuer grimaced. "How should I know? They're your gifts. It's your head."

That was less than illuminating. But it was apparent that his companion knew him – why else would he have come to his rescue? – so maybe he was right that the prisoner could indeed control how he saw and heard. He fervently hoped so.

The prisoner mustered his willpower and commanded his eyes to take in less. His surroundings grew dimmer, and a smear of murk obscured what had been agonizingly clear a moment before. He then attempted to dampen his hearing. Many sounds, like the small man's heartbeat and his own, disappeared entirely, and those that remained faded to a tolerable volume.

He smiled at his rescuer. "You were right. I could do it once you told me I could."

His companion didn't return the smile. Rather, he looked concerned, as if he'd only now realized something dismaying. "But you didn't *remember* you could do it. Do you remember who you are?"

"Well... no," the prisoner said. He felt another pang of shame because he was manifestly dismaying his companion. "Nor who you are, come to that."

"You're Heimdall, thane of Asgard. I'm Kamorr of the Blackhammer clan, a dwarf of Nidavellir."

The prisoner shook his head. "I'm sorry. None of that means anything to me."

"But it has to! I can't get us out of here all by myself! Look, I'll remind you how we met and how we came to be here as we make our way along. It'll rouse your memory."

"I hope so."

"It must! Because if you don't remember who you are and what you can do, we might not get back to Midgard in time. And if we don't, your world and everyone in it will die."

TWO

MIDGARD:
BEFORE THE DESCENT

The dead giant sprawled inside one of the enormous tents he and his fellows had brought when they and their masters showed up at the work site. Perhaps, Heimdall thought, the giant had gone in to escape the afternoon sun, although in these mountainous northern climes, it didn't shine so hot even now in the midst of summer. It was more likely he'd grown bored and decided to neglect his responsibilities in favor of some solitary drinking. The wineskin in his outstretched hand with its mottling of old burn scars suggested as much.

To a degree, the behemoth reminded Heimdall of the frost giants who were the eternal foes of Asgard, but there were clear differences as well. Notably, the style of the tunic and sandals and, obviously, the one great eye in the center of the face where a Jotun had two. Which was to say, the giant was a cyclops, and his death could only mean trouble. Heimdall silently cursed his luck.

Such ill fortune had begun when Odin approved the sorcerer Ulbrecht's plan to create a "rainbow bridge" that would facilitate travel between Asgard and the other eight Realms. It was an enormous undertaking that would require excavating and consecrating gigantic runes beneath the surface of Midgard itself. Midgard because, to the limited extent that Heimdall understood arcane knowledge, it had special properties. It was the "nexus" world shared by many realities. That was why it was spread out flat when viewed perched on a branch of Yggdrasil but round when a person was inside it.

Heimdall hadn't realized it was ill fortune at the time. He was happy when the All-Father assigned him the task of protecting the work. Why not? It was an honor. He got along well with Ulbrecht, who'd stood on the battlements with him when the frost giants laid siege to the royal city, and the Blackhammer dwarves who were doing much of the tunneling under the Asgardian warlock's direction. At first his task itself seemed easy enough, largely a matter of shooing away curious mortals who lived in nearby villages without harming or terrorizing them. He hadn't even needed to draw the magical two-handed sword Hofund strapped to his back or sound the Gjallarhorn hanging at this hip.

Then, however, Odin advised him to expect visitors – none of the human mortal variety – and extend them every courtesy. For reasons of his own, the All-Father had been vague about where these strangers hailed from or what they wanted. Eventually, however, Heimdall gleaned that two were gods in their own right. The revelation astounded him. He knew Midgard was the nexus world, but for all his reading and conversations with learned sages, he hadn't realized that it had deities and pantheons other than those holding sway in Asgard and Vanaheim.

He'd had little time to reflect on the discovery, though, because the dignitaries weren't just gods. They were suspicious gods, come to ensure that Bifrost, as Ulbrecht had named this rainbow bridge, wasn't a way for the All-Father and his kin to extend their influence unduly and steal worshippers from these other deities. And the crotchety, taciturn sorcerer had left it largely to Heimdall to make them feel welcome and attempt to allay their misgivings.

In the days that followed, Heimdall had discovered a little more. With his grim demeanor and somber armor and attire, balding, burly Pluto seemed to be a death god. Pluto seemed particularly concerned about the rainbow bridge because one of its principal uses would be to help the Valkyries transport the spirits of fallen warriors from Midgard to Valhalla. Maybe he thought that would enable the Valkyries to steal spirits that by rights should come to his domain. His divine companion was Hephaestus, who wore iron leg braces, carried a hammer around even when there was no obvious reason to do so, and forthrightly declared himself a god of artificers and as such, capable of inspecting the work to see if it was just what Odin claimed. His half dozen cyclops retainers were skilled smiths and would assist him in this oversight.

Despite feeling woefully hindered by his ignorance of the visitors – a novel feeling for him – Heimdall fancied he'd done a reasonable job of reassuring these new deities and their followers… until this. Drawing a deep breath, he tried to believe that, tragic as it was, the cyclops's death represented an opportunity. If he could determine the circumstances quickly and honestly, perhaps that would further demonstrate that he and his fellows had only good intentions.

"Do you think it was murder?" Uschi asked.

Uschi was the only other person he had thus far allowed into the enormous tent, although it was only a matter of time until Pluto and Hephaestus turned up, whereupon it would be impossible to keep them out. Lean and long-legged, as was Heimdall, clad in leather and mail with her enchanted sword, the Brightblade, hanging at her side, Uschi had been his trusted comrade in many a perilous mission and was his lieutenant in the current enterprise, an assignment she'd requested in part because she and her sister Valkyries had a vested interest in seeing Bifrost completed.

"By the Odinsword, I hope not," Heimdall answered. "But we have to look into the possibility. Will you fetch Amora inside?"

Uschi scowled. "*Her?*"

Heimdall understood how his friend felt. Amora had betrayed Asgard and sided with the frost giants during their invasion of the Realm Eternal. She'd since served her sentence of a hundred years in exile, after which Odin permitted her to return to court. But many people disapproved, and disapproved again when the All-Father tasked her to work on Bifrost under Ulbrecht's direction, though few voiced their misgivings in Odin's presence.

"I don't trust her either," Heimdall said. "But she's a skilled sorceress, and of all the mages here, who do you think best understands how to kill someone surreptitiously?"

Uschi smiled a grudging, crooked smile. "All right, when you put it that way. If she did it herself, maybe she'll say something to give herself away." She strode out of the tent and soon reentered with Amora the Enchantress at her side.

The contrast between the two was striking. Uschi's mouth was set in a stern line, and she tramped along looking every inch a warrior carrying out an assignment in the field. Amora smiled an amused, coquettish smile, and although she kept pace with her companion, something about her insouciant way of moving nonetheless conveyed that she was here because she chose to be, not because anyone had commanded her presence. She'd spent a long time brushing her long golden hair to shining perfection, the close-fitting green garb encasing her slender form would have been appropriate for an appearance at court, and as she drew near, Heimdall caught a whiff of rose-scented perfume.

"Well," she said, surveying the enormous corpse on the ground, "this is interesting."

"I need to know how the cyclops died," Heimdall said. "Can you tell me?"

"Of course," Amora said.

Facing the dead giant, she opened the pouch on her belt and brought out a handful of tiles with runes engraved on them. She tossed them into the air, and they popped out of existence with small flashes and sounds like muffled drumbeats. Most left nothing behind, but three gave birth to runes of fire floating in the air. The burning symbols shifted, arranging themselves in a certain order, hung in front of the enchantress for another moment, and then faded away.

"Do you know?" Heimdall asked.

"Patience," Amora replied. "I'm not done yet." She walked to the huge hand gripping the wineskin, stooped, and took a deep breath, breathing in the smell of the spillage. She then murmured a brief incantation and twirled her left hand in a casual-looking mystic pass. Jagged, tangled strands of maroon light flickered up from the puddle. Heimdall was no diviner, but upon beholding the display, even he experienced a cold, creeping feeling of malevolent intent.

"It was murder," the sorceress said. "Someone poisoned him."

"Who?" A suspicious part of Heimdall's mind added, *if it truly wasn't you.* But he could think of no reason why it should have been, and if it had, wouldn't Amora then have attributed the death to natural causes?

"Orien!" The anguished voice boomed from the direction of the flap granting access to the tent. When Heimdall looked around, Hephaestus rushed forward, his bald, beardless countenance a mask of distress. Glowering, his breastplate and other trappings adorned with graven skulls and other symbols of mortality, Pluto strode along behind his companion. As Heimdall had expected, no one had dared to keep these two personages out.

"What happened?" Pluto growled.

Hoping to avoid a complete breakdown in relations between the Asgardians and their guests, Heimdall wondered if he should play for time by saying something in the order of, *that's what we're trying to find out.* Before he could decide, though, Amora said, "Somebody poisoned the giant's wine."

She then gave Heimdall and Uschi a smirk as though to say this was revenge for foiling her scheme so long ago. Or maybe it simply amused her to see the situation become as difficult as possible as quickly as possible. Either way, there was no delaying the inevitable now.

"What?" Hephaestus cried. "Who?"

"I knew you people were up to no good," Pluto said. "I *knew* it!"

"My lord," Heimdall said, "I swear on my mother's life that I had nothing to do with this outrage, and I won't rest until Orien receives justice." He turned to Amora. "I asked you before: who's responsible for this?"

She spread her hands. "That, the divination couldn't tell me. Even magic has its limits."

"Then we'll search the camp," Pluto said. "Look for evidence to identify the killer."

Inwardly, Heimdall bristled. It was *his* role to give such orders. But Pluto and Hephaestus were true gods who Odin had directed were to receive every courtesy, and a search was a reasonable idea.

"Of course, my lord," he said. "Please let your retainers know we'll be searching their belongings as well."

Hephaestus glared. "Why?"

"I could answer, just to be thorough. But instead, I'll ask you: don't you think it's possible that someone who actually knew Orien harbored a grudge against him? Your people knew him, but he was a stranger to all us Asgardians." Heimdall realized it was also possible an Asgardian had decided to poison a random cyclops and Orien had simply had the bad luck to be the one. But alluding to that possibility wouldn't help him mollify Hephaestus.

The god of artificers grunted. "None of our people would have done this. But I understand the need to be fair. So yes, search everyone and everywhere."

Heimdall let out a sigh of relief. At least the new gods seemed somewhat reasonable.

They recalled everyone from their labors, and when the dwarves returned from their immense diggings scattered through the surrounding mountains, the hunt commenced. Through the early stages, Heimdall hoped his notion was correct and they would indeed find proof of guilt on the persons or among the possessions of a cyclops or one of Pluto's servants. That would put an end to the visitors' present hostility and perhaps even make them reluctant to suspect the worst in the future. But that wasn't what happened. Ill fortune still followed Heimdall.

The Asgardians and the visitors had pitched tents and pavilions to serve their needs. But Ulbrecht had recruited warlocks, smiths, and miners from Nidavellir as well, and the dwarves of the Blackhammer clan had taken a different tack. They'd excavated interconnecting burrows in the mountain earth.

An Asgardian warrior found a corked silver vial hidden in a bedroll in one of the smallest of these living spaces, a mere cubbyhole in a tunnel wall. When the finder brought it forth to the clear area among the various temporary habitations, Amora opened it, sniffed the insides, and cast the same spell she'd worked over the spillage from the wineskin. The zigzagging, crisscrossing strands of red-purple light that flashed up from the neck of the bottle revealed it contained a residue of the same poison that had killed the cyclops.

"Whose burrow was it?" Pluto demanded. "Bring him forth!"

A group of Blackhammers watching the proceedings grabbed one of their number and shoved him out into the open. "It was Kamorr's hole!" one of them shouted, and then, turning to the dwarf in question, added, "Wretch, you've brought dishonor on us all!"

Heimdall had rarely met a dwarf who stood taller than his waist. Kamorr was shorter than most and lacked the typical broad shoulders and barrel chest as well. He likewise lacked the telltale accoutrements of a mage, the weapons and armor of a warrior, or the tools and badges that would have proclaimed him a smith or miner. A menial, then, whom the contingent from Nidavellir had brought along to do chores that were beneath the others.

Despite his lowly status and current predicament, though, Kamorr wasn't cowering. Rather, he tried to meet the accusatory stares directed at him with a mien both calm and defiant. His voice only quavered slightly when he said, "I've never seen that vial before, and I didn't poison your aide, Lord Hephaestus."

"Liar!" roared the god of smiths. With his clenched fists and ruddy countenance, he looked ready to exact vengeance with the hammer hanging at his side.

Such being the case, Heimdall presumed to lay his hand on the deity's shoulder. "Easy, my lord," he said. "We still have questions needing answers."

"I can't think what they might be," Pluto said. "Not when the murderer stands revealed before us."

"I'll show you," Heimdall said, and despite the guest's divinity, it took effort to keep annoyance from sounding in his voice. As far as he was concerned, a wise man made sure he understood the facts of a situation before acting, even when some would say there might be a practical advantage to punishing this Kamorr to put the incident behind them as soon as possible.

Heimdall looked over at the Blackhammers and spotted the three mages he'd come to know well during his sojourn in their underground city: skinny Gulbrand with the shaven, azure-tattooed scalp; merry, matronly Bergljot; and boyish Ailpein with the wispy whiskers. He beckoned them over.

"You three know the workmanship of your people," he said, keeping his voice low. "Does the vial look like something a dwarf would have?"

Ailpein took it, gave it a close inspection, and then passed it along for the other two mages to do the same. Afterward, Gulbrand, his long beard decorated with dyed blue and yellow streaks and with iron and silver trinkets knotted in, delivered what was evidently the unanimous verdict. "Dwarves didn't make this," he said.

Pluto sneered. "Naturally, you'd claim that."

But Hephaestus had been looking over the tops of the dwarves' heads, conducting his own close examination. "No, I've seen the style of these people's gear and effects, and I concur. To be honest, the container looks like something from *our* home. Or something a skilled silversmith among our worshippers might have fashioned here on Earth."

"Well, that proves nothing," Pluto said, clearly vexed that his fellow god hadn't supported him. "People trade. Goods pass from place to place and even world to world."

"But Kamorr is poor," Heimdall said and internally winced at his undiplomatic phrase. "Would he have such a costly item?"

"He would if he stole it," Pluto said.

"Maybe," Heimdall said, "but if he used the contents to poison Orien, wouldn't he then dispose of it? This is wild country, by and large. If he'd simply hidden it in the brush down the mountainside, there's a good chance we would never have found it."

Pluto glowered. "You yourself already provided the answer to this question. The vial is valuable. Too valuable for this lowly creature to throw away when he imagined that hiding it in his hole would suffice to protect him."

"I'm not convinced." Heimdall waved Amora over. "You said before that the poison in the vial is the same one that was in the wineskin. Can you tell us what poison that is?"

She regarded him with an expression of surprise, one hand pressed to her sternum. "Me, captain? What makes you think *I* know anything about poisons?"

"Witch," Uschi growled, "this isn't the time."

"Oh, all right," the enchantress said. She uncorked the vial, sniffed at the neck, and whispered words of power. Though even Heimdall couldn't see it, nor did he truly hear or feel anything, he nonetheless had the unsettling impression that *something* joined the circle of deliberators long enough to whisper briefly in Amora's ear.

"It's hemlock," she said afterward. "It scarcely grows in our Realm or the dwarves'. It's more plentiful in this world, but still, not so much in the region where the All-Father's worshippers live."

"But you *do* have it," Pluto said, pouncing on her words, "and I said before, trade goods pass from one people to another. Enough of this pointless delay. We have our culprit. We have our proof. Let justice be done."

Despite his best efforts, Heimdall felt the situation slipping out of control. What made things even worse was his own suspicion that, had he been consulted, Odin would have directed that the single menial be sacrificed if that was what it took to keep the creation of Bifrost on track. But Heimdall's every instinct rebelled at the prospect of seeing Kamorr executed when his guilt was in doubt.

"What's this?" said a new voice. "Why has the work stopped?"

Feeling a renewed sense of hope, Heimdall turned. A gaunt fellow with a goatee had come up behind him. As usual, Ulbrecht's high-collared cloak with its embroidered stars made him look like an evil sorcerer from some masque or puppet theater, but Heimdall knew such looks meant nothing. Maybe he could salvage the situation where his deputy was failing.

Heimdall gave a terse summary of recent events, concluding with, "So you see, there are details that don't seem to fit, notably that Kamorr would appear to have had no reason to murder any cyclops, let alone this one in particular."

Ulbrecht frowned and fingered his beard as he pondered what he'd heard. At length he said, "We have the proof–"

"It may have been planted," Heimdall said.

"We have the murder weapon," Ulbrecht persisted, "and there are no other suspects. We must demonstrate that we as a people intend no harm to any of Lord Hephaestus and Lord Pluto's people, else they'll take steps to see that our work, the work the All-Father entrusted to us, cannot continue. Thus, I believe summary justice is in order." He looked down at Gulbrand, Bergljot, and Ailpein. "Kamorr is one of your folk. Do you concur?"

None of the trio looked happy about the way events were proceeding, but none spoke out to object, either. They were in the midst of a great work like no other, and it appeared that the lowliest among them had jeopardized its completion and brought shame on the Blackhammers in the bargain. If executing Kamorr would resolve the matter, so be it.

For just a moment, bitterly disappointed by Ulbrecht's attitude, Heimdall too felt tempted to acquiesce to the seeming inevitable. But no, curse it, no! They mustn't kill someone who could be innocent no matter how inconvenient the harder course might be.

He took a deep breath and looked Ulbrecht in the eye. "Sir, you are the designer and leader of this work, and I understand that. But Odin put *me* in charge of maintaining order and keeping everyone safe, and that responsibility includes identifying malefactors and punishing them. Accordingly, no one will be executed until *I'm* satisfied guilt has been established."

"What will it take to satisfy you?" Pluto asked. "Above and beyond the proof we've already uncovered."

"First," Heimdall said, "we must know the last time Orien drank from the wineskin without harm." He raised his eyes to the surviving cyclopes, standing in a semicircle to view the proceedings behind all the other onlookers. Their towering forms would have blocked people's view if they'd stood any closer. "Do any of you know?"

The cyclopes exchanged glances with their single eyes, and then one said, in a voice even deeper than a dwarf's, "I saw him tipple at noontime, and he took no harm from it. He was out and about later, watching the workers like he was supposed to."

"Then the murderer," Heimdall said, "must have sneaked into Orien's tent and poisoned the wineskin at some point after noon. We need to account for Kamorr's whereabouts during that period."

Because no one had been in the servant's company continuously, Heimdall had to elicit information from a number of dwarves. Stomachs were rumbling for want of supper, and the setting sun was staining the fjords to the west with its crimson by the time he finished.

Raising his voice, he then addressed the gathering at large. "You see how it is. Kamorr was working in that excavation well to the north, pushing out barrows of rock the miners broke away. No one had his eyes on him every moment, but people saw him frequently enough that he couldn't possibly have hiked all the way back here and then returned to the digging without being missed."

"In short," Uschi said, resting her hand on the hilt of the Brightblade, "he's innocent, and no harm will come to him."

"Thank you," Kamorr said. He'd sought to maintain his calmness and dignity through all that had transpired since his fellow dwarves manhandled him out into the open, but now his relief was apparent.

Heimdall turned to Hephaestus and Pluto. "I swear to you this isn't the end of the matter. We'll find the true killer, and justice will be done."

Hephaestus grunted. "See that it is." He and Pluto walked away muttering back and forth. Plainly, neither god was content with how things had turned out, but they hadn't demanded an immediate stop to the work, and Heimdall supposed that was something.

As the crowd dispersed, Uschi whispered, "How will you find the real murderer?"

Heimdall sighed. There were six hundred people in the camp, and with Kamorr eliminated, none was a more plausible suspect than any of the others. "Right now, I don't have the slightest idea."

"I still think it's Amora."

"We'll keep an eye on her." And everyone else? Even for one possessed of the sight of Mimir, it seemed an impossible task.

THREE

THE UNDERWORLD:
FIVE DAYS UNTIL BIFROST

After some wary experimentation, Heimdall – he supposed he must be Heimdall if Kamorr said so – found he could do more than dampen his extraordinary sight and hearing. He could use them at need, sifting through what had formerly been a painful, chaotic barrage of impressions to focus on what was required.

Thus, he could now discern that he and the dwarf were on the floor of a huge pit with a scatter of fires flickering in the darkness and a tinge of eye-stinging, pungent smoke fouling the air. Kamorr was leading him toward one rim, at which point they would presumably climb one of the few trails switchbacking up the towering, rocky cliff face. High above the abyss arched an irregular stone ceiling with stalactites hanging down. Even after they left the abyss, they'd still be in a cavern.

That gave Heimdall one more reason to feel uneasy. Though

he didn't remember why, he had the impression the man he'd been hadn't much liked venturing underground.

Of course, he scarcely needed another reason when he comprehended so little of what was happening. At length, he posed one of the questions weighing on his mind. "Why was I being tortured? Did I do something wrong?"

The question manifestly surprised Kamorr. "What? No, of course not. I told you, you're a thane of Asgard."

"But I still have no idea what that means."

"Please, keep your voice down! I don't see any sign that anybody's chasing us yet, but they will be as soon as someone notices your escape, and even now, we can't risk attracting attention. Just be patient. Look, let me go on telling you what happened, and I promise, everything will make sense by the end. Soon, probably, when your memory comes streaming back."

That answer failed to assuage Heimdall's anxiety. But when he himself understood nothing, he supposed he had to accept that his companion knew best.

As he and Kamorr crept along, they continued to follow a winding course to avoid coming too close to any of the other prisoners, some normal-looking men and women, others gigantic, all undergoing some ghastly torment. A man chained to a perpetually burning wheel screamed. A colossus writhed on a stone slab while a pair of vultures tore at his insides.

Their agonies sparked a guilt that troubled Heimdall no less than his trepidation. He felt the urge to free his fellow sufferers as Kamorr had freed him. But he had no idea how to go about it with the reptilian guards standing watch over the prisoners, and the dwarf insisted an attempt to liberate everyone could only result in their own recapture. Heimdall supposed he was right.

Kamorr continued his story, "Though you proved I was innocent, afterward, it turned out that some of the other Blackhammers didn't believe it and gave me reason to suspect they'd take matters into their own hands. So, I came to you and asked to be your servant."

"I guess I said yes," Heimdall replied.

Kamorr nodded. "I didn't think you would. After all, my own people didn't think I was anything much, because I didn't have the knack for any of the crafts they valued or fighting with the heavy weapons and armor they favored."

Heimdall frowned. "You fought well enough when you overcame my guard."

"Well, I can fight some in my own fashion. My people have a system of empty-handed fighting for when a warrior's weapon breaks or slips from his grip. When I saw that being practiced, something about it spoke to me. I trained at it, pondered what worked and what didn't and why, and got good at it."

"But mastering it didn't make your people esteem you any more highly?"

"No," Kamorr said, bitterness in his voice, "because they continued to believe a true dwarf warrior fights with battle-axe or war hammer and only resorts to his empty hands in moments of desperation." He sighed. "I suppose they have a point."

"You say I accepted your offer of service," Heimdall said, "so I must not have agreed. Or I saw something in you that made me think you would be useful."

"Or else you just felt sorry for me. Anyway, now do you remember?"

"No," Heimdall said. "I believe what you've told me, but it's like a story that happened to someone else. My memory is as blank as before."

"By Thor's hammer!" Kamorr snarled. Then, clamping down on his frustration, he continued, "But it's all right. I'll just keep telling you how we came to be here. There'll be *something* in the tale that jogs—"

Back the way they'd come, something roared, the bellow echoing off the steep, stony scarps that bordered the pit. Startled, Heimdall pivoted and sharpened his sight. The gloom scarcely hindered his vision, but the drifting veils of smoke from the various fires of torment did. Still, he could make out a huge figure possessed of a dozen arms and a relatively tiny head standing over the guard Kamorr had strangled and the vacated site of his own torture.

"I was hoping we'd have more time," Kamorr said. "But something discovered you escaped, and they'll be after us now. We should keep on trying to sneak, but at some point, we may have to fight."

"Fight," Heimdall repeated with dismay. He had more respect for Kamorr's wrestling prowess than the dwarf evidently had himself, but he doubted it would prevail against something as big and dangerous as the twelve-armed giant. Even so, the Blackhammer's expertise made him seem more formidable than his companion. "Was I any good at it?"

"You were one of the best," said the dwarf. "*Are* one of the best. I'll wager your body remembers even if your head doesn't. Now come on. We should keep moving."

They did, changing course repeatedly to avoid creatures that Heimdall spotted searching in the distance. The deviations meant they were only approaching the cliff face slowly. Sometimes they had to backtrack and actually give up ground.

Meanwhile, Heimdall's mouth and throat were dry, and a hollow ache flowered in his belly. When he reflected on how long he'd been skulking around already, it seemed he must be hardier than a mortal of… Midgard, was it? But it was becoming apparent that he, too, had needs.

He held out as long as he could, then finally said, "I need water and food. Otherwise, I'm not sure I'll make it out of here."

Kamorr grunted. "Right. I could do with a drink and a bite myself, and I didn't undergo torture and lose blood like you did. We'll look for something."

Happily, with Heimdall's sight to guide them, it didn't take an inordinate amount of time to find it. Lying prone behind the top of a low hill they hoped would hide them, they peered down at a skinny naked man standing knee deep in a pool with the branch of an apple tree growing on the shore hanging over him. He held himself clenched with eyes closed as though resisting some powerful temptation. Periodically, though, his resolve gave way.

Then, when he stooped to snatch up a double handful of water, the liquid receded from him and left him standing on bare earth, revealing a fetter like the one Heimdall had worn. When he reached up to snatch an apple, the creaking, rustling limb lifted out of reach.

Heimdall scowled in disgust at the mocking cruelty manifest in the torment. It struck him as vile even if the prisoner had done something heinous, and it seemed entirely possible he hadn't. After all, Kamorr claimed that Heimdall's own imprisonment had been unjust.

Well, unshackled people should be able to obtain water and apples despite the magic, but first he and Kamorr would have to deal with the snake-man sentry. For a moment, he deemed it bitterly unfair that the guard hadn't abandoned his post to join the search for him, and then he thrust the useless feeling aside. Matters were as they were, and he and his companion would just have to deal with them.

Maybe, he thought, he had something of the iron of a warrior inside him after all.

"I doubt I can sneak up on the creature," Kamorr whispered. "Too long an approach and not enough cover. I'll run at him and hope for the best. Who knows, it might even be true that death doesn't mean the same thing down here. I don't believe it for a heartbeat, but I guess it could be possible."

Heimdall put a hand on the Blackhammer's shoulder. "You aren't going. I am."

Kamorr frowned. "What? No!"

"Tell me this. You were running around loose before you freed me. Do the creatures even know you're here?"

The dwarf hesitated. "Well, no. Maybe not."

"Then if I don't defeat the guard, you can sneak away, and he'll be none the wiser. You didn't lose any of your blood and can press on until you find water and food somewhere else."

"If you're hell-bent on going down there, let's at least tackle the snake-man together."

Heimdall shook his head. "Normally, that would make sense. But you said that if we don't make it out of here quickly, a world and everyone in it is going to die. I still don't understand how that's possible, but if it's so, then someone must survive to carry the warning or whatever it is we need to do. Also, you said we'll likely have to fight eventually, and I'm a fighter. It's time to test whether that's still true. If I can't defeat that one guard, I won't be any use in whatever battles are coming. I'll only be a hindrance, and you'll do better trying to escape without me."

Kamorr grunted. "I can see there's no talking you out of this, and I do believe in you. But I'll be ready to charge down if you need me."

Heimdall drew his stolen sword. He hoped that this time the hilt would feel natural, familiar in his grip, but there was no burst of recognition. He might never have touched such a thing until his companion told him to appropriate it from the strangled sentry.

He rose and crept down the long shallow slope leading to the pool. At the moment, the guard had his back turned to watch the prisoner, and Heimdall wondered if he might take him by surprise, kill him from behind, and so avoid the battle that seemed a more reckless idea with every step he took. The hope that he'd escape a fair fight felt vaguely shameful, but he couldn't repress it entirely.

In any case, it was a hope that would go unfulfilled. The prisoner in the pool didn't have his back turned, and he happened to open his eyes when Heimdall was still well out of striking distance. He gasped and goggled at the stranger, and the snake-man turned and snatched for his sword.

Heimdall faltered for a moment and then broke into a sprint, though there was a part of him that wanted to do anything but. He hoped that where stealth had failed him, all-out aggression would prevail.

In that, too, he was disappointed. The snake-man had his

blade drawn and ready when his attacker was still several strides away, and as Heimdall closed the distance, the guard shifted to the side and thrust. Heimdall's own slash missed, and he sensed more than saw his adversary's counterattack stabbing at his flank. He leaped, and the snake-man's sword point merely grazed him. If not for his frantic attempt at evasion, though, it would have driven deep into his body.

As it still would if he didn't defend himself. He wrenched himself around and came on guard. Or at least he hoped it was a reasonable semblance of a fighting stance.

The guard hissed like the reptile he was, advanced, and jabbed at Heimdall's face. Heimdall simultaneously stepped back and raised his blade to deflect the attack. The snake-man spun his sword away from the attempt at a parry and into another thrust to the midsection. Fortunately, Heimdall's instinctive retreat made the stab fall short by a finger-length. He hacked at the guard's extended sword arm, but the creature pulled it back in time to avoid the cut.

So far, Heimdall realized, he had at least managed to stay alive. There was something inside him that remembered how to fight even if his conscious mind didn't.

"Kill him!" cried the prisoner in the pool, his voice a croak from who knew how many days or years of thirst.

I'm trying, Heimdall thought, though he was by no means certain of success. His trained reflexes notwithstanding, judging from the first couple of exchanges, the fight seemed all too likely to go the other way.

It was a fear that continued to swell as the guard pushed him back to the water's edge. Evidently sharing the same fear, Kamorr jumped up and started running down the slope, but

Heimdall doubted the dwarf's short legs would close the distance in time for it to make a difference.

An unexpected surge of anger – at himself, for thinking the duel already lost – couldn't erase Heimdall's dread entirely, but it did blunt it. After all, though the snake-man was pressing him hard, the creature hadn't actually scored on him since that initial scratch. He was still successfully parrying and retreating.

If his body remembered how to fight even if his mind didn't, maybe he should stop trying to think what to do next and simply react. Maybe then it would remember well enough to win the battle.

So, he tried to calm himself, to relax to the degree he was able, and fight by reflex. Blade rang and scraped repeatedly on blade, and then he and the guard were pressed up against one another, swords locked together. Heimdall drove in and shoved the gaunt snake-man stumbling backward. In that moment of vulnerability, before the creature could recover his balance, he slashed at the bit of exposed throat between helmet and cuirass. Blood sprayed, and the guard collapsed.

Kamorr stopped running now that there wasn't any need. "That ended better than it started," he said.

"Maybe you were right," Heimdall panted. "I am a warrior. Not as able as I once was, but possibly still able enough to be useful."

"Help me!" said the prisoner in the pond.

Now that the moment had come when Heimdall could free at least one of his fellow captives, he felt more uncertain as to whether he should. For all he knew, the fellow truly had committed some monstrous crime. But no. His original inclination had been the right one. Given his own torture, he wasn't inclined to simply assume justice had been done, and in any case, surely not even the most diabolical offense merited endless agony.

He rummaged in the guard's belt pouch, found an iron key, waded into the pool, and put it in the prisoner's trembling hand. "Here," he said.

When the captive stooped, the magic meant to torment him actually helped him. The sibilant drawing away of the water made it that much easier to unlock the fetter. Afterward, Heimdall supported him as he hobbled to shore.

The water couldn't stop the prisoner from drinking, either, when Heimdall scooped up some of it for the other man to slurp out of his hands. Nor did the apple tree stir to protect itself when he picked all the ripe red fruit within reach.

He and his companions then positioned themselves between the tree trunk and the pool. The apple tree provided cover against anyone looking from one direction, anyway, and the dimness, irregular terrain, and drifting veils of smoke should help, too. Besides, eating should only take a little while, and they were all too eager to satisfy their hunger to put off doing so while they sought a more concealed location.

When, sitting cross-legged on the shore, everyone had drunk and crunched his fill, Kamorr looked at the prisoner and asked, "Who are you?"

"King Tantalus," the man replied, sitting up straighter in an attempt at regal dignity. The litter of apple cores around him diminished the effect considerably. "You've probably heard of me."

"No," Kamorr said.

"Forgive me," Heimdall said. "At the moment, it's as if I'd never heard of anybody."

Tantalus's eyes narrowed at that, but if he meant to question the comment, Kamorr forestalled him with another question of his own. "Why are you down here?"

"A misunderstanding," Tantalus said, "between my father Zeus and myself."

Kamorr grunted. "We don't know who Zeus is, either, but *we've* done nothing to deserve being chained or tortured."

"So, we're making our escape," Heimdall said. "You're welcome to come with us, but you should know that the creatures that guard this place are already on our trail."

"And we'll leave you behind if you slow us down," Kamorr said.

Heimdall shot him a surprised, reproachful glance.

"I won't like it either," said the Blackhammer, "but I told you, there's more at stake here than just you and me."

Tantalus drew himself to his feet. "Thank you for freeing me and for the offer," he said to Heimdall, "but if the guards are already looking for you – looking hard, from what I gather – I'm better off on my own. Which way are you heading?"

Heimdall pointed. "That way."

"Then I'll go this way." Tantalus collected most of the picked apples that remained uneaten, stuffed them in his tunic, and hurried away.

"I didn't trust him," Kamorr growled.

"I didn't either," Heimdall replied. "That's why I told him we were going one direction when it looks to me like we'd be better off heading in another. That way, if the guards catch him, he can't betray us."

Kamorr grinned. "Those famous wits of yours aren't gone any more than your skill with a sword. They're just... stifled. Good to know."

Heimdall stood up. "We should grab what apples we can and keep moving."

"Right," Kamorr said, "and while we do, I'll tell you more about who you are and how we landed in this fix."

Four

Midgard:
Before the Descent

"Should I go with you?" Kamorr asked.

Heimdall considered. He'd taken the dwarf on as a servant as much to protect him from anyone not yet persuaded of his innocence as because he expected the Blackhammer to be of any great use. Yet Kamorr had proved intelligent and industrious. Still, in this instance…

"No," he said. "People are more inclined to discuss sensitive matters with one person than two. I'll tell you later how I fared."

"As you wish," Kamorr said. He turned and strode toward Heimdall's tent, where the dwarf had moved his meager belongings and was staying for the present.

Heimdall walked on through the benighted camp, filled with the murmur of conversation after another day's labor and the scent of the roast mutton from the evening's supper lingering in the air. The blackness of nearby peaks cut a sawtooth rim from the dome of a sky where the *nordrijos* – the northern lights – made a green and purple curtain.

In the gloom, Pluto's somber-hued tent looked ominous, especially with the two reptilian sentries stationed in front of the entry. Their red eyes shining inside their helms, they crossed their spears in front of the flap when Heimdall drew near.

The Asgardian had had a long, fruitless, exasperating day and felt a momentary urge to remove the creatures from his path with a stunning blast from the Gjallarhorn. He was, after all, the officer in charge of the camp's order and safety, and as such, in theory had the authority to go wherever he liked.

But knocking the guards insensible wouldn't be diplomatic nor likely to produce any helpful result. Instead, he halted a couple of paces away from the gaunt, scaly guards and said, "Please tell Lord Pluto that Captain Heimdall wants to see him."

One sentry disappeared into the tent. The other positioned himself squarely in front of the flap until his fellow reappeared a few moments later to beckon Heimdall inside.

Within, the black pavilion was even gloomier than it looked from the outside. Only a brazier of coals glowed to relieve the darkness, and the gloom heightened the disquieting effect of furnishings fashioned in the form of monsters or decorated with macabre imagery. A horned, squatting figurine of a demon held its three pairs of arms crooked before it to provide a rack for scrolls. Carved in bas relief on the lid of a trunk, a muscular man in agony tore off his shirt, and his flesh came away with the tattered cloth, exposing the bones beneath. A skeleton provided a stand for Pluto's armor.

The god himself appeared to be lounging in a thronelike chair, a cup fashioned from a human skull cradled in one large, powerful hand. Heimdall had never seen Pluto out of his dark metal armor before. The Asgardian noticed, however, that Pluto still had his battle-axe leaning against the side of the seat within easy reach.

"Good evening, my lord," Heimdall said.

"Have you figured out who killed the cyclops?" Pluto asked.

"No. Captain Uschi and I have spent the past three days investigating with every means at our disposal, but the killer did an excellent job of covering his tracks."

Pluto's lip curled. "Or else you're just not the clever fellow you're supposed to be."

Heimdall took a steadying breath. "Be that as it may, my lord, it occurred to me there's one thing we haven't tried yet."

A bit of Pluto's contemptuous demeanor fell away. "What's that?"

"It has to do with you being a death god."

"Why would you assume I'm any such thing?"

Heimdall sighed. Unless Pluto was stupid – something the Asgardian doubted – he was being willfully obtuse simply to annoy his visitor. "The morbid decorations everywhere I look? By the Tree, I know our respective monarchs have decided for whatever reason that our two groups should conduct their business without learning anything much about one another, but it's pointless to deny what's obvious to everyone."

Pluto scowled. "For the sake of argument, let's suppose I am what you say. What follows from that?"

"When the followers of the lord of Asgard die, their spirits journey to one or another of the Realms where death gods hold dominion. I infer the same holds true for the followers of yours."

"What if it does?"

"Then at this very moment, Orien is in a place to which you can grant access. You can take me there, and I can question him."

"Impossible for the very reason to which you have already alluded. You couldn't undertake such a journey without learning more about my pantheon than my ruler *and* yours wish you to know."

"They made that decision before the murder."

"Do you think the death of a single underling would cause them to change their minds? Even if it did, the cyclops wouldn't know who put the hemlock in his wine. That's the point of poisoning. It's murder by stealth."

"My lord, one of the difficulties I'm having with my inquiries is that I haven't been able to identify anyone who even had a motive for killing Orien. His spirit may be able to shed light on that. Or, if not, provide some other clue."

Pluto sipped his wine as he sat and pondered. At length he said, "I'm not convinced by anything you've said. But just in case there's something to it, *I'll* find and question the cyclops the next time I visit my kingdom. Me, not you."

Heimdall wondered how much further he could push. Once again, the thought came to him that Odin would regard the placating of Pluto and Hephaestus and the successful completion of Bifrost as far more important than the solution of a single murder possibly committed for petty, personal reasons. Still, his agent was unwilling to let the matter go. He wanted the truth, and the cyclops deserved justice. "My lord, I truly think it would be better if we both questioned him."

"And we've already covered the reason that's impossible.

You're starting to bore me, captain. I suggest you take your leave."

The appointments in Heimdall's tent looked sparse and utilitarian but considerably less grim compared to the various items in Pluto's pavilion. When the Asgardian entered, he found Kamorr perched on a campstool, his feet in their worn-out leather shoes dangling above the ground.

"How did it go?" the Blackhammer asked.

Heimdall shrugged the scabbarded Hofund off his back. "It's too early to tell."

FIVE

MIDGARD:
FIVE DAYS UNTIL BIFROST

When night fell, Uschi made one of her frequent visits to the paddock to see how Avalanche was faring. Well, to all appearances. The white Valkyrie stallion with his folded wings was sleeping standing up when she arrived, but he woke, came to her, and enjoyed a scratch on the neck behind the ear. He then gave her a look that seemed to ask if they were about to go flying together.

"Soon," she murmured. "In a week, if not sooner." According to Ulbrecht, that was when the work would be done, and the Rainbow Bridge would spring to glorious life.

She might not have checked on Avalanche quite so often if not for the two shaggy black, red-eyed horses at the other end of the pen. They pulled Lord Pluto's chariot and had a vicious look about them that prompted other animals to keep their distance. She was confident of Avalanche's ability to hold his own in a fight, but still, if one broke out, it would be two against one, and her steed's ability to fly might not protect him if the tide ran against him. Despite the lack of wings, Pluto's horses could fly too.

She felt easier in Avalanche's company, as she often did, but soon succumbed to the urge to resume prowling through the camp. She could feel the festering suspicions, the tensions waiting to erupt. The strangers blamed the Asgardians and dwarves for the murder. Despite Heimdall's proof to the contrary, some still suspected Kamorr in particular, believed his defender had used glib words to obscure the Blackhammer's guilt, and regarded the current absence of the two as evidence their suspicions were correct. Meanwhile, many of Uschi's people conjectured the visitors had turned on one of their own, or that some lone rogue Asgardian had committed the crime. The fact that no one could adduce a plausible reason for anybody to poison Orien only fed the wildest speculations.

She thought wistfully of Bodil with her green eyes and her braided auburn hair coiled on the top of her head, a sister Valkyrie with whom she'd grown close of late. I could be back in Asgard with her, she told herself, instead of trying to keep a lid on all this.

Not that she was *truly* sorry she'd taken on the responsibility she had. If Bifrost functioned as promised, it would be a fine thing for Asgard in general and the Valkyries in particular. But when she'd come to assist Heimdall, she hadn't expected him to go running off with Kamorr to question Orien in some land of the dead or to stay gone as long as he had. Her exasperation at being deserted existed in concert with a growing fear that something terrible had befallen her friend.

She came to an entrance to the Blackhammer burrows, a tunnel sloping downward into the earth. The ceiling was too low for any but the shortest Asgardian to stand straight, precisely because the clannish dwarves wanted to discourage others from entering. Stooping, she did so anyway and groped her way along until she came within earshot of a chamber where, by the sound of it, a number of workers were talking and drinking together. She eavesdropped, heard much resentment of the stranger gods and the cyclopes but no actual statement of hostile intent, and withdrew when the Blackhammers launched into a song about the clink of the picks, the heat of the forge, and yellow, yellow gold. If she'd lingered, it was conceivable she might have heard something requiring her intervention, but she had the whole rest of the camp to try to monitor as well.

She scowled as she approached Amora's pavilion. Striped with colors that would shine green and yellow in the daylight, it was as big as the tents the two stranger gods had brought and no doubt furnished with every comfort. Maybe the luxury was no more than was appropriate for a lady of the court of Asgard, but as far as Uschi was concerned, it was far too grand for a one-time traitor.

Assuming it was only the one time. Unless it was pure malicious pleasure in the spreading of chaos, Uschi couldn't see what the enchantress would have to gain by poisoning Orien. But the witch was certainly capable of that and worse, and her playful mockery after Heimdall sought her help hadn't done anything to allay the Valkyrie's suspicions.

Accordingly, she felt a certain sympathy when she spied a shadow skulking toward the entrance of the striped pavilion.

All was dark inside the tent, and even the most powerful sorceress might be vulnerable while she slept.

Let the fellow do his work, a part of her whispered. It's only justice, for Orien's death and for all Amora's wicked deeds in the past, those we know of and those that have yet to come to light.

But she realized she couldn't really stand aside. Another killing without proof might only enflame tensions further, even if it was only Amora who died. And, looming just as large in her mind, she knew Heimdall would be appalled if he ever discovered she'd chosen not to intervene.

Besides, her suspicions and dislike notwithstanding, the enchantress might actually be innocent. This wasn't war, where the essential thing was often to strike and stride quickly. This was an effort to produce justice, and Heimdall was right that the truth mattered.

"You there!" she called. "Bide a moment!"

The shadowy figure gave a guilty start and lurched around. A nearby cookfire had burned low, but what light remained sufficed to reveal the round face of Fritjof with his snub nose and eyebrows so pale blond they were sometimes hard to see. Fritjof was a young Asgardian warrior under Heimdall's command. And hers, come to that. He was eager to prove his mettle and do whatever was needful to help the work succeed. Maybe, in this instance, too eager.

"Captain," he said, his baritone voice steady. He had yet to draw his sword or dirk. Maybe he thought he looked innocent, and that helped him maintain his composure.

The lack of proof of murderous intent made what Uschi was about to do more awkward, but she had to let Fritjof know she was on to him. Otherwise, he was apt to sneak back here tomorrow night or the night after. "What are you doing?" she demanded.

"Just out for a walk," he said. "Thinking about home."

"It looked like more than a walk," she said. "It looked like you were creeping toward the entrance into Lady Amora's tent."

Fritjof did his best to put on the appearance of a man astounded by a false accusation. "Captain, whatever it looked like, I wasn't. I'm no thief, I swear!"

"I didn't think you were," she said. "I don't believe theft was what you had in mind. Swear to me on your honor as a warrior of Asgard, swear by the Spear and the Hammer, that you weren't going to hurt Lady Amora."

She stared into his eyes for several moments, until he could hold her gaze no longer. He looked down and muttered, "Would it have been so bad if I did?"

"Of course it would!" she snapped, hoping the vehemence of her response concealed that she herself was of two minds about the matter. "It would be cowardly, despicable, to murder someone sleeping in her bed."

"If Amora were a warrior, I'd challenge her to an honorable fight. But do you think I'd be any match for the enchantress unless I took her unaware?"

Uschi sighed. "Either way, that's not really the point. I assume you came here because you believe Lady Amora poisoned the cyclops. But there's no proof of that, and we – I mean, you – can't simply kill her without it."

"There isn't going to *be* proof as such," Fritjof replied. Initially, he'd dissembled, but now that he knew it wouldn't serve, he was offering an increasingly spirited defense of his intentions. "The enchantress is too wily for that. But we can look at her history. She betrayed Asgard once. Why not again?"

"She has nothing to gain this time."

"We don't know that. Some people are saying, what if she's working with the frost giants again? What if she poisoned the cyclops to outrage the strangers and prompt them to demand an end to the work? After all, anything that's bad for Asgard is good for Jotunheim."

"Odin is wiser than either of us and he plainly didn't suspect her of bad intent. Otherwise, he wouldn't have sent her here."

"All praise to the All-Father. Still, Amora fooled him before, and if we allow it, who's to say what harm she'll do next or what the consequences will be?"

Uschi was growing increasingly frustrated with the argument, especially considering that Fritjof's justifications echoed her own private misgivings. She was groping for something else she might say to persuade him when sickly green light flickered at the periphery of her vision.

She pivoted to see that at some point Lady Amora had emerged from her striped pavilion. Maybe she and Fritjof talking back and forth woke the witch. At any rate, it seemed plain Amora had heard at least some of what was said.

Now she was murmuring sibilant words of power and sweeping her hands through mystic passes. The magic produced the bilious glow around her and a cold, crawling sensation on Uschi's skin, as though ants made of ice were skittering there.

Fritjof drew his broadsword and ran at Amora. The enchantress flung out her hand, and a yellow beam flashed from her fingertips and bashed the warrior, who reeled backward. As he fell to the ground, she resumed casting the lengthier spell.

Fritjof gave a croaking cry. He thrashed, struggling to spring back to his feet, but it appeared his legs had gone rigid and would no longer obey him. Grayness crept up his neck, the unnatural hue supplanting the color of normal skin.

Uschi realized the magic was turning him to stone. "Stop!" she cried.

Amora left off her spellcasting to turn, give the Valkyrie an enquiring smile, and arch her eyebrows. The green glow and the itchy chill in the air remained, however, like a hound awaiting its mistress's permission to gobble a morsel. "Whatever for?" she asked.

"He's done nothing," Uschi replied.

"He was about to slip into my tent and murder me in my sleep. He confessed as much to you, and I heard it too. You surely can have no objection to my acting in self-defense."

"The need has passed," Uschi said. "I was handling the situation."

"Well, now I am, in a manner that ensures he won't try again."

Uschi put her hand on the hilt of the Brightblade. "*I* guarantee he won't. Restore him."

Though the Valkyrie had no intention of backing down and made sure her demeanor conveyed as much, she hoped the enchantress would. Fritjof had been correct about one thing. Amora was a formidable sorceress and might well neutralize even a Valkyrie before the latter could draw her sword and close to striking distance. What's more, even if Uschi could best the other woman, given the circumstances, it was far from certain that afterward, Odin would believe she'd done the right thing.

Fortunately, though Amora could defend herself at need, she notoriously preferred striking by surprise or at a distance to anything approximating a fair fight. She might also have decided it wasn't in her best interests to escalate the situation further. She snapped the fingers of her left hand and the green light blinked out. Fritjof groaned and shuddered as the stony grayness and rigidity left his body.

Uschi glared at the young man. "Get up and go. If you come within twenty paces of Lady Amora ever again, she has my permission to do anything she likes to you."

Fritjof scrambled up and ran. As he disappeared into the darkness, Amora said, "Well, Valkyrie, we were at odds for a moment there, but I suppose I must still thank you for preventing our would-be assassin from slipping into my tent."

Uschi scowled. "I didn't do it for you."

"I didn't imagine you had. Be that as it may, please believe me when I say that despite any past peccadillos and misunderstandings, I didn't poison the cyclops, nor am I conniving to cause Ulbrecht's grand design to fail."

"The truth will come out in due course. Whomever it implicates."

"I assume you mean when your shrewd friend ferrets it out. Where *is* Captain Heimdall, anyway? I haven't seen him in at least a week. I know that before that, he entered Lord Pluto's tent for a private conversation. Did he learn something that sent him wandering off?"

"That's none of your concern."

Amora heaved a sigh. "There's just no talking to you, is there?

I'll bid you good night, then, return to my tent, and cast some wards. Should anyone else seek to enter without permission, he – or she – won't survive to do so a second time."

The threat set Uschi's teeth on edge, especially since she suspected the *or she* part was aimed squarely at her. But she could scarcely object to the enchantress taking precautions after what had just happened.

"We'll make sure everybody knows what you've done," Uschi said. "Deterrents don't work unless people know they exist."

Six

The Underworld:
Four Days Until Bifrost

"After you asked Lord Pluto to bring you here and he refused," Kamorr continued, "nothing much happened for a while. Well, nothing except the mood in camp souring further. Some people still suspected me of poisoning Orien, and when I was running errands for you, I was careful about ill-wishers coming up behind me or cornering me. Some suspected Lady Amora of killing the cyclops as a roundabout way of halting the work, and I imagine that for all her power, she was being careful too. A number of the strangers made no secret of believing the Asgardians or Blackhammers as a whole murdered Orien for some nefarious reason, and many in our company resented it. They apparently made it more difficult for Lord Hephaestus and the one-eyed giants to inspect the work, or at least that was the complaint. I could see you and Captain Uschi worrying that everything was about to fall apart, and I understood why."

"So do I," Heimdall said. Kamorr's story fascinated him. How could it not when it was an account of the resourceful, capable fellow he had apparently been? But it was as maddening as it was engaging because he felt so inadequate compared with the warrior of yore. Moreover, the story still felt like a tale told about someone other than himself. He sifted through the details, vainly seeking one that would stir his memory.

Maybe he would have fared better if he'd felt able to give the Blackhammer his full attention at every moment of the telling. But there were reptilian searchers and guards to be avoided while still navigating a winding course toward one of the paths up the scarps, and with his heightened sight and hearing – Kamorr called them *the gifts of Mimir*, whatever that meant – the responsibility fell primarily on him.

Kamorr looked up to study his companion's face. After a moment, his mouth twisted at what he saw there. Heimdall evidently wore a glum expression that reflected his continuing lack of memory.

The dwarf's disappointment inspired a twinge of guilt. "I'm sorry," Heimdall said. "The story hasn't been entirely in vain. I now have an inkling of where we are. But that's inference, not recollection."

Kamorr dredged up a smile. "Well, I'm not giving up. Eventually–"

"Hold on," Heimdall said.

The trek across this gloomy, smoky pit, lit mainly by the occasional fire of torment and what wan illumination shone down from high above, had shown him that oases like the one that had served as the prison of Tantalus were rare and generally infused with some evil magic to bedevil the prisoner. Heimdall now believed the apples he and Kamorr had carried away would stave off hunger until they either escaped the underworld or met with disaster trying, but thirst was somewhat more of a concern.

They had occasionally encountered a stream, but the shallow waters were dark with ash, offal, and other filth. Sometimes they stank or even steamed and bubbled with the run-off they accumulated from the various sites of torture. They appeared so likely to be toxic that neither of the fugitives had deemed it safe to drink.

Ahead, however, a spring flowed from the side of a hump in the barren earth. No doubt the rill it fed soon became contaminated as it flowed away across the pit, but here at the source, the water was clean.

Heimdall wasn't all that thirsty yet, nor had Kamorr complained. He supposed he had his Asgardian hardiness, and the Blackhammer his dwarf resilience, to thank for that. Still, it seemed foolish to pass up the chance to drink when they had the chance.

He explained what the vision of Mimir had enabled him to see, and then he and Kamorr skulked toward the spring. As they approached, he peered for any sign that snake-men were lurking in the vicinity. They didn't seem to be.

Though he hadn't felt especially thirsty, the awareness that he *could* drink made him eager to do so, and it took willpower to continue creeping up to the spring as slowly and cautiously as he intended. Finally, he and the Blackhammer reached the trickle, knelt over it, scooped up handfuls of water, and drank their fill. The liquid was as cold and refreshing as he'd hoped it would be.

Kamorr swiped water on his face, and stray droplets hung in

his beard. "It's too bad we don't have some kind of bottle," he said. "We can carry a couple of apples stuck inside our tunics, but–"

A thunderous roar sounded behind them. For an instant, it startled Heimdall into passivity, and then fear screamed that he had to move and move now. He started to do so, then registered that Kamorr, still frozen with shock, had yet to do the same. He grabbed the Blackhammer by the forearm and jerked him along as he dodged.

Splashing up water from the start of the rill, a massive something pounced into the space the fugitives had just vacated. Struggling against panic, Heimdall backed further away from it, let go of Kamorr, and grabbed for his sword. He thought he'd evaded barely in time. Then, at the periphery of his vision, he saw to his horror it hadn't been in time. Kamorr's tunic was torn and bloody, and more blood welled from the three gashes – claw marks – over his ribs. Teeth gritted, the dwarf clutched at the wounds in an effort to stop the bleeding.

Now that it was too late, Heimdall fancied he knew what had happened. After the raid on Tantalus's pool, the snake-men had reasoned the fugitives would avail themselves of clean water when available. So, they'd laid a trap here, and, given that they'd already lost two of their number, had chosen a creature more formidable than a reptile-man to take down their prey. The uneven ground had allowed the beast to hide where even Heimdall's extraordinary eyesight couldn't pick it out.

The creature itself was so grotesque that Heimdall's first good look at it nearly shocked him into a second paralysis. The greater portion of its body was that of some fearsome hunting cat with tawny fur, glaring amber eyes, and a snarling mouth full of fangs. Midway down its back, however, sprouted the shaggy horned head of a goat that twisted and glared back and forth, wisps of smoke leaking from its mouth and nostrils. At the hindquarters, fur gave way to dusky scales, and a relatively thick neck writhed and shifted where one might have expected a slimmer feline tail. The neck terminated in a wedge-shaped head with slit-pupiled eyes, a flickering forked tongue, and long, pointed teeth oozing venom. Now that it was no longer creeping up on its prey, the beast's three heads made a growling, bleating, hissing cacophony together.

It was possible that before losing his memory, the notable fighter Heimdall had faced ghastlier foes, but the frightened, diminished fellow he was now found that difficult to credit. Despite his recent drink, his mouth was dry, and his sword hand would shake if he allowed it. But much as he yearned to run, he was certain turning tail would only make it easier for the beast to kill Kamorr and himself.

"Stay behind me," he said to the wounded Blackhammer.

Crouching, the triple-headed creature advanced. To Heimdall, the approach looked as if his foe would charge or spring and so bring him within reach of its fangs and claws. That, he judged, could well be the end of him, but, he sensed, it could also make the beast vulnerable to a potentially lethal cut or thrust to the cat head and the brain inside it. He strained once more to quell his fear and let trained reflex choose the proper moment.

Unfortunately, the beast had its own tricks to employ. It glided two more paces forward, but then, instead of the final lunge Heimdall anticipated, turned slightly and abruptly to the side. Now the goat head was looking straight at its adversary.

It opened its mouth wide and belched a stream of crackling yellow fire.

Reflex hurled Heimdall to one side, but even so, only the fact that the flames shot out in a relatively narrow flare saved him from incineration. As it was, the fierce heat seared and blistered his side.

Nor was that the end of the attack. As he lurched and stumbled away from the fire, the creature kept pivoting, and the serpent head arced around to meet him. The reptilian jaws gaped as it struck.

Off balance and unable to arrest his forward momentum, frantic to stop the attack, Heimdall slashed wildly. The first venomous strike stopped short to avoid the blade, but the long neck immediately lifted, prepared to deliver another. Meanwhile, Heimdall was all too aware that the other portions of this hodgepodge horror might be about to assail him while he was barely able to see what they were doing. He didn't dare take his eyes off the menacing snake head for a good look.

Kamorr rushed past him, sprang into the air, bellowed, and delivered a side kick to the hock of a scaly hindlimb. The kick jolted the beast off balance, and it needed an instant to recover.

After that, the serpent head struck, and the hind paws clawed at the Blackhammer dwarf. Kamorr somersaulted out from under the attacks. Heimdall took advantage of the creature's distraction to cut into the reptilian neck, but the scales served as armor, and the result was less damaging than the severing stroke he'd intended.

At least, he told himself as he hurried backward, he and Kamorr had both managed to retreat to a slightly safer distance. That wouldn't save them for long, though, and he was grimly certain neither of them had yet succeeded in seriously injuring the creature. Most of the blood spattered on the ground was the Blackhammer's, shed when he exerted himself despite his wounds.

Kamorr scrambled, circling wide to put Heimdall and himself on opposite sides of the beast. Heimdall wanted to tell him again to stand back or, better still, get away entirely, but he didn't. He was now sure he needed the help and that his comrade wouldn't abandon him anyway.

Because he and Kamorr were now causing the creature to watch in two directions, he no longer had to contend with all three heads focusing on him at once and consequently fared a little better. It was meager encouragement at best, but he cut and thrust whenever he saw an opening, and his sword gashed the beast's body in the moments before he had to leap back to avoid its reprisals. Some of his adversary's own blood came to streak the dull yellow fur, and one of the feline ears was clipped off short.

Thick muscle and bone armored the creature's vitals, however, and all the wounds he inflicted were superficial, as his own would surely not be when his foe managed to score on him. He and Kamorr weren't turning the tide. They were simply delaying the inevitable, and it seemed horribly plain they wouldn't delay it much longer when, despite the dwarf's determination, fatigue and blood loss started getting the better of him. Apparently recognizing that he'd lost the stamina and dexterity to attempt kicks and strikes, he hung back and threw rocks, which plainly failed to trouble the beast as much.

Frightened though he was, Heimdall suspected that fierce aggression represented the only real hope of survival. He dodged another stream of fire, and then, as the beast pivoted to threaten him with cat fangs and cat claws, sprang in, feinted to the head, and stooped low to slash at a foreleg. The creature hopped back out of range, lunged forward again the instant the cut fell short, and clawed. Heimdall snatched his arm back in time to keep it from being shredded into uselessness, but the swipe still slammed against the flat of his sword. Gripping with all his strength, he only barely managed to prevent the weapon falling from his hand. Now the snake head was there, striking at his flank. He jumped away and avoided it by just as narrow a margin.

As he retreated, breathing hard, he recognized his assault had failed, and for a moment he came close to despair. Then, however, it occurred to him that while letting ingrained reflex attend to the fighting would suffice to overcome a snake-man guard, it wasn't enough here. A truly expert swordsman possessed such reflexes but was also evidently capable of making a plan to defeat a genuinely formidable foe.

Heimdall had apparently been such a warrior before the loss of his memory diminished him. Please, he thought, please, let some of what I was return to me! He strained to think of a stratagem, and after several more desperate dodges and retreats, he hit on something.

The beast had three heads. Did three heads mean three brains, and was it possible that they could be made to react independently of one another? If so, maybe there was still a chance.

"Circle back around behind me!" he called.

Kamorr frowned at the seemingly stupid notion of relinquishing the slim tactical advantage they'd gained by flanking the beast. But he didn't shout back to argue or question. Swinging wide once more, he instantly dashed back around.

"Now throw rocks at the goat head," Heimdall said, "and the goat head only." That way, all the attacks would come from the same direction. With luck, maybe it would even feel like they all came from the same infuriating source.

Kamorr hurled his stones whenever the Asgardian wasn't blocking his target, or when he wasn't dodging a retaliatory spray of yellow flame. Meanwhile, Heimdall concentrated his own attacks on the goat.

Springing into the distance and out again, thrusting and cutting, he bloodied the black nose and bearded muzzle and nearly succeeded in stabbing out an eye. His focus on the goat made him even more vulnerable to attacks from the cat and snake just as his own strength was flagging, but somehow he evaded snapping fangs, raking claws, and glistening venom for a few more heartbeats.

Was the goat head becoming more and more agitated at the punishment it was receiving? It seemed to Heimdall that it was screaming and spitting its fire more wildly, and flinching whenever he started a threatening move, but truly, in the midst of a desperate fight with an unfamiliar monstrosity, how could anyone be certain?

He *was* sure, however, that he couldn't last much longer. If he was ever going to make his stratagem work, it had to be now. Evading another snake strike by springing forward, he hacked at one of the curling goat horns. The blow snapped it in two. He kept lunging forward and dived across the creature's back between the goat head and the feline one.

The goat head swiveled, tracking him. It shrieked fire but was too slow. He tumbled off the creature's back an instant before the flare would have caught him and set him ablaze.

He landed awkwardly, hard enough to knock the wind out of him. He scrambled around and up anyway. He didn't dare lose track of his foe even for a moment. It was only when he had his eyes on it again that he knew his idea had worked.

The flame had splashed across a portion of the creature's own body, and the furry feline head and shoulders were burning. Roaring, screaming, and hissing in distress, the beast reeled about, then flung itself to the ground and rolled in an apparent effort to extinguish the blaze engulfing it.

Heimdall couldn't permit that, lest the attempt succeed, and the monstrosity still prove combative afterward. Grinning now that he finally had the upper hand, heedless of the heat and the risk that the fire would burn him, too, he advanced and stabbed repeatedly.

"Look out!" Kamorr cried.

Possibly because it was furthest from the flames and so felt the pain less, the serpent head was still capable of resisting Heimdall and had stretched around to strike. Kamorr's warning enabled him to pivot and meet it with a cut that hacked it in two. The scaly neck thrashed, writhing in its death throes. The rest of the creature had stopped moving at all.

Coughing, withdrawing from the haze of malodorous, eye-stinging smoke, Heimdall had only a moment to take satisfaction in his victory. Then, his face ashen above the beard and clutching his bloody side again, Kamorr sat down heavily on the ground.

Heimdall ran to his companion's side. "How bad is it?"

The Blackhammer forced a smile. "Only scratches. I just need a moment to catch my breath."

"Keep holding the wounds. I'll help you back to the water, and we'll get you cleaned up."

Kamorr snorted. "Might as well. We fought hard enough for the use of the spring, didn't we?"

With Heimdall's assistance, the dwarf clambered back to his feet. Once water from the rill washed some of the blood away, it appeared to the Asgardian that the cuts needed bandaging, and cloth torn from his own upper garment would have to serve as the wrapping. Glad his stolen sword belt would hold up the lower portion regardless, he started ripping.

As he worked, something in his expression or manner made Kamorr's face crease in concern. "Hey," he said, "none of that. It's not your fault I got nicked up a little. Old Three Heads had a hiding place. Even you couldn't see the beast as we were coming up."

The Blackhammer's refusal to blame him made Heimdall feel even guiltier, even more a pitiful shadow of the man he'd once been and urgently needed to be again.

"No. It *is* my fault, and I ask your forgiveness. If I'd sharpened my hearing, I would have caught the creature's heartbeat wherever it was lurking. But I didn't think to use my ears as well as my eyes." Heimdall sighed. "I feel like with my memory gone, I can barely think at all."

"You'll be all right," Kamorr said. "You'll be, I'll be, and Asgard will be once we get back to Midgard. So let's have another drink and get away from here. What with all the commotion the beast was making and all the fire it was spitting, that was a noisy fight and a well-lit one, too. Our pursuers will come to find out what happened."

"You're right," Heimdall said. "But you weren't right about something else. Before, it seemed like you thought your fighting skills were nothing much. But you saved my life. I could never have beaten the beast alone."

"Huh," Kamorr replied. "Well, maybe. Anyway, if the fight with the snake-man didn't do it already, this battle proved that whatever else you've forgotten, you still know how to use a sword."

Heimdall smiled. "Well, maybe."

The fugitives did hurry on their way, and once they left the spring behind, Kamorr resumed his story. Heimdall wondered if the Blackhammer took up the telling less because he was still certain it would help and more because it might distract him from the ache of his wounds.

SEVEN

MIDGARD:
BEFORE THE DESCENT

Like most of the colossal runes the Blackhammers were creating, this one east of camp was a set of tunnels excavated to Ulbrecht's exacting specifications and consecrated by the various rituals the sorcerers performed. That meant that while the god of smiths Hephaestus could periodically fit inside the diggings to inspect them firsthand, the enormous cyclopes couldn't. They had to rely on charts, the miners' and warlocks' explanations, and what they could glean from their own divinations practiced aboveground.

Kamorr remembered when that hadn't posed as much of a problem. Since the murder, though, the one-eyed giants had been increasingly reluctant to take a dwarf's or Asgardian's word for anything.

The scene he was watching from a stand of pale-barked mountain birch was a case in point. In a space cleared to facilitate the work, with piles of excavated earth and rock rising like mountains in miniature here and there, a cyclops was arguing with several of the senior miners. It was clear from the rising volume and the annoyance and frustration on everyone's faces that the discussion was growing increasingly acrimonious.

Kamorr wondered if he should head down the slope and try to mediate. After all, following his visit to Pluto's tent, Heimdall had asked him to check on the work. That responsibility arguably encompassed trying to resolve disputes when possible. Kamorr actually doubted his ability to do the latter. His fellow Blackhammers had never thought highly of him to begin with, and many now continued to regard him with suspicion. Shrewd fellow that he was, Heimdall surely realized that as well. But matters in the camp had grown so tense that the Asgardian might be depending on all his helpers to do everything they could.

Which made a certain amount of sense. Not, however, if Kamorr interceding would only make things worse, and it might. He resented his fellow dwarves turning on him and worried that he might not be able to keep that resentment from coloring any attempt to intervene. He decided that, for the moment at least, he would simply continue to observe and hope the situation resolved without him.

Suddenly, though, it appeared he'd waited too long. The cyclops bent down, grabbed one of the miners, and lifted him high, perhaps to pulp him in a crushing grip, fling him off the mountain, or the Fates only knew what. Kamorr gasped in dismay.

The dwarves around the giant cried out and snatched for

weapons, either proper ones they carried, or the makeshift arms provided by picks and shovels. Dodging trees, springing over roots, Kamorr sprinted down the steep slope toward the clearing. He feared he'd held back too long, and now it was too late to avert a disaster.

Before anyone could hurt anybody else, however, and when his frantic charge had covered only a fraction of the distance, a burly figure in dark metal armor appeared among the scrambling miners. Kamorr couldn't tell where the new arrival came from, or how. Lord Pluto was simply not there one moment and present the next.

The death god possessed far more influence and authority than Kamorr could ever hope to exert. Hoping Pluto would use them in the service of a peaceful resolution, the dwarf stumbled to a halt.

"Put him down!" the stranger god shouted up at the cyclops.

Despite what was, from Kamorr's perspective, the grotesque appearance afforded by the single enormous eye, the giant's features fell in a recognizable expression of sheepishness. His hugeness notwithstanding, at that moment he resembled a child caught misbehaving.

"I wasn't going to hurt him," he mumbled. "I was just trying to make him listen."

"Put him down," Pluto repeated, and then rounded on the Blackhammers. "And you lot, put up your weapons."

His scowl was so fierce that the dwarves complied, albeit not without a bit of resentful whispering back and forth. A god Pluto might be, but not *their* god, or even their employer.

When the captured miner was back on the ground and

straightening his garments with furious little tugs, the stranger deity asked, "Now, what's this all about?"

The cyclops and three of the miners started jabbering at once. Pluto ended the babble with a sweep of his battle-axe and required the disputants to speak one at a time.

Even afterward, however, though he listened attentively, Kamorr could only follow the broad strokes of the debate. The details were too technical. But evidently the giant's divinations suggested a minute deviation from the dimensions the subterranean rune was supposed to have while the Blackhammers claimed they were digging the tunnels precisely as directed. And even if they hadn't, the change was too trivial to matter.

Pluto listened to everyone argue for a time and then declared, "I'm satisfied that the work is proceeding properly. Miners, resume your labors. Bernus, return to your master. I imagine he'll find some other task for you."

The cyclops hesitated. "My lord, if Lord Hephaestus came here, he could actually look around *inside* the tunnels, and then–"

"I, too, am a god possessed of power and wisdom that a servant like you could never even imagine, and *I* say there is nothing here to concern us. Do you doubt my judgment?"

Bernus swallowed. "No, my lord."

"Then do as I bade you."

The cyclops turned and tramped away. The trail up the mountainside was too narrow for him to pass comfortably, and his shoulders brushed and rustled the branches of pines and spruces as he passed. Kamorr was glad he himself was a goodly distance off the trail. With his ruddy, mottled countenance,

Bernus still looked angry enough to kick or step on a stray dwarf as he made his way along.

After watching the departure for a moment, one of the miners turned, possibly to speak some grudging words of thanks. But Pluto was gone, too, as mysteriously and swiftly as he'd arrived, as though the Blackhammers were thralls who didn't merit courtesy or another instant of his time. Knowing his clan brothers and sisters as he did, Kamorr suspected resentment of the seeming disrespect would soon efface any gratitude they might otherwise have felt.

He regretted that Pluto had squandered an opportunity to improve relations but wasn't surprised. He'd seen enough of the death god since the latter's arrival to know that haughty brusqueness was Pluto's usual manner. It was something else that had surprised him, and he resolved to report it to Heimdall in due course.

The opportunity came at the conclusion of the evening meal, when the western sky was red and purple with the final traces of the vanished sun, and the interior of the Asgardian's tent was shadowy and dim. Heimdall sat on his cot with the Gjallarhorn and the greatsword Hofund resting beside him, the magical treasures doffed and dropped without ceremony in the interests of comfort. Uschi and Kamorr sat on campstools.

Heimdall spooned the last of his millet porridge from his wooden bowl, then washed it down with a sip of ale. "Well," he said, wry humor in his tone, "another day has passed, and apparently the work is still proceeding. What near-disasters does everyone have to recount?"

"I witnessed something odd," Kamorr said. He'd learned not to be diffident with Heimdall and Uschi. It only made the two Asgardian warriors impatient. He described the altercation between Bernus the cyclops and the miners and Pluto's subsequent intervention.

By the time he finished, Uschi had narrowed her brown eyes and was touching the knuckle of her crooked forefinger to the corner of her mouth. This, he'd observed, was often her unconscious habit when thinking something over. "That is peculiar," she said. "We've been taking it for granted that the strangers suspect we're up to no good and are happy to hinder us whenever possible. Yet here we have Pluto siding with your folk, Kamorr."

"Right," Kamorr said. "It's like his overlord – whoever that may be – is suspicious, and, carrying out his master's orders, Lord Pluto has no choice but to play along. Really, though, he *wants* Bifrost created."

"Or maybe he was just trying to be fair and do the right thing," Uschi replied.

Heimdall grunted. "Possibly, and I shouldn't assume the worst of him without proof any more than I was willing to do so with our friend Kamorr here. Still, that said, has Lord Pluto impressed either of you as the kind of person who greatly cares about being fair and doing what's right?"

"No," Kamorr and Uschi said, nearly in unison.

"That's my feeling as well," Heimdall said. "If I had to wager, I'd bet that if he wants the Rainbow Bridge finished, it's because he stands to gain something thereby. But I can't imagine what that something would be."

"Nor can I," Uschi said. Kamorr spread his hands to signal that he didn't have any idea either.

"So maybe any suspicions are groundless, and we should

certainly keep them to ourselves for now," Heimdall said. "I do notice, though, that the *specific* effect of Pluto's intervention was to allow the work to go forward without Hephaestus inspecting that particular excavation on this particular day."

"So, what, then?" Uschi said. "Are Pluto and Hephaestus actually at odds?"

"I've seen no sign of it," Kamorr said, "but if they are, I'd wager on Pluto. He's more cunning." In contrast, the god of smiths and artificers had a brusque, straightforward manner not dissimilar to that of the typical dwarf.

"Agreed," Heimdall said. "Let's hope he's not more cunning than we are."

"So, you *do* think he's our enemy," Uschi said.

Heimdall sighed. "I truly have no idea. Maybe he and his fellow god are exactly what they purport to be. Maybe Amora murdered Orien just as you've suspected all along. Maybe a fellow cyclops poisoned him for making eyes at his wife."

Kamorr snorted. "Or making eye."

Heimdall flashed a grin. "I stand corrected. Making eye."

"It sounds," Uschi said, "like all we can do is continue as we have been. Watch everyone, throw water on fires when they break out, and try to shepherd Ulbrecht's great work to a satisfactory conclusion."

"Maybe there's a little more," Heimdall said. "Aiding Ulbrecht is the mission Odin gave us. He didn't specifically charge us with trying to unmask Orien's murderer – obviously, it hadn't happened yet – but there's little doubt it would help. It would dampen the suspicions and hostility everyone is currently feeling, and it would rid us of a scoundrel who might otherwise commit further mischief."

Uschi gave an impatient nod. "Of course. That's why we've run ourselves ragged poking around. But we've gotten nowhere."

"Maybe because I still haven't been able to question the spirit of Orien."

The Valkyrie cocked her head. "I thought you told us Lord Pluto said he was going to question him. I assumed he did, and the cyclops provided nothing useful."

"Maybe we shouldn't assume that. What if Pluto didn't truly think Orien was worth questioning and only said he did to placate me? Or didn't think to ask the right question? Or really does have some secret agenda of his own…" Heimdall turned his hands up. "I know it may not help, but I still want to talk to the cyclops myself."

Uschi shook her head. "Pluto was right about one thing. Odin didn't want us learning too much about the strangers."

"But what he cared most about was having Bifrost built."

"Unless it wasn't."

Heimdall paused, plainly considering the idea, then smiled. "So, all the work here is only a gambit, a sham in the service of some deeper game? No. I know the All-Father is cunning, but that just seems too unlikely. I truly believe I should talk to Orien if it will help us finish our task. I promise, I'm only after what we need."

"Have you discussed this idea with Ulbrecht?" she persisted.

"No. If things go wrong, it's better if he can say honestly that neither he nor the All-Father had any idea I meant to overstep. But they won't go wrong. If I learn nothing, I'll be back before I'm missed with no one any the wiser. If I do have the answer, those above us will pardon my transgression."

"*Perhaps,*" Uschi said. "Just because you've gotten away with this kind of thing before doesn't mean you will again. Anyway, aren't you forgetting something? You don't know how to pass in and out of the kingdom of the dead that Pluto rules."

"You're right," Heimdall said. "But from time to time, the god hitches those two black horses of his to his chariot and flies off to the south. My guess is, he's returning to his domain to make certain all's in order there. I'll wager Golden Mane can fly just as fast as his team, and the vision of Mimir will enable me to hang well back and still keep track of him. He won't know I'm following."

"You hope," Uschi said. "He's a god, and you have no way of knowing what he can sense." She smiled a rueful smile. "But all right. I can tell there's no arguing you out of this any more than I was able to argue you out of haring off to Nidavellir."

"Which worked out."

"Which worked out," she acknowledged. "In the end, we defeated the Lurking Unknown. So, I'll hold myself ready to saddle up when you are."

"That's exactly how I would wish it," Heimdall said. "But someone has to stay here and watch over things. It won't help if I return with answers, but the camp has already exploded into violence, and in consequence Bifrost can never be finished."

Uschi shook her head. "Leave Kamorr in charge. He's proven himself shrewd and able."

Though gratified by the Valkyrie's assessment, the Blackhammer drew breath to explain why what she'd proposed was a bad idea. Heimdall spoke before he could, however, and said pretty much what he'd intended to say.

"Kamorr is everything you said. But he doesn't carry the

imprimatur of Odin like you do. The Blackhammers never valued him as he deserved, and now some on every side still suspect he's the murderer. Many wouldn't heed him, and so it has to be you."

"You're right," Kamorr said. "The truth is that, though I've done my best, I'm of little use here." And he realized he very much wanted to be useful to these friends who had faith in him. It had been a long, long while since anyone had expressed any such thing. "Maybe I can justify your belief in me if I accompany you on your journey."

Plainly surprised by the suggestion, Heimdall blinked. "Thank you," he said, "but no. It's too dangerous. I have no idea what I'll be facing."

"Moments ago, you said nothing would go wrong and you'd be back before you were missed."

Uschi snorted. "He's right. You did."

"And if it does turn out to be dangerous," Kamorr continued, "it will be good to have a comrade watching your back. And I can truly repay you for saving my life when my own clan was ready to give me up."

Heimdall pondered for a few moments. At length, he said, "As far as I'm concerned, you don't owe me anything, but if you're putting yourself forward, so be it. We'll want to keep a watch on the chariot or the horses that pull it, so we'll know when Pluto's making ready to depart. It will be easier than trying to shadow the god himself."

EIGHT

MIDGARD:
FOUR DAYS UNTIL BIFROST

It was after midnight when, as usual, Pluto slipped into Ulbrecht's tent with the invisibility afforded by his helmet shrouding him and the dark of night providing further concealment. In addition to all that, he suppressed a momentary childish impulse to creep on tiptoe. It would manifestly be beneath his dignity as god of the underworld, but once, just once, it would be gratifying to surprise his fellow conspirator as by rights he should have every time.

Ulbrecht greeted his entry with the usual sly, almost mocking smile that looked out of place on his wrinkled, dyspeptic features. He waved a hand weighted with rune-engraved rings at the earthenware bottle and silver cups waiting on his cluttered table. "You've probably never tasted mead," he said. "Try some. It's good."

Willing himself visible, Pluto ignored the invitation. "How much longer?"

Ulbrecht sighed. "You already know the answer. A few more days."

"A few more days if the two groups don't go to war. You could do more to help manage the situation."

"No," Ulbrecht said. "The man I'm impersonating would have been glad to concentrate on his sorcery and leave suppressing conflict to Captains Heimdall and Uschi. Besides, do you have any idea how demanding it is to subvert the original design without your smith god, the cyclopes, or any of the other warlocks noticing what I'm doing? I truly do have to spend a great deal of time working subtle magic alone in this tent. At that, the one giant did realize something was amiss."

"And I had to silence him," Pluto replied. "It's not easy for me, either, pretending I'm suspicious of the work but actually keeping it moving forward. Keeping anyone from detecting your alterations."

"But you're doing splendidly. The one cyclops – Or-something, was it? – was a fluke. No one else will realize what we're doing."

"Don't underestimate Hephaestus. He's a god like me."

"Hephaestus may know how to hammer a piece of hot metal, but otherwise, he's a dullard. Far too straightforward a fellow to ever unravel our deceptions."

"You hope."

Ulbrecht spread his upturned hands. "Did you think the task I entrusted to you would be altogether easy? How could it be, when we stand to gain so much? Once the All-Father's kingdom and all its people perish, I can lead my folk on a conquest of other Realms on the World Tree's branches.

And when Odin's pantheon dies, other gods can extend their influence here on Earth, and as the god who understands what's happened, you'll be poised and ready to enhance your power considerably."

Pluto scowled. It was, to say the least, an appealing prospect, but he was in no mood for his partner's blandishments. "There's no need to remind me why I joined forces with you. But answer me this: can you still finish Bifrost if Hephaestus goes to my king and says it mustn't be allowed to happen? If there are no miners left to dig or lesser warlocks to cast the spells you tell them to cast?"

Ulbrecht tapped the fingers of his two hands together as he thought it over. Then he said, "Perhaps you have a point. We should ease the tensions in the camp. Possibly your instinct was even correct that the way to do that is to provide a scapegoat for the cyclops's murder."

"Kamorr again?" It occurred to Pluto that he hadn't seen the dwarf lately, but presumably he was still in the encampment somewhere.

"No," Ulbrecht said, "particularly since Heimdall proved the Blackhammer's innocence already to anyone with the wit to understand. I have a far more plausible miscreant in mind."

After brushing and arranging her blonde tresses and accenting her green eyes with kohl, Amora inspected her face in her looking glass and decided the results of her efforts were satisfactory. She then exited her tent. The morning sun had already cleared the peaks to the east when she did so. The Blackhammer miners and other common laborers might rise early to resume their tasks, but she saw no reason to do the same. A lady of the court had her privileges and, in her view, was a fool if she didn't take advantage of them.

As she made her way through the camp in search of breakfast, people scurried to clear her path. She would have liked to regard this as the deference that was her due, but the truth was manifestly otherwise. Once she'd passed, a pair of dwarves muttered insults. An Asgardian warrior surreptitiously crooked his fingers to ward off the evil eye. Even a towering cyclops, who must have heard people complain and conjecture about the wicked enchantress, turned and hastily tramped away, not stopping until he was a long bowshot away.

Plainly, it was fear, not respect, on full display.

Amora frowned. She'd always had her share of ill-wishers expressing dislike in one fashion or another. Occasionally, she'd reveled in their hostility. But she'd generally preferred to pretend goodwill for all around her until there was some advantage to be had from plunging in the knife, so this naked and nigh-universal suspicion was unfamiliar, and she found it unpleasant.

It was particularly galling given that she hadn't poisoned the cyclops and had no intention of ruining Ulbrecht's design. To the contrary. She was diligently casting any spells he directed her to cast. Perhaps one day – who knew? – she'd pursue some new illicit scheme to enhance her position in the world, but for now, she was obeying Odin's commands like a faithful subject. Why couldn't people see that and forget the past?

The ground shuddered under her boots and distracted her from her disgruntled musings. Off to the northeast, something rumbled.

Surprised, she peered in that direction. The Blackhammers

were digging one of the huge underground runes over there. She knew because she'd been at the site performing one of Ulbrecht's rituals only yesterday.

Had something gone wrong? If so, no one had directed her to sort it out, but she had to admit, she was curious. She recited a charm of flight and soared into the air, above the rows of tents, above even the heads of the cyclopes. People exclaimed and pointed as she hurtled away through the brisk morning air.

In moments, she arrived at the excavation and paused to survey it from overhead. A coughing dwarf was stumbling out of the tunnel mouth while his fellows who'd remained aboveground clustered around to help him. Some of the nearby spruce trees now leaned precariously against one another, evidence that deeper inside the excavation, a collapse had been serious enough to partially uproot them. Serious enough, too, she suspected, to bury some miners alive.

It was odd. The Blackhammers were supposed to be expert diggers who knew how to avoid such a calamity. That was one reason the All-Father hired them.

The enchantress reflected again that this was no problem of hers. But she wasn't entirely heartless, no matter what some people thought, and in any case, the sooner the work was done and Bifrost came into being, the sooner she could return to the pleasures and luxuries of Asgard. Like a goshawk swooping to catch a hare in its talons, she dived into the tunnel entrance and resumed standing on her own two feet.

A couple of crystals shed ruddy light from niches in the wall, evidence that even dwarves couldn't see in total darkness. Not all of them, anyway. Further ahead, though, the way was black. She conjured a will-o'-the-wisp to float before her as she cautiously made her way forward. The luminous orb pulsed green at certain moments, yellow at others.

The throbbing light illuminated increasing amounts of drifting dust in the air that scraped her nostrils and throat when she inhaled. In time, she came upon the source: a plug of earth and stone sealing the way before her.

Her first impulse was to blast through the obstruction. With the magic at her command, hurling beams of concussive force was easy enough. But it might dislodge more of the ceiling to rain down on her head. It might also damage the bodies of dwarves trapped but still clinging to life in or behind the mass, and, curiosity aside, succoring them was the reason she was down here choking on dust. She'd have to cast a more precise and thus more taxing combination of spells to accomplish her purpose.

First, crooning words of power, she visualized additional supports around her, and gradually they came into being and hardened to hold up the ceiling above her come what may. No one else could have seen them, and they were like congealed mist, ghostly, even in the sight of a sorceress, but they'd accomplish their purpose nonetheless. They'd make sure *she* stayed safe. That, after all, was more important than rescuing a thousand miners, though had anyone questioned her priorities, she could have pointed out that she couldn't rescue anyone else if she was dead or incapacitated herself.

Once the support columns were finished, she cast a different spell, one to grant her awareness of living beings before her, irrespective of obstructions in the way. Like smaller will-o'-the-wisps, sparks glowed before her inner eye. The nearer ones were faint, flickering, and evidently represented Blackhammers buried by the collapse but still clinging to life. Shining more brightly and steadily, those further away must be miners trapped on the far side of the plug.

There were twenty-two survivors altogether, which meant Amora had her work cut out for her. She took a deep breath, spat away more of the ambient dust, and cast a third spell.

The new magic conjured a disembodied hand as big as a frost giant's. Like the pillars she'd created, it would have been invisible to anyone else and was a spectral, semitransparent manifestation even to her. But what mattered was that it obeyed her. She made scraping, grabbing, and pulling motions with her hand of flesh and blood, and the huge materialization mimicked them as it dug away at the collapse.

So far, so good, but it became apparent almost immediately that simply shifting the dirt and rock wasn't going to be good enough. She couldn't just let it pile up to form a new plug.

Amora had long ago mastered the secret of transporting herself from one of the Nine Realms to another. With more effort, she could open a portal for anyone or anything to pass through as she had when she brought the ice giants from Niffleheim to the siege of Asgard. Declaiming rhymes of transition and linking, she opened a gate to the first place that occurred to her, her country estate outside Ljosalfgard, the capital fortress city of Alfheim. Her light elf groundskeepers wouldn't be happy with her for dumping dirt and rock on the immaculately kept lawn, but they were just going to have to cope. She tossed piles of earth through as the giant hand dislodged them.

She sensed the conjured hand was nearing the first buried survivor. She had to slow down and dig more carefully now lest the magic grab him roughly and kill him itself. Eventually she drew him free and discovered he was unconscious. But presumably she would eventually reach some who weren't, and the ones who were able could carry the others out into the daylight. She laid the miner on the floor behind her and resumed her digging.

She freed a second trapped miner, then a third. The third was conscious, and it irked her that he didn't greet his liberator with a profuse expression of gratitude. Plainly, she deserved one. But apparently the accident had left him too stunned and dazed, or he was too intent on reaching the surface to say anything. She told herself the important thing was that he carried one of the unconscious dwarves with him as he headed on up the tunnel.

The dust stung her eyes, and tears streaked what were surely her grimy cheeks. Even with sorcery doing the work, she had no doubt she was becoming filthy and felt sorely abused in consequence. It was likewise irksome that the most beautiful woman in Asgard should have her appearance so besmirched.

A rumble and more dirt spilling down from the ceiling of the section of newly cleared tunnel snapped her attention back to the task at hand. Additional phantom support columns were necessary to keep the recalcitrant earth from producing another collapse to undo her work. She growled the incantation, and the pillars duly appeared, but at the same moment, she felt a stab of headache.

Amora was a powerful sorceress. When in a good mood,

she had occasionally conceded that Karnilla the Norn Queen, her first teacher, *might* be even more powerful, but surely no other witch in Asgard could claim the same. Yet even the enchantress had her limits. The will-o'-the-wisp, her awareness of the locations of the surviving miners, the support columns, the digging hand, and the portal to Alfheim were all products of her willpower and attention, and she was trying to maintain too many spells at once.

She considered exiting the tunnel and leaving the rest of the miners to their fate. After all, she'd rescued several of them, and what were the remaining Blackhammers to her anyway?

But even Amora's detractors had never claimed she'd abandoned a task because it was difficult, and she didn't intend to give them reason to say so now. She drew herself up straight, focused her will anew, and went back to her digging, shoring up the passage as needed. Her head pounded. Sweat trickled down her face and dampened her armpits.

In time, she heard the clink of picks and scrape of shovels. Only a relatively thin layer of the plug remained, and dwarves were attacking it from the other side. A final swipe of the conjured hand broke it away.

Blackhammers stumbled up the tunnel through the floating dust and the gloom, some helping their injured fellows along. To her annoyance, none of the new ones paused to thank or even acknowledge her, either. Ingrates! She'd long regarded the people of Nidavellir as deficient in grace and courtesy, and while she recognized this was an extreme situation, the miners' behavior was doing nothing to improve her opinion. She grudgingly told herself that the important thing was that they were at least stopping to pick up the unconscious dwarves she'd unearthed previously and bear them to safety as well.

Amora permitted all her conjured apparitions except the nearest support columns and her floating orb of luminescence to wink out of existence. The pounding in her head abated somewhat, but her body felt as devoid of strength as a ragdoll's. Reflecting that her attire was surely grubby beyond salvaging anyway, she sat down on the floor.

She only remained that way for a brief time, however. She didn't want anyone else to come down the tunnel, see her that way, and realize how sorely the magic she'd just performed had taxed her. She clambered to her feet, ran her fingers through her dirty, sweaty hair to restore it as best she could, and strode back out into the sunlight to what she assumed would finally be the cheers of grateful Blackhammers.

No one cheered, however. Instead, a sudden silence fell.

She had little sense of how long she'd spent in the tunnel. Evidently there'd been time enough for other dwarves and some Asgardians, including Captain Uschi, to assemble aboveground. Many were holding shovels and picks, evidence they'd been organizing a rescue attempt before stopping to gape and glower at her.

She inferred that the ones who hadn't been trapped belowground didn't understand what she'd done. Evidently, the dwarves she'd rescued – the conscious ones – hadn't yet informed the others. Apparently that chore, like the rescue itself, fell to her. So be it, then. Having done the work, she was by no means inclined to dispense with the accolades that were her due.

She gave everyone a smile and drew breath to speak. Before she could, however, someone threw a stone and struck her in the temple.

The unexpected jolt sent her stumbling back a step, but even in her spent condition, she was capable of protecting herself from such crude attacks when need be. She reflexively raised her hand in a warding gesture, snarled a magic word that rattled the branches of nearby pines and spruces, and a transparent shield of swirling green and yellow light flared into existence before her. More stones clattered against the barrier and rebounded.

"What's the matter with you all?" Amora cried. She was angry, but bewildered, too.

"You caused the cave-in!" a miner shouted.

"You killed three of our people," yelled another, "and hurt more! And now you dare to stand before us? Why, to gloat?"

"That's mad!" Amora said. She felt blood dripping down from the small cut the stone had inflicted and brushed it away. "Why would I do such a thing?"

"Everyone knows you work for Jotunheim!" an Asgardian warrior called.

"Only once, and not for a long while," Amora said. "Odin trusts me again. His subjects should as well."

In the front ranks of the crowd slumped a Blackhammer supported by two others. He was filthy like the enchantress herself and was plainly one of the injured miners, his right leg bent and broken. Yet he'd prevailed on two of his fellow dwarves to help him forward, the better, evidently, to confront her.

"We *might* trust you," he gritted, "if we hadn't seen your

green and yellow magic flickering in the digging right before the collapse."

"You're confused," she said, straining to be conciliatory. Her instinct was to lash out, but there was little point in saving the miners only to slaughter them moments later. "Small wonder that you are, considering what you've been through. But I didn't work any spells in the tunnel until *after* the ceiling fell in. When I was saving your lives."

"Liar!" the Blackhammer said. "I know what I saw! We *all* saw it!"

Other miners clamored in agreement.

"And did nobody see me rescuing you?" Amora asked. "I was right there in the tunnel as you hurried out. You must have seen me even if you didn't say anything! Why would I turn right around and help you if I'd only just worked magic to do you ill?"

That quieted the crowd for a moment, just long enough for her to imagine they'd begun to see reason. Then the dwarf with the broken leg said, "I didn't see you there."

"Nor I," said another miner.

"Nor I," said a third, his pick still in his hands. "We dug ourselves out."

Amora was incredulous. True, the tunnel had been dark, the air full of floating dust, the freed miners intent only on reaching safety. Yet even so, *someone* should have seen her.

She was still standing stunned with disbelief when a number of the dwarves and Asgardians started forward, the fools fanning out as though they imagined they need only circle around the edges of the shield she'd created to overwhelm her. Well, she decided, her patience at an end, she'd recovered at least some of her mystical strength and would be happy to show them just how wrong they were. She drew breath and raised her hands to conjure.

She'd only spoken the first words of her incantation, however, when Uschi broke through the front ranks of the crowd-turned-mob. For an instant, Amora wondered why the Valkyrie hadn't intervened sooner.

Uschi sprinted to interpose herself between the oncoming Blackhammers and Asgardians and Amora, turned, and whipped the Brightblade from its scabbard. The blade of the enchanted broadsword burst into flame as she brandished the weapon. "Stop!" she shouted.

Amora wouldn't have credited it. But something – wariness of the Brightblade's magic, perhaps, or of the determination manifest in every aspect of its Valkyrie wielder's demeanor – balked even the angriest members of the mob.

Evidently certain she had them cowed, Uschi then turned her back on them to round on Amora. "And you," she said, "stop your spellcasting!"

Somewhat reluctantly, Amora lowered her hands and allowed the wave of mass heart failure she'd been about to unleash to dissipate with a sound like pork sizzling in a pan. "I only meant to protect myself," she said. "It appears that once again, I must thank you for doing it for me."

"And once again," Uschi said, stalking closer, the unsheathed Brightblade still burning in her hand, "I don't want your thanks. I'd be happy to take your head myself. But first your guilt must be proven beyond doubt."

Amora smiled. "Else Captain Heimdall would be disappointed in you."

Uschi ignored that. "If you didn't collapse the tunnel, explain the green and yellow lights the Blackhammers saw before the ceiling fell in."

"Obviously," Amora replied, "green and yellow are my favorite colors." She waved her hand, indicating her now-grimy attire to emphasize the point. "And sometimes, when a sorceress *has* a favorite color or two, the visible manifestations of her magic may take on the same hues. But the truth is that any skilled mage could, with a bit of effort, tinge his workings to look the same."

"So that's your explanation? Another witch or warlock collapsed the tunnel and wanted to put the blame on you?"

"It's one hypothesis."

"Why would anyone do that?"

"I don't know," Amora said. But, she thought grimly, she would very much like to. If someone had caused the cave-in and tried to put the blame on her, that was an injury she needed to avenge.

"Why did none of the miners see you in the tunnel if you were really inside helping people?"

"The same mage cast an enchantment to prevent it? Let me go back in the tunnel and investigate. If I cast divinations, I can likely identify the sorcerer or witch who truly caused the collapse."

"Whereupon I would have only the word of a notorious deceiver that your spells revealed what you claimed they did," Uschi said. "Clearly, that would prove nothing. So, here's what's going to happen. I'm going to gag you, bind your hands, and take you back to Asgard for judgment. Odin can sort this out."

Amora bristled. Perhaps she hadn't always comported herself like the king's most dutiful subject, but she'd paid for her missteps. This time, she was innocent. Indeed, twenty-two among the ungrateful rabble before her owed her their lives. Yet here they were, howling their hatred, intent on destroying her, and Uschi was scarcely better.

Amora resolved that neither the Valkyrie nor anyone else would subject her to the humiliation of hauling her back to Asgard as a prisoner. She no longer cared about the All-Father's commands or opinion of her or Ulbrecht's great work, intriguing though the latter was. Plainly, the Fates meant her to walk her own path again, recognizing no law or authority except her own.

"I think you'll find," she said to Uschi, "that is *not* what's about to happen." She rattled off the first words of the spell that would whisk her from one Realm to another.

Uschi hesitated for an instant, perhaps deciding whether it would be better to attempt to breach the barrier separating her and Amora or dodge around it. The Valkyrie opted for the former, raising her burning sword high and sweeping it down. To Amora's surprised dismay, the Brightblade's magic proved the stronger. The shield of shimmering green and yellow luminescence shattered like stained glass, the shards winking out of existence as they tumbled through the air. Uschi poised the Brightblade to deliver a potentially lethal slash to the torso.

Instead of making the cut immediately, though, she snarled, "Surrender!"

Which gave Amora time to recover from her surprise and work more magic. Smiling a mocking smile, she slipped between worlds. At the same time, she visualized the guise she wore when enchantment cloaked her in the image of the light elf lady who supposedly owned the palatial mansion in Alfheim. She was confident that once the disguise was in place, even Odin, with all his power, ravens, and whatnot wouldn't be able to find her.

NINE

Uschi turned back around to find the assembled Blackhammers and Asgardians regarding her reproachfully, if not with outright disgust. Her assertion of authority augmented by a show of the Brightblade's fire had intimidated them for a moment, but the moment had passed, and the worst part was that she wasn't even certain they were wrong. She felt disgusted with herself, too.

Why hadn't she cut the enchantress down without hesitation? She'd wanted to.

But really, she knew the answer. Amora might not be guilty of causing the collapse, and if she wasn't, she didn't deserve to die for it any more than Kamorr had deserved to die for the poisoning of Orien. The enchantress's death might even have hindered efforts to discover the truth.

Which, in retrospect, didn't make Uschi feel any better about holding back. Because it did seem all too likely that Amora was guilty, and now she was alive and free to strike again.

The Valkyrie took a deep breath and tried to let the matter go. She'd done what she'd done, and it had worked out as it worked out. Now she had the outraged Blackhammers to deal with. Heimdall – once again, she worried what had become of him even as she felt another twinge of frustration that she had to deal with problems that were properly his – was counting on her to keep the workers working, come what may.

A woman among the miners shouted, "You let the enchantress get away!"

"You would have fared no better," Uschi replied. "She would have struck you all down with witchcraft if I hadn't intervened." And though she said it partly in an effort to justify her actions, it seemed to her it was likely true.

"She might have gotten some of us," shouted an Asgardian warrior, "but the rest of us would have gotten her!"

Members of the crowd clamored in agreement.

"Either way," Uschi said, "it's over. Lady Amora fled. Whatever she was doing, she won't cause trouble anymore." She hoped. "Now the healers must tend the injured, and everyone else should get back to work."

Some of those she was addressing turned away grumbling. A number of the Blackhammers, however, shifted their grips on the spades and picks in their hands. It looked like they meant to serve her as they'd intended to deal with Amora, and she wondered if she'd have to call on the Asgardian warriors who were present to subdue them. She even wondered if every one of those warriors would still obey her orders.

Fortunately, she didn't have to put the matter to the test. Scowling Gulbrand, motherly Bergljot, and Ailpein with his wispy whiskers and generally boyish appearance, had belatedly arrived at the back of the crowd. The mages pushed their way out of the mass of their fellow Blackhammers and came to stand beside her.

Gulbrand sneered at the members of the crowd who, in their belligerence, had chosen to linger. "Well, what are you waiting for?" he asked. "Do as the Valkyrie bade you! Or do you think you'll dig better if I turn you into cave rats?"

"He can do it," said Bergljot, beaming as though teasing her beloved children. "I've seen it."

"And if you force the issue," Ailpein said, "we'll help." He snapped his fingers, and an onyx wand appeared in his hand.

The rest of the crowd dispersed. Either they weren't angry enough to dare the power of three mages, or the Blackhammers decided that if their own wonder-workers supported Uschi, maybe they should relent. They'd long known and respected Gulbrand, Bergljot, and Ailpein, and besides, Maarav, their clan lord, had set the warlocks and sorceress in authority over them.

Feeling the tension leave her body, Uschi managed a smile for the dwarves. "Thank you. I hope I deserve your help. Meaning, I hope I was right to keep everyone from attacking Amora." And to balk at striking down the enchantress herself.

Gulbrand shrugged.

"Better the enchantress should run away," Bergljot said, "than that she should rain death on us all. I'm not sure even we three working together could have stopped her once she got going, and we only just arrived here."

"I agree with that." Uschi realized the Brightblade was still burning like a torch, extinguished the hissing flame by willing it, and slid the broadsword back in its scabbard. "Still, I wonder if people were right to accuse her in the first place."

Ailpein cocked his head. "By all accounts, she's ruthless enough to collapse a mine or cause any evil."

"She certainly is," Uschi said. "But she said some other mage could have produced green and yellow light to give the impression she caused the cave-in and addled the minds of the miners to hide the fact she was in the tunnel to save them. Is that possible?" The Valkyrie knew nothing of witchcraft. But it belatedly seemed to her that Amora's claims, coupled as they were with the peculiar circumstances surrounding the disaster, had a certain plausibility. If so, she'd been right not to cut her down. That thought, however, did little to assuage her regret over not taking the enchantress's assertions more seriously before the latter fled. Or over her failure to manage the situation more deftly in general. She suspected Heimdall would have done a better job.

Gulbrand fingered one of the iron trinkets knotted in his dye-streaked beard. "That mage would also have had to keep his eye on her to trigger the collapse when she'd be sure to notice it. Then he would have either had to trust her to go and help or given an accomplished sorceress a psychic push without her realizing. It's all a lot. Still, for a powerful sorcerer who made preparations in advance, theoretically possible."

"Here's what I keep coming back to," Uschi said. "Apart from an alliance with the frost giants, which may well be long over and done with, I don't see what motive Amora would have for collapsing the tunnel. Or poisoning Orien the cyclops, if we're trying to hang that on her as well."

"What discernible motive does anyone have?" Ailpein asked.

Uschi sighed. "That's part of the problem. We don't know. But I also wonder why, if Amora was up to mischief, she'd collapse the tunnel in a way that instantly brought suspicion down on her head. Back when she was conspiring with the Jotuns, she had more guile. Heimdall and Sif had to penetrate her secret lair in Skrymir's Tower of Sorcery to find out what she'd done."

"So where does that leave us?" Ailpein asked. Like Uschi, he no longer had an immediate use for the weapon in his hand. He tossed the onyx wand into the air and it disappeared like a bubble popping, returning to wherever he kept it when not in use.

Uschi shook her head. "I don't know. Maybe with Amora gone, our troubles are over. But I'd feel more confident if it was possible to examine all the magic at play in the camp and the area around it. We might spot the enchantress if she's still lurking about. Or, if there truly is another powerful mage working against us as she suggested, we might catch him."

Gulbrand grunted. "That's asking a great deal. You have plenty of warlocks and witches hereabouts. Ulbrecht. The Asgardian sorcerers he brought with him. We three. The stranger gods and the cyclopes, and their magic is unfamiliar to us. Then there are the giant underground runes, ablaze with power because we've been working hard to make them so."

Uschi sighed. "So you can't do it. I understand."

"I didn't say that," Gulbrand growled. "We'll think about the problem and let you know."

TEN

THE UNDERWORLD:
THREE DAYS UNTIL BIFROST

"We did keep watch on the black horses and the chariot," Kamorr said, continuing his story, "and things happened as you said they would. In time, Lord Pluto flew away to the south, and once he was gone, you saddled your Valkyrie horse." The Blackhammer paused for a heartbeat. "What's his name again?"

Heimdall sighed. Kamorr had taken to interrupting his narrative periodically with these unexpected questions. Apparently, he had some notion that if he took his companion by surprise, it might shake something loose in his memory, but so far, the tactic hadn't worked.

"I wish I could tell you," Heimdall said.

"Golden Mane," Kamorr said, as if he'd only just recalled. "That's the name. Because he's got one, and golden eyes, too, though the rest of him is black. As far as I know, you and your sister Sif are the only people who aren't Valkyries ever to be given mounts from the herd. As rewards for your service to Asgard during the war with the frost giants."

Heimdall grimaced. "I seem to have been an impressive fellow before my mind was broken."

"You were," Kamorr said. "I mean, you *are*! It will all come back to you, I know. Anyway, when Golden Mane was ready, you tried again to talk me out of coming with you, but I'd have none of it. So off we–"

Heimdall raised his hand for silence. Though still attending to the Blackhammer's tale, he'd also sharpened his hearing to monitor the ambient sounds of the abyss – wailing, shrieking, clinking chains, crackling fire – for signs that pursuit was drawing nigh. He was doing it periodically, and with practice, the use of the gifts of Mimir at least had become habitual and easy.

At the moment, he heard a complicated thudding like the sound of several enormous horses if they were all galloping along together. It wasn't the first time he'd caught it, but now it seemed louder and closer.

He peered in the direction of the sound, and a chance thinning of the underworld's veils of drifting malodorous smoke afforded him a relatively clear look at one of the giants he regarded as the most fearsome searchers. Moles and dangling string warts covered its naked hide, its black eyes seemed all pupil, and the fanged jaws gnashed and foamed. Though the head was small in proportion to the rest of it, its jaws were yet large enough to bite and snap prey Heimdall's size to bits. Bent far forward, the creature was loping along using its dozen long arms as well as its legs, a way of moving that made its quarry think of a colossal spider.

"It's one of the giants," he told Kamorr, "and it's coming straight at us. It must have picked up our scent or tracked us somehow."

"But we've finally made it almost to the edge of the pit and a path," the dwarf replied. "Maybe, once we're high enough, it won't be able to follow. The trail could be too steep and narrow. Or maybe it just never leaves the pit."

Kamorr was right. After days of hiding, dodging, and backtracking, it might at last be possible to escape this ghastly place. Heimdall ran his gaze up the narrow zigzag trail. At the top, the wrinkled, hook-nosed face of a haglike woman looked down over the edge of the abyss. Only for an instant, though, and then she withdrew beyond his view.

Heimdall didn't know if she was guarding the way up or had even spotted him if she was. Given the distance and the ambient gloom, it was reasonable to doubt the latter, and in any case, a normal-sized woman seemed a less formidable adversary than the giant rapidly approaching. Moreover, Kamorr insisted time was running out to save an entire world, and at long last the two of them had a real chance to climb out of the abyss.

Unfortunately, since receiving his claw wounds, presently wrapped in their bloody improvised bandages, the dwarf had been moving stiffly, occasionally grunting and hissing through gritted teeth, and taking more frequent rests. "Can you run to the foot of the trail?" Heimdall asked. "And keep on running until we're beyond the giant's reach?"

Kamorr grinned, a fierce flash of teeth inside his beard. "Try me."

Abandoning any attempt at stealth, they dashed toward the

cliff face. Heimdall was ready to pick up the Blackhammer and carry him if the latter's strength gave out, ready, too, to turn and fight if such an expedient resulted in their many-handed pursuer catching up to them. He suspected Kamorr would urge him to keep running and save himself, but even with the life of a world apparently at stake, Heimdall realized it just wasn't in him to forsake a friend who'd risked everything to rescue him.

To his relief, Kamorr's strength didn't give out. Somehow, despite his short legs and the fresh blood seeping through the bandaging, the dwarf kept pace with him. Still, the giant was catching up. They reached the foot of the switchback path barely ahead of the creature and scrambled frantically upward. The giant glared at its prey but didn't follow them up the path. When Heimdall was satisfied that it wasn't going to, he and Kamorr slowed down. They wanted to catch their breath and clambering at maximum speed up the treacherous ascent posed a danger in and of itself.

Even proceeding more slowly, the dangers of the climb were in fact considerable. The trail was so steep and narrow that in places it was best to press one's back to the cliff face and sidle along. In other spots, the path sloped down from the stony wall to the drop beside it or was wont to crumble beneath a climber's feet. Still, Heimdall felt safer than he had when he feared the giant was about to catch up with them.

That peril, at least, appeared to be behind them. Their pursuer was still glaring up after them but taking no other action. Kamorr controlled his wheezing long enough to stick his head out over the drop and hawk a gob of spit down into their pursuer's upturned face.

Heimdall grinned at the gesture and then urged his

companion to climb a little higher before taking a rest. The relative smallness of the giant's head, its twitching features and foaming mouth, gave the appearance of rabid imbecility, but the creature might possess sufficient wit to start throwing rocks.

It didn't, though, nor did the crone reappear for another look down into the pit. When they were halfway up the trail, at a point where one could sit without constant fear of slipping over the edge, Kamorr slumped against the wall and then flopped down on his rump. "I think I will take that rest," he gasped, "just for a moment."

"Take as much time as you need," Heimdall said. Invoking his heightened senses, he once again checked the top of the ascent.

He didn't see anything. The hag was still up there, though, her breath hissing in and out of her lungs and her heart thumping. Well, one sentry, if in fact that's what she was, shouldn't be impossible to overcome. She almost certainly had to be less formidable than the giant or the cat-goat-snake beast he and Kamorr had already bested. It was a reassuring thought until he caught the rustle of feathery wings.

Heimdall had already noticed that a bit of the light ameliorating the darkness of the pit shone down from high overhead. The source of that illumination was a pearly phosphorescent mist, cleaner looking than the malodorous smoke below but equally capable of blocking sight. Consequently, he didn't get a clear look at the creatures that came soaring and circling overhead. They were mere winged shadows in the fog.

The hag at the top of the trail gave a shrill, harsh cry, and the newcomers answered in kind. Then came the snap of another pair of wings as she rose to join her sisters. Whatever manner of creature the others were, she was too.

Wincing, Kamorr clambered to his feet. "I can't see what you're seeing," he said, "but judging from the look on your face, rest time's over."

"I'm afraid so." Heimdall drew his sword. The Blackhammer picked up a stone in either hand.

The creatures flew lower, and when they burst through the luminous mists overhead, Heimdall could finally see them clearly. There were eight altogether. Each possessed the head of some spiteful if not demented crone and a pair of spindly human arms as well. The fingers, however, bore long claws, and below the head and arms, any semblance of humanity warped into the form of a vulture, the pinions clothed in gray-black plumage and the talons on the feet a larger counterpart to those on the hands.

Heimdall had gleaned from what Kamorr had told him that when his memory was intact, he'd been quite the slayer of horrors. Moreover, the fights he'd already won at the bottom of the pit had bolstered his confidence a little. Still, he wondered if he'd prove equal to this new challenge.

"Do you have any pointers?" he asked.

"No," Kamorr replied. "Whatever those things are, we don't have them where we come from."

"Well, then," Heimdall said, trying to sound unconcerned, "we'll just have to learn as we go along." He hoped that if he looked and sounded brave on the outside, it would help him feel the same way on the inside.

Even at a distance, the reek of the vulture-women was strong and vile enough to roil Heimdall's stomach. Their eyes were milky as though clouded by cataracts, and matter had seeped from them to congeal on the cheeks beneath. Still, the manner in which, circling and shrieking to one another, they oriented on the fugitives showed they could see perfectly well.

Kamorr threw his first stone, and one of the nearer ones dodged it. A flick of her wings lifted her just high enough for the missile to fly harmlessly by underneath her.

More cries rasped back and forth. Then the sisters hurtled down, driving at the duo on the trail like a cloudburst streaking at the ground.

Heimdall felt a jolt of fear. A part of him, however, the part that had awakened when he faced the cat-goat-snake thing, remained cool and calculating, and in that final moment, it told him that all eight vulture-women couldn't attack at once. With the scarp at his back, there wasn't room. He simply had to deal with the creatures one or two at a time as they came within reach of his sword.

He raised his point to impale the lead vulture-hag when she plunged down at him, but she veered in flight and avoided the blade. He resisted the impulse to pivot and slash as she dived past him and away. She wouldn't be a threat until she rose and circled to come at him again. Her sisters, however, were swooping at him right now.

He cut furiously as they did, and for the most part they, too, broke off their initial attacks to avoid injury. One, however, succeeded in coming close enough to snatch at his head. He ducked, and the talons merely gashed his scalp instead of tearing his face off. He struck back, and the sword caught the creature's feathered torso. It shrieked, pulled itself off the blade – which came away fouled with black ichor – and plummeted down the cliff face and out of sight. Heimdall couldn't tell if he'd hurt it badly enough to take it out of the fight.

Nor did he get the chance to glance down and see. A weight slammed onto his back and talons dug into his shoulders. He was trying to fight with his back to the wall but striking at the attackers necessitated some stepping and turning, and he must have provided just enough room for one of his foes to take him from behind. As it turned out, a vulture-woman wasn't as heavy as a person of the same size would be, but momentum made up for that. It sent him stumbling toward the edge of the drop-off.

A shout rang out, one of the cries Kamorr was wont to roar when making a hand-to-hand attack. Facing the other way as he was, Heimdall had no way of knowing exactly what his companion had done, but, wings flapping, the creature on his back let go of him and returned to the air.

It seemed unlikely to matter, though. Balance lost, Heimdall was already tottering on the edge of the trail. He started to topple into space, to fall toward the waiting dozen-armed giant and all the fires, smoke, and gloom of the pit. He felt a jolt of fear, and then hands gripped his sword belt from behind and yanked him backward.

All the vulture-crones had swooped on past and would have to rise and circle to renew the attack. There was time enough for him to look around at Kamorr and say, "Thank you."

The dwarf was breathing hard, but still looked game to fight. "I told you I'd repay you for saving me from the mob."

Heimdall shook his head. "I still don't remember that, but I am sure that by now, the debt's on the other side."

Kamorr stooped to pick up another pair of rocks. "We can talk about it if we make it out of this."

As Heimdall looked out at the vulture-women, still clamoring back and forth to one another, he realized he and his friend might not. There were only seven winged creatures in the air now. His sword, or maybe a thrown stone or the Blackhammer's hand-to-hand attack, had taken one out of the battle. But the rest were still manifestly intent on fighting, and both fugitives were wounded.

The trail, moreover, made a poor battleground. He and Kamorr had chosen one of the wider spots at which to stop and rest, but it was still narrow enough that a person couldn't scramble about without risking a tumble over the edge. And when Heimdall's body, if not his mind, remembered how to fight, it had become clear that footwork – advances, retreats, circling, sidesteps – was as much a part of his manner of swordplay as bladework. He judged Kamorr's style of empty-handed combat was much the same.

Deprived of nearly all ability to maneuver, Heimdall could only cut and thrust as the vulture-crones swooped down and crowded around him again and again. Kamorr threw rocks and punched and kicked when an unwary adversary came within reach.

The fugitives managed to fend off their assailants and escape further injury a while longer. But they didn't succeed in eliminating any more of the vulture-women. There were still seven of the vile-smelling creatures in the fight, all as indefatigable and intent on their prey as ever.

Though neither side had yet succeeded in defeating the other, Heimdall felt a cold, growing fear he and Kamorr wouldn't emerge from the battle alive and free. Even if they did ultimately succeed in killing or routing all the vulture-crones, surely, if they were pinned down here much longer, the commotion would draw additional pursuers.

Panting, wiping away some of the blood from his gashed scalp that threatened to flow down into his eyes and blind him, he didn't see how the situation could get much worse. But then it did.

Throughout the battle, the twelve-armed giant had lingered at the foot of the cliff peering upward. Now it decided to enter the fray. Either it had always been the plan to trap the fugitives between attacks from two sources, or else watching the combat whetted the creature's bloodlust until it had no choice but to join in. Heimdall deemed the latter possibility more likely, not that it was apt to matter.

He'd reckoned the trail too narrow and steep to accommodate the giant, and in that, at least, the brute proved him correct. Ignoring the path, it sought to scale the cliff face itself. With its dozen arms working, it once again resembled a colossal spider making its way upward.

The giant didn't skitter up with the ease of a spider, though. It moved cautiously, as though it had seldom, if ever, climbed before. Periodically, its toes slipped off a narrow foothold, or its weight broke away a lump of rock to which it sought to cling. Then its body lurched downward, but with multiple hands gripping handholds, it never dropped back to the foot of the cliff.

"Fall, you bastard," Kamorr growled. "Fall!"

"Look up," Heimdall said, taking a fresh grip on the hilt of his sword. "The vulture-women are coming around again." So they were, and if he and the dwarf didn't pay attention, it wouldn't matter what the giant did when it finally dragged itself high enough.

The pair repelled another swooping assault, another frenzy of ear-splitting shrieks, ripping talons, and dark, lashing wings. Afterward, the dwarf looked over the edge to check on the giant's progress. Despite its caution and the occasional near-fall, it was higher. Closer. Kamorr cast about, clearly seeking something to drop in the upturned slavering face, but he'd already thrown all the stones in the immediate vicinity, not that such small missiles were likely to stop such a huge creature anyway.

But it occurred to Heimdall that they did still have something else to drop, and it might provide the answer to both aspects of their twofold problem. He doubted he'd survive the tactic, but maybe Kamorr would.

"Hang back," he told the Blackhammer. "Fight only if you have to protect yourself and run for the top of the trail if you get a chance. With luck, at least some of the vulture-women will stay focused on me."

"But–" Kamorr began.

"Please, do it!"

An instant later, the first of the vulture-hags was on Heimdall again, and it would have been death to look away from the swooping attackers to see if Kamorr had heeded him. This time, bellowing his defiance, he fought more aggressively than before, assailing the winged creatures as though nothing mattered but that his sword stroke should kill its target even if other foes struck him down the moment after. He lunged and sprang as best he could on the steep trail as though he no longer cared about blundering off the edge either.

Luck was with him. Despite his maneuvering, he didn't fall over the drop, and his reckless onslaught took the vulture-hags by surprise. He evaded slashing, scrabbling talons, and his sword split a gray-haired, milky-eyed head clear down to the nose. The creature's body flopped onto the path, and as he yanked the blade free, he was certain that this one foe wasn't just wounded but dead.

The other six sisters knew it too. Consternation made them draw back, breaking apart the screaming, reeking cloud of lashing dark wings and scrabbling claws that had surrounded him. Only for a moment, though, and then shock and wariness gave way to fury. Crying to one another, they came at him once more.

The drop-off was only a step away. Heimdall peered over the edge and verified that the ascending giant was pretty much where he'd estimated it would be. Then he leaped into space. Kamorr shouted to deter him, but by then he was already plummeting.

He landed hard on the giant's rounded shoulder, struggled to remain there, and rolled off anyway. Now, frightened, he was tumbling down its chest and had only one chance and one moment to save himself from smashing to the ground far below. He let go of the sword – even now, he hated to relinquish his only weapon but needed both hands to clutch at something, anything, to arrest his fall – and managed to grab one of the long brown string warts sprouting from the creature's hide. The growth was like a rope to someone his size, and to his relief, the jolt as it took his weight didn't tear it loose.

Heimdall was now helpless, however, with no way to resist if the giant opted to pluck him loose and crush him in one of its hands, chew him up in those jagged-toothed, drooling jaws, or simply drop him to his death. As it surely would have done, if not for the surviving vulture-women diving down in wild pursuit of the swordsman who'd slain their sister.

From the giant's general aspect, Heimdall had guessed it was little better than an animal, a brute driven by bloodlust and instinct. Startled, it reacted that way now, and half a dozen vulture-hags suddenly swooping close to its face were as unbearable as a swarm of flies would have been to a person Heimdall's size. Whereas the mite presently hanging from its chest was a lesser annoyance to be dealt with afterward.

The giant released all but one of its handholds, the better to flail at the vulture-hags. A swat pounded one to a bag of shattered bones and flung her tumbling and falling. Another blow from a different hand smashed one of the sisters against the cliff face, where the wet, flattened remains stuck for an instant before slipping free. Huge fingers grabbed a third winged creature out of the air and squeezed. Inky ichor leaked from between the digits.

Then, with a *crack*, the lump of stone that was the giant's sole remaining handhold broke away from the scarp. It hadn't been strong enough to support the creature's entire weight, nor, intent on killing the vulture women, had the twelve-armed brute paid much attention to its balance or the slight, rounded extrusions of rock that were its toeholds. It roared as it toppled outward.

When the giant's body tilted back, Heimdall managed to plant his feet against its chest. In the moment before the brute dropped away, he leaped at the cliff face, and, reaching it, clutched for handholds. He found a pair and clung there, gasping for breath.

Gasping, and waiting for the three remaining vulture-hags to claw his flesh to rags or jerk him from his perch to plunge after the giant. Clinging precariously as he was, he could do nothing to prevent it.

They didn't assail him again, though, and when he twisted his head around, they were winging away across the pit. Evidently the losses they'd taken had finally persuaded the survivors to withdraw. Maybe they didn't comprehend that Heimdall's situation was now such that they could easily have disposed of him. At any rate, he and Kamorr had won another battle, although in retrospect, he felt less like a cunning tactician than a lucky one.

Lucky or not, he needed to get off the cliff face before his strength ran out. He hauled himself upward toward the nearest stretch of the ascending trail. The sight of Mimir enabled him to distinguish solid outcroppings from those that might crumble upon taking his weight, and to his relief, he discovered climbing was like swordplay. He'd apparently learned at some point, and his body remembered his training even if his mind didn't.

Despite his instructions, Kamorr had descended partway down the path to find him and helped him crawl onto it. That didn't surprise him. "I thought for sure you were dead," said the dwarf.

"So did I," Heimdall panted. "But I hoped I was giving you a chance."

"How in the name of forge and fire did you even think to do it?"

Heimdall shrugged. "It just came to me."

"It was mad." Kamorr hesitated, his dark eyes narrowing.

"Or maybe not. You're a giant-slayer, after all. You've killed dozens over the years."

Heimdall sighed. "You should have told me that before I jumped. It might have felt less suicidal."

For a moment, he'd been happy about his unlikely victory, but satisfaction soured into frustration as he once more contemplated the contrast between the master warrior Kamorr insisted he'd once been and the shrunken fool remaining. The old Heimdall – curse him! – would probably have been too canny to ever end up trapped between monstrosities on the trail. And if it had somehow happened to that paragon, he would have devised a tactic that didn't depend on blind, stupid luck to see him through.

Kamorr frowned at whatever he saw in Heimdall's expression. "What's wrong now?"

Heimdall tried to shake off the gloom that had overtaken him. It might be justified, but it wasn't helping, and his friend deserved better of him. "Nothing. I was just thinking we should finish the trek to the top before the vulture-women come back with reinforcements, or something else happens. I mean, if you're able."

"I could use a little more rest," Kamorr replied. "By the looks of it, you could too. But after that, I'll be ready."

The Blackhammer proved as good as his word, although his pale, sweaty face, stiff, hobbling gait, and occasional grunt of pain or effort gave Heimdall reason for concern. They reached the top of the trail without anyone or anything else trying to stop them, whereupon he used the gifts of Mimir to survey the country surrounding the abyss.

He'd previously marked the pale, luminous mists that

drifted and billowed here. Now he could tell that some of the clouds floated at ground level. They blocked sight like the smoke below and kept him from taking in every aspect of the geography. What he could observe, however, made this portion of the immense cavern seem a pleasanter place than the pit he and Kamorr had just escaped. Albeit not every aspect of it was cheerful.

In one direction, he could make out a cluster of buildings. Even the least of them was palatial, with stepped bases and long lines of columns topped with entablatures and pediments. The builders, however, had fashioned them out of a stone so dark that even up close, normal eyes could scarcely have made out the figures in the ornamental friezes.

In the opposite direction, about as far from the grim palaces as it was possible to get, was an area where the mists were scarcer but glowed brighter, the light revealing buildings almost as grand as the dark palaces but made of pale marble. Nearby, youthful, happy-looking people were strolling, talking, feasting on fruit from the orchards that dotted the land, or playing at wrestling, running races, and throwing the javelin and discus.

In the fugitives' immediate vicinity, however, in the fields that ringed the ragged mouth of the abyss, the light was dimmer, the atmosphere somber despite the long clusters of white, pink, and yellow flowers growing in abundance. Here, the inhabitants wandered aimlessly, restlessly, their faces empty of expression.

Heimdall smiled a crooked smile. "I still don't remember, but I have a hunch the way out is not toward the happy people and the white houses."

"Your instincts are good," Kamorr replied. "It's in the opposite direction."

"And me without a sword, and people still hunting us, I imagine. Still, now that we're out of the pit, maybe the worst is behind us."

The Blackhammer snorted. "You truly don't remember anything, do you? But when you hear the next bit of the story – *our* story – you'll understand. I'll tell it as we make our way along."

ELEVEN
THE DESCENT, PART ONE

Golden Mane galloped a few paces, unfurled and lashed his black-feathered pinions, and climbed into the air. Snow-white Avalanche looked on with what Heimdall could readily believe was envy, and common horses whinnied as if to express a wish that the fence of uprights and stacked, trimmed, horizontal branches comprising the pen were no impediment for them, either.

If Heimdall sharpened his hearing, he could tell that a couple of the karls who tended the animals and other folk who'd noticed his ascent were exclaiming as well. They were surprised if not dismayed to see the warrior who bore ultimate responsibility for the safety of Ulbrecht's great work and the workers involved making an unexpected departure.

"Back before you know it," he murmured, and then said in a louder voice, "Are you all right back there?"

"Fine," Kamorr replied, seated just behind him. "This is fun. Makes me wish I had a winged stallion of my own. Do you see

Pluto's chariot?" To his eyes, the death god and his conveyance were no doubt lost in drifting white clouds and blue sky.

"Yes," Heimdall said, "I've got him." He urged Golden Mane higher and into the south on the stranger deity's trail.

For the moment, his concern was to keep Pluto in sight while avoiding detection himself. The vision of Mimir notwithstanding, he could still lose his quarry behind a cloud, and, moreover, Uschi had been correct: He didn't know what the god could perceive and what he couldn't. He was relying on guesswork to tell him how much distance to leave between the two of them while also trying to think of a convincing excuse for following if Pluto should turn his chariot around and accost him.

He never hit on one he believed would satisfy the deity, but fortunately never had to put the matter to the test. They flew far enough into the south that the sun shone warmer, and trees and plants unfamiliar to an Asgardian warrior appeared in the forests and river valleys. Despite the importance of the task at hand, Heimdall's curiosity compelled him to scrutinize them more closely at moments when he deemed it safe to do so.

The blue waters of an inland sea appeared before the deity in the chariot and those who followed him, and Pluto urged his team hurtling down a large peninsula that jutted out into it. Heimdall continued his pursuit.

When they'd flown nearly the length of the landmass below, Pluto guided his chariot down toward a rocky cape. Heimdall lost sight of the black horses, the dark two-wheeled vehicle they were pulling, and the burly figure in armor holding the reins in one hand and a whip in the other when they all passed behind a mountain. He urged Golden Mane onward until the far side of the peak came into view. There was no sign of Pluto, but to his relief, it was easy enough to infer where the stranger deity had gone.

A cave opened near the base of the mountain, and gray-white vapor swirled around it. For an instant, Heimdall imagined the mist was billowing forth from underground, but then he discerned the truth was otherwise. Entities were coming to the mouth of the passage. As they approached, they were invisible even to his sight, but upon arrival, they gradually materialized. First, they became vague transparent figures, and the vapor was a byproduct of this stage of their transformation. They continued to take on substance and definition until they looked just like living men, women, and children, at which point they walked into the mouth of the cavern. Heimdall watched the process with a mixture of wonder and wariness.

"Well," Kamorr said, and for once, Heimdall could hear the uneasiness the Blackhammer sought to hide, "I think we found the strangers' realm of the dead. Those are ghosts passing in."

"I think so too," Heimdall replied, although the process was unlike what happened to the souls of newly dead worshippers of Odin and his kin. It was the most disquieting sign so far that he and Kamorr were trespassing on territory that was altogether strange to them.

"So do we just fly on into the cave over their heads?" the Blackhammer asked.

Heimdall was glad his companion had focused on practicalities. It helped him shake off both his marveling and his misgivings to do the same. "I'd rather not. Pluto doesn't strike me as a fellow who wouldn't bother posting guards, and even if there aren't any, surely someone would notice two odd-looking intruders on a winged stallion."

"What do we do, then?"

"To me, the phantoms look like sleepwalkers, oblivious to everything except going where they're supposed to. What's more, once they put on substance, they look just as they did when alive. If we don the same kind of clothing they're wearing, what's to stop us from joining the procession and just walking in like they are? There are men of Midgard who stand no taller than one of your folk."

"Good," Kamorr said. "Even if you could convince me to shave my beard, I'm not sure I'd make for a particularly convincing human child. Where do we get the right kind of tunics, sandals, and whatever?"

"I noticed a little town on the cape, and the town has a marketplace. There'll be someone to sell us what we need."

Kamorr grunted. "Do you think the people there know they live so close to the entrance to the land of the dead?"

"You'd think someone would have noticed. The All-Father's mortal followers wouldn't be comfortable with it, but these are different people with different beliefs, and maybe they are. Anyway, for our purposes, it doesn't matter."

"Fair enough, but here's something that does. Can we make ourselves understood well enough to make our purchases?"

Heimdall smiled. "Leave that to me. One advantage of being an Asgardian is that we possess the Allspeak."

Matters in the town proceeded smoothly enough. At first, the unexpected arrival of two such peculiar-looking strangers, one a tall man in armor with a greatsword hanging down his back, occasioned alarm, but once Heimdall made their peaceful intentions known and demonstrated he and Kamorr could pay well for what they needed, the marketplace became more welcoming, with several eager merchants competing for their custom. The coinage of Asgard was unfamiliar to them, but silver was silver.

It wasn't until, clad in his new white linen tunic, belted and secured at the covered shoulder with a bronze clasp, and concealing his gear and Golden Mane's tack in the forest near the entrance to the underworld that Heimdall truly felt a pang of trepidation. He stood looking at the scabbarded two-handed blade in his grip, reluctant for that moment to lay it down in the patch of thick brush with the Gjallarhorn and everything else.

As was often the case, Kamorr sensed something of what he was feeling. "Afraid it won't be here when we come back?"

"No," Heimdall said, "not that. I pity the thief who tries to make off with it while Golden Mane is in the area looking after it. It's that I hate to go in unarmed, especially given that Hofund can change the bearer's appearance. That means it could hide the fact that I have it. But no. We don't know how long we'll be in Pluto's kingdom, and using the blade takes a toll on a person's strength. I don't want to be wandering around the cave, tire, and have Hofund appear when somebody's looking. None of the true dead are going in with weapons, and if I'm seen with one, it's all too likely to rouse suspicion, especially if it suddenly pops out of nowhere."

"Makes sense." The Blackhammer grinned. "Besides, you've got me to look after you, and I don't need a piece of cutlery to deal with a foe. There is one thing that worries me, though."

Heimdall smiled a crooked smile. "Only one?"

Kamorr grinned back. "One that I'll mention now. All the

dead we saw going in were human. Are you sure that's where a cyclops would go when he died?"

"Honestly, no. But when I suggested that Orien would come to his domain, Pluto didn't deny it. My guess is that there are fewer cyclopes in this world than humans, thus fewer dying on any given day, and that's why we didn't see any going in. If Orien is there, it could work to our advantage. Once we enter the underworld, it might be easier to spot a giant than it would be to find any other soul. And maybe there'll be someone we can ask where the cyclopes are."

Kamorr nodded. "Makes sense. Let's get to it then."

Heimdall rubbed Golden Mane's neck and shoulder and told the stallion to wait for him. He and Kamorr then made their way to the mouth of the cavern, where the scene remained essentially unchanged. The dead coalesced from nothingness to phantoms and swirls of mist to tangibility, then proceeded into the depths.

"We can't do what they're doing," Kamorr whispered. "We're already solid."

"They won't notice," Heimdall replied. "They only have eyes for the path they're about to take." He hoped. It certainly appeared to him that the dead were essentially oblivious to everything except their own entry into the underworld, but the only way to be certain was to put the notion to the test.

As it turned out, he was right. None of the silent spirits gave him or Kamorr a second glance as the two of them tramped toward the cavern mouth with everyone else. Heimdall felt grateful these ghosts were nothing like the draugr, the predatory undead that had once threatened Vanaheim.

Veins of greenish rock shed a sickly phosphorescence to

light the way down. Periodically, the path led past a niche in the wall, each containing an apparition that, Heimdall came to realize, embodied some terror or misery of mortal existence, misfortunes and horrors the righteous dead were presumably leaving behind. Here was Disease, covered in pustules and seeping, gangrenous flesh; here, War, sword red with gore from point to hilt and a trampled corpse beneath its sandaled feet; and here, Fear, shaking and weeping, cowering on its knees at the back of its alcove.

Some of the apparitions were disturbing enough that, had Heimdall encountered them without warning, he might have recoiled in alarm, raised his hands to defend himself, and so given himself away. But he'd noticed the dead trudging along ahead of him passed the niches with sometimes a wince or a shudder but nothing more; had observed, too, that nothing actually sprang out to attack them. He whispered to Kamorr to do as the ghosts were doing, and they too passed without harm.

Eventually, the tunnel opened out into a cavern so gigantic Heimdall suspected he wasn't really in Midgard anymore, at least not entirely. There existed, he knew, so-called "pocket realms," smaller satellite worlds in addition to the primary ones, sometimes occurring naturally and sometimes created by some powerful being. This was likely one such. Evidently, like the Nine Realms, Pluto's reality had them too.

Still maintaining their silence and haphazard queue, the newly dead were descending a slope toward a river and waiting for a ferryman to row them across in a long narrow boat with a high prow and stern. The ferryman himself was tall, his bare limbs knotted with muscle, and dressed in a ragged, grease-stained, rust-colored tunic. He had the face of some bitter old man, his white hair and beard shaggy and unkempt, his dark eyes glaring as though in resentment of the spirits he carried over the river or the endless labor their passage required.

In the field on the other side of the river stood a colossal three-headed hound with bristling red fur and yellow eyes. Heimdall had faced his share of huge foes in his time. Of necessity, he'd even played a game of hnefatafl with the dragon Nidhogg, with his life and his sister's forfeit if he lost. The triple-headed beast wasn't *that* big, but still plenty big enough to daunt even a warrior who'd faced King Skrymir and the Jotun army in his time.

Headed for a cluster of imposing black buildings, the dead who'd crossed the river were marching past the three-headed hound without much concern, and the gigantic creature wasn't bothering them. Still, Heimdall found that only partly reassuring. Who was to say that the hound couldn't smell the difference between the spirits who actually belonged in this place and interlopers like Kamorr and himself?

"I don't like the look of the dog either," the Blackhammer whispered, "but we've got a more immediate problem. Take another look at the ferryman now that he's taking on more passengers."

Heimdall did. The boat had returned to the near shore, and the spirits in the front of the queue were climbing aboard and seating themselves on the benches. Before the ferryman permitted each to do so, however, he held out a callused hand for payment, whereupon the dead person opened his or her mouth, took out the small copper or bronze coin inside, and handed it over. Maybe the need to carry the coin was as responsible for the ghosts' silence as their more or less somnambulistic state.

Heimdall's new belt had a small pouch attached to it, and reasoning that even in a kingdom of the dead there might be someone to bribe, he'd stowed a few of his remaining Asgardian coins inside. He didn't know if they'd pass muster, though. As they were silver when the true dead were using copper or bronze, the difference should be readily apparent even if the ferryman was a dullard.

Well, he could think of no better plan than to try to use the coins graven with an image of two wolves on one face and a pair of ravens on the other and see what happened. Trying to be surreptitious about it, he opened the pouch, extracted two of the silver pennies, and dangled his hand behind him. Kamorr took one of the coins, and Heimdall slipped the other under his tongue. If any of the nearest dead even noticed what had just happened, they didn't see fit to react.

After that, Heimdall's anxiety made it seem to take forever to reach the front of the queue, and then a second eternity for the ferryman to row his now-empty craft back to the shore on which the next batch of passengers stood waiting. The Asgardian sought to control his breathing, to slow his heartbeat and make his face as expressionless as that of any of the dead.

When it was his turn to proffer his coin, the ferryman grunted, scowled, held it close to his eyes, and considered it for several moments. Straining to mask his growing fear that the ploy was about to fail, Heimdall wondered if there was any hope of turning tail and making it back up the tunnel alive. Then, however, the oarsman thrust the silver round into a bag hanging from his own belt and made an impatient jabbing gesture for the Asgardian to board. Next it was Kamorr's turn, and the ferryman accepted his offering with no hesitation at all.

On the far side of the river, the dead made their way across the misty field where the gigantic triple-headed hound regarded them with little interest. For their part, the spirits chose a course that avoided coming too near the ruddy paws and the furry legs that looked as big as tree trunks, although they still didn't appear overtly frightened as they made their way toward the cluster of dark colonnaded buildings beyond.

But Heimdall remained uncertain the hound would likewise ignore living trespassers, and he was equally worried about what might happen if he and Kamorr continued trudging along with the spirits. He suspected the dead were presenting themselves for some sort of scrutiny, if not from Lord Pluto himself then from deputies apt to prove equally discerning.

"I think it's time to split off on our own," he murmured.

"I don't like this either," Kamorr replied, likewise keeping his voice low. "But won't somebody – or something – notice?"

"The dead still don't seem to care about anything but their own journey," Heimdall said. "The hound isn't interested in us so far, but the closer we get, the more likely it is to smell something funny about us. Even if we get by it, I doubt it would be wise to face what's waiting in those dark temples or whatever they are."

"So, we run," Kamorr said. "No, too likely to make the dog chase us. We *amble* off on our own and start looking for giants."

"That's what I was thinking too."

The dead weren't in a tight group anymore, and for the first few steps, as Kamorr and Heimdall began the process of veering off, the Asgardian could tell himself the deviation from the course everyone else was taking looked random and unremarkable. Before long, though, it surely became apparent to any observer who cared that they were no longer headed for the cluster of black stone buildings.

The ghosts didn't care – they still seemed like sleepwalkers unaware of anything but the vague imperative to reach their destination – but maybe the hound did. With its three heads each capable of peering in a different direction, it was difficult to be sure, but it appeared to orient on the pair of trespassers and then lope in their direction. Heimdall frantically cast about for something, anything he could use to defend himself. Then he heaved a sigh of relief when the beast stopped well shy of them and started digging at the ground, the huge, clawed feet throwing up showers of earth as it sought whatever lay buried. As far as the Asgardian could see, no one in the vicinity of the black buildings had noticed his and Kamorr's departure from the customary path either. Not yet, anyway.

Sweating, heart pounding, making sure he walked at the same unhurried pace as before, he kept moving, and Kamorr moved with him. As they reached the top of a rise, a gentle one but sufficient to conceal them once they descended the other side, he glanced back at the black buildings.

At this point, they'd left the dark stone structures well behind. The drifts of mist partly veiled them, and the luminescence the vapors shed was dim as twilight. Yet even so, the sight of Mimir revealed a black-haired woman in a somber gray gown, a rod or scepter capped with green crystal in her hand. She was looking out from between two pillars, and Heimdall had the odd, unsettling feeling she could see him, or had at least watched as he and Kamorr made their escape.

"What's wrong?" the Blackhammer asked.

"Nothing," Heimdall said, telling himself he must be mistaken. For if a lady of Pluto's court had noticed them wandering off the prescribed path, surely she would have raised the alarm.

"Good. I thought for sure that red beast was going to gobble us up for dinner." Kamorr grinned. "I have to say, it *looks* fearsome, but truly, it's not much of a watchdog."

"Don't be too sure."

The dwarf's eyes narrowed. "Meaning?"

"I've been thinking... maybe its job isn't to control who enters Pluto's domain. Maybe it's to keep people from getting out."

"Then how in Hela's name are we supposed to get out?"

"We'll have it figured out when the time comes." He hoped. "For now, we need to find Orien."

TWELVE

MIDGARD:
THREE DAYS UNTIL BIFROST

Uschi slipped into Gulbrand's burrow under cover of darkness to find that Bergljot and Ailpein had arrived before her. As the senior among the three Blackhammer mages, the irascible dwarf had the largest hole dug out for him, a retreat unconnected to the rest of the tunnel system his folk had excavated in their portion of the camp.

When not performing rituals with Ulbrecht in his tent or down in one of the immense subterranean runes, the trio generally worked their magic here, and accordingly, Gulbrand had given over most of the space to sorcerous paraphernalia. On a stand reposed the skull of some draconic creature, the bone graven with runes and a candle burning inside to set the empty eye sockets aglow. Three battle-axes floated over a stylized representation of Yggdrasil carved on an ivory tabletop, one axe head of flint, one of steel, and one of Uru that gleamed like gold. Blue, red, green, white, and black marbles lay on a section of the floor. Occasionally, they rolled around and changed position. The resulting arrangements seemed random and meaningless to Uschi, but presumably the warlocks could interpret them.

Gulbrand appeared to have brought only a few non-magical effects along from Nidavellir and stuffed them all in one little corner. Surveying the clutter, arcane and otherwise, Uschi sought in vain for something that looked safe to sit on. She supposed she should be grateful that here, in contrast to many another dwarven excavation, the ceiling was high enough that she didn't have to stoop.

Ailpein looked up from reading whatever was written on a piece of parchment. Uschi had the disquieting feeling that the eyes drawn at the top of the page and down the margins were looking back at him. "Glad you could make it," he said.

"I'm not," Gulbrand said. He was prowling around the burrow seemingly conducting an inspection, making sure his preparations and those of the other mages were in order. "There's no reason for her to be here distracting us."

Well, this whole thing *was* my idea, Uschi thought, but she was still wondering if it would be useful to remind him when Bergljot spoke first:

"I'm sure the Valkyrie understands we need to concentrate, don't you, dear?"

"Of course," Uschi said. "I'm just going to stand quietly by the entrance to the chamber and make sure no one else disturbs you while you survey the area for hostile magical forces."

"If you must," Gulbrand said.

Over the course of the next little while, he continued his stalking and peering about, Ailpein pored over a couple more parchments – the runes on one glowed like red-hot coals and sizzled away to nothing as he ran his gaze over them – and Bergljot closed her eyes, folded her hands, and whispered to herself. Uschi couldn't distinguish the words, but the repetitive cadence led her to believe it was the same phrase over and over.

Eventually, Gulbrand said, "Stop dawdling and let's get on with it." Uschi was unable to tell how he knew his colleagues had finished their preparations, but they evidently had. They gathered around the shifting marbles and stared down at them. Their breathing slowed, their eyelids drooped shut, and the Valkyrie inferred they were entering a sort of shared trance that afforded them some manner of arcane sight.

For a time – long enough for any wonder Uschi felt at witnessing an unfamiliar form of sorcery to give way to impatience – nothing more happened except the periodic stirring of the marbles. Then, at last, Bergljot spoke, so faintly that the warrior almost missed it. "I think I see something."

"So do I," Ailpein mumbled just as softly. His tone was dull, inflectionless, but Uschi suddenly felt excited enough for both of them. "We should take a closer look."

As he sipped from a silver cup at the end of another long, taxing day of working complex and demanding high-magic rituals, the lord who'd stolen Ulbrecht's life and identity was happy to relax with a measure of tart white wine and contemplate triumphs and pleasures to come. Battles won, he'd select the most annoying of his captured enemies and subject them to protracted torture. Eventually, of course, the torment would kill them, but that needn't mean an end to the entertainment. He didn't anticipate running out of prisoners anytime soon.

He smiled to imagine cranking the rack. He could almost feel the handle in his fingers, hear the clink of the chains and the frantic pleas of a captive whose body was about to be stretched beyond endurance, when a different phantom sensation, this one unexpected, impinged on his awareness. For the first instant, it was simply a jolt of shocked alarm such as a lesser person might experience on hearing a shout of "Fire!" Then his magical perceptions made more sense of it.

Creating Bifrost according to an altered design while simultaneously concealing that anything was amiss was the most difficult mystical task he'd ever undertaken. Still, he fancied he'd accomplished it. Despite the occasional hiccup, the subordinate mages had done their work as he bade them without questioning the plan itself.

Now, however, matters were otherwise. When he invoked the proper sort of supernatural awareness, he beheld what amounted to a map of the surrounding country with the huge runes blazing with power that shone up through the ground. Superficially, the symbols appeared as the original, murdered Ulbrecht had intended them to be, but if one looked deeply enough, the subtle deviations and subversions became apparent.

And somebody else was on the verge of peering deeply enough. The astral forms of Gulbrand, Bergljot, and Ailpein were converging on one problematic portion of the design like hounds attracted by an interesting scent.

Snarling incantations, Ulbrecht sought to drive them back into their bodies, and, when that failed, to create some illusory phenomenon to distract them from their purpose. That didn't work either. They didn't even notice. Ulbrecht was certain he could have bested any of the Blackhammers in a fair magical battle. But here, it was one against three, and the three had made preparations while the one was improvising on the fly. In consequence, his audacious scheme was about to come apart.

He scrambled out of his chair and grabbed what had appeared to be Ulbrecht's staff, and the rod resumed its true form, a gleaming broadsword, in his hand. He'd whisk himself across camp, enter Gulbrand's tunnel, and butcher the Blackhammer mages while they were absent from their bodies. Even as he rattled off the first phrase of the spell of translocation, he was aware of all the ways in which this desperate throw of the dice could go awry, but he could see no other option.

Then, however, the tent flap stirred, and, just visible as blur and shadow to his eyes despite the helmet of invisibility, Pluto entered the tent. No doubt he'd once again come to complain or seek reassurance that the scheme was still on track, but Ulbrecht didn't even give him time to announce himself. "Come here!" he snapped. "I need you to lend me your mystical strength!"

The death god scowled. "What? No!"

"Do it right now," Ulbrecht said, "or I swear to you, the plan is ruined!"

Pluto hesitated an agonizing moment longer, but then his fellow conspirator's urgency must have persuaded him. Allowing the veil of invisibility to dissolve, he strode across the tent and extended his weapon. "Take hold of the Midnight Axe," he said. "It can channel my power."

Ulbrecht laid his sword on the table, gripped the edge of the adamantine axe head with both hands, and felt the sharp metal cut his palms. He could have taken hold of the weapon in some other way and avoided hurting himself, but his sorcerer's instinct told him that allowing it to taste his blood would establish a stronger connection. He'd tend to the gashes later.

Energy, a god's might, surged up his arms and made him shudder. It had a tang to it unlike any power he'd ever tapped into while traveling about the Nine Realms, but he could still add it to his own. Grinning, he once again hurled maledictions at the astral forms of the three Blackhammers.

Now that the two warlocks and the sorceress appeared to be getting somewhere, it was a temptation to watch them every moment. Uschi, however, was too seasoned a warrior for that, too mindful of her duty as self-appointed sentry to neglect it. She divided her time between looking at the dwarves and peering up the sloping passage that led into the chamber.

She was doing the latter when a small *crack* sounded at her back. Her hand reaching for the Brightblade's hilt, she wheeled but at first saw nothing different. A second snapping noise drew her gaze to the floor.

Gulbrand's colored marbles were rolling about faster and without pause, but the frantic motion didn't save them. One at a time but in quick succession, they were shattering into powder and flecks of glass.

That, Uschi suspected, was bad, but she was no witch and had no idea how to spare the remaining marbles from destruction. She raised her eyes in hope of guidance.

She didn't get it. The dwarves still seemed entranced, and none of them spoke to her. Their aspect was different, though. Gulbrand's fingers crooked, making mystic signs. Bergljot softly hummed – no tune, just two notes shifting monotonously back and forth – and Ailpein's boyish face clenched as though he was lifting something heavy. Uschi had the feeling they were either trying to counter the force destroying the marbles or continue their probing regardless of the breaking of the orbs.

The final marbles burst despite any effort the trio might have been making to save them. Then vague black forms, like shadows cast by nothing and existing in midair, leaped up from the patch of floor containing the rubble. Orienting on the three mages, they raised murky hands whose too-long fingers ended in claws.

Uschi drew the Brightblade, willed its fire to spring forth, and bellowed, "Asgard!" Her intention was either to startle the shadows into faltering or to make them whirl around and face her. She succeeded in the latter, and as they lunged at her with talons outstretched, she met them with a sweep of the burning sword.

The blade passed through the shadows without resistance, and they vanished at its touch. More of the phantoms leaped up to take their place, however, and she had to cut and dodge furiously to prevent any of them from plunging its claws into her body.

The several exchanges required every iota of her attention, and so she didn't realize the Blackhammers had roused from their trance until they used their magic to aid her. Gulbrand snarled, "Kill!" and the three levitating axes flew across the chamber and chopped shadows into nothingness. Bergljot blew out a long breath, and from that exhalation formed a dozen ghostly phosphorescent bats. The luminous flyers swarmed other murky attackers, and they too vanished.

Ailpein distanced himself from the fray and chanted. At the end of the incantation, Uschi didn't actually hear anything, but she had the impression that somewhere, massive doors were booming shut, one after another after another, and once a slash of the Brightblade destroyed a final pair of phantoms, no more sprang up from the floor.

The Valkyrie turned in a circle, peering for other threats. There didn't appear to be any, which didn't necessarily mean there were none when magic was at play. "Are we safe now?" she asked.

"We seem to be," Ailpein panted. Despite his avoidance of anything approximating physical combat, he seemed more winded than the rest of them.

"Thanks to our guardian," Bergljot said, giving Uschi a smile.

"Whose blade would have done nothing if a Blackhammer swordsmith hadn't rekindled its enchantments," Gulbrand growled. Then, to Uschi's surprise, his sour demeanor slipped just long enough for him to give her a wink.

"Well," she said, "it appears the investigation stirred up *something.*"

"Yes," Ailpein said. "There's evil magic somewhere in the vicinity, and its creator doesn't want anyone looking into it."

"So, who is it?" Uschi asked. "Is Amora still lurking nearby?" She'd welcome a second chance to take the enchantress into custody or slay her outright if the dwarves had established her guilt. "Or is it the stranger gods and the cyclopes?" Maybe the delegation had moved on from asking endless questions and slowing the creation of Bifrost to preventing it altogether.

Bergljot sighed. "We can't say. The enemy power drove us away before we could get a good look."

"But you can get one now," Uschi said, "now that you know what to expect."

Ailpein waved a hand at the shattered marbles. "As you can see, our foe broke our tools."

"But we have other tricks," Gulbrand said. "Give us a chance to ponder and we'll try again."

Ulbrecht let go of the Midnight Axe, so breaking his connection to Pluto's godly power. Blood dripped from his gashed hands, and he knew he should close the cuts with the healing ointment stowed away in a trunk. That could wait a moment, though. For now, he wanted to sit down. He walked around his worktable on rubbery legs, flopped down in his chair, picked up the silver cup, and drained what was left of his wine.

"Well," Pluto demanded, "did it work?"

Ulbrecht felt a stirring of contempt, though he made sure it wasn't reflected in his borrowed features or voice. His collaborator might possess the strength of a god, but if he hadn't been able to witness what had just transpired, Pluto's powers of mystical perception were manifestly inferior to his own. Of course, that was for the best.

"Yes," the sorcerer said. "I diverted the Blackhammer mages from discerning what we're up to."

"So they're dead?"

"No." Ulbrecht saw no point in admitting that in the heat of the moment, he'd tried and failed to kill them. "I still need them to help me finish Bifrost." It was true even though he'd briefly lost sight of it.

Pluto frowned. "But… everything is all right now?"

"No," Ulbrecht said. "The dwarves now know for certain

something is wrong. After they've had a chance to rally, they'll surely try again to discover what. Meanwhile, if they communicate what they've already learned, the suspicions festering in camp can only grow worse. It's possible work could even grind to a halt."

The death god raised the Midnight Axe. "You *promised* the plan would work! That's why I poisoned the cyclops and saw to Heimdall's imprisonment! Better you should die here and now than that it should fail, and my brother get wind of my involvement!"

Pluto's attitude was threatening enough that Ulbrecht considered springing up from his seat, grabbing the broadsword he'd set aside to take hold of the battle-axe, and assuming a fighting stance. But no. He might still have use for the death god's power, and he could probably mollify Pluto with persuasive words as he had before. If not, surely his magic would protect him even if he was seated empty-handed.

"The plan won't fail," Ulbrecht said. "We simply have to arrange it so the dwarves see no reason to come sniffing around a second time."

The deity scowled. "And how do we do that?"

"Simple. We give everyone the villain they've suspected all along and a glorious victory over said villain. In the fight, the Asgardians, the dwarves, and your folk will stand together, and afterward, with all suspicion and hard feelings eliminated, the workers will push ahead until Bifrost comes to life. It will only take a couple more days of effort."

THIRTEEN

THE UNDERWORLD:
TWO DAYS UNTIL BIFROST

Kamorr had the feeling the kingdom of the dead had cheated the pink, yellow, and white flowers of their splendor. Under the sun, the colors might have shone brilliantly, but in the perpetual twilight of the gigantic cavern, they were muted and dull.

Had some kindly deity or warlock granted his wish, however, it wouldn't have been for the blooms to receive their due. It would have been for them to grow tall enough to provide cover as he and Heimdall made their way across the fields containing the plants. As it was, only the gentle unevenness of the ground and the drifting veils of luminous mist provided concealment, or at least the hope that he and his companion would be mistaken for two of the dead spirits aimlessly wandering this space.

Or, Kamorr thought, maybe he would have wished for the healing of the claw wounds in his side and the restoration of his vitality. Thanks to the innate hardiness and grit of a dwarf and the discipline he'd acquired training at unarmed combat, he'd thus far managed to dig deep and find strength when he sorely needed it. Heimdall may have imagined he could continue doing so indefinitely, and that was the impression he'd tried to create. Blackhammer pride demanded it, and anyway, the Asgardian had enough to worry about. The truth, however, was otherwise. He wasn't sure how much longer he'd even be able to trudge along.

Just keep putting one foot in front of the other, he told himself, and keep telling the story. Maybe it will still wake Heimdall's memory, and even if it doesn't, it will take your mind off the weakness and the pain.

"So that was our first look at the same fields of flowers we're crossing now," he said.

Heimdall made a sour face. "Crossing and heading toward the same black stone buildings you tell me we were careful to avoid before."

"But not *straight* toward them," Kamorr said. "We can swing wide and still reach the river."

"But even if we manage that, we still have to get by the giant three-headed watchdog I thought was there to keep people from escaping?"

"We're swinging wide around it, too. With luck, it won't pay any attention to us and we'll swim the river. And if it does notice us, well, you were confident you'd think of a way to deal with it when the time came."

"Well, I'm not confident now. I can't imagine how we'd manage it."

Kamorr had done his best to be a staunch comrade, but

with his side aching and his body stiff and weary, his patience finally crumbled. "Well, you'd better think of something! This journey was *your* clever idea, and it's not my fault you lost your memory!"

Heimdall looked taken aback by the outburst and then ashamed. "Of course it isn't, and I'm sorry for whining to someone who's been a true friend through all this. It's just frustrating to have so much of myself locked away!"

Kamorr sighed. He, too, felt ashamed for momentarily losing control. "I understand, and we'll say no more about it. Let's get around the dark temples or whatever they are and take the rest as it comes."

They walked a little further, crossing paths with one of the aimlessly drifting dead who, as usual, didn't acknowledge them. Heimdall scratched the mostly healed scratches on the top of his head, prompting Kamorr to wish dwarves had the recuperative powers of Asgardians. Then his companion lifted his head and peered around at the expanse between them and the cavern ceiling.

The Blackhammer was sure his friend had heard something that was inaudible to him. The Asgardian likely saw it too, now that he was looking. "More vulture-hags?" Kamorr asked.

"No," Heimdall answered. "Something else, but they might mean us harm. Keep your head down and drift along like the spirits hereabouts are doing."

Kamorr did his best to comply even when he too could hear the flutter of approaching wings and shrill voices calling to one another, and it took an effort of will not to peer and see what new menace was drawing near. There might be men of Midgard who stood no taller than a dwarf, but he doubted there were many, and if he looked up, his bearded face was unlikely to pass for that of a child.

Directly overhead now, the flyers called back and forth in their high, grating voices. Kamorr couldn't tell what they were saying, but, no doubt thanks to the Allspeak, Heimdall could. The Asgardian shouted, "Look out!"

Kamorr made haste to do so. Above him, dark wings beating, hovered a creature just as ghastly as a vulture-crone. The wings were membranous and batlike, though, and in place of hair, the thing had writhing, hissing serpents growing from her scalp. Save for those features, however, her form was entirely that of a woman, albeit one snarling with malice and glaring with bloodshot eyes. Instead of claws, she bore a brass-studded whip, which she now lashed at him.

The Blackhammer tried to dodge out of the way, but, as he'd feared, his weakened body finally proved too slow and clumsy. Pain exploded across his back, and he fell to his hands and knees.

He told himself he'd been taught to transcend pain. That he could rise and fight. The whip, however, didn't allow him the chance. It lashed him again and again, agony compounding agony until it beat all the struggle out of him.

He did, however, have just enough strength left to look around, and what he saw through eyes blurred with tears gave him a glimmer of hope.

Heimdall had taken a whip-strike across the chest. A red welt attested to it. He was still on his feet, though, and the fighting skill he'd recovered was enabling him to evade further attacks. So far, so good. It was difficult to see how he was going to strike back at a foe flying out of reach, however, let alone deal with two now that the creature who'd lashed Kamorr into helplessness was winging his way as well.

Fortunately, it turned out that the Asgardian knew how. As his first attacker struck at him again, he didn't just dodge the length of brass-studded braided leather. He grabbed it and yanked so forcefully that his bat-winged assailant bobbed down low enough for him to leap and seize her by the ankle. He then slammed her into the ground as if her body itself was a whip. Bone crunched, and she didn't move thereafter.

Heimdall scrambled to snatch the whip from his fallen adversary's hand before the other winged woman flew into striking distance. He just made it and whirled to face her. They used their weapons at the same time, the lengths of braided leather cracking, but neither found its target.

The flying woman circled, and Heimdall turned to keep her in view. Though she was on the wing and he on the ground, he now had a weapon as long as hers, and that diminished the advantage altitude might otherwise have afforded her. He was ready to grab her lash with his off hand, too, and serve her as he'd served his first attacker. The way he mostly let the hand hang at his side would have concealed his intention from most, but Kamorr had learned to read every subtle shift in a combatant's fighting stance.

For a time, though, as he and his adversary traded cracking whip strokes that all missed, Heimdall wasn't able to use the tactic. The winged woman whirled her lash beyond his reach too quickly. Then a moment came when her aerial maneuvering seemed to catch him off guard. She flitted behind him and at once committed to a savage whip-stroke.

Heimdall pivoted and caught the lash in midflight. Kamorr

realized the hearing of Mimir had allowed his friend to know the exact trajectory of the brass-studded lash even when he couldn't see it. He jerked the startled winged woman earthward as he had his first adversary, released her whip to snatch hold of one wing of hide and bone, and hammered her on the side of the head with the butt of his own weapon. She stopped struggling. Even the writhing tangle of snakes she had in place of hair went limp.

For one wonderful moment, Kamorr imagined the fight was over. Then, no doubt detecting the approach with his keen hearing, Heimdall pivoted. His pain diminished now that the savage whipping had stopped, the dwarf managed to turn his head and look where his comrade was looking. And felt a pang of mixed fear and frustration when he discovered what had drawn his friend's attention.

It appeared that before her sisters even launched their attack, a third winged woman had gone in search of reinforcements and found them, too, maybe searchers on the fugitives' trail or simply a patrol Lord Pluto had assigned to monitor this portion of his domain. At any rate, flapping along above their heads, she was leading five earthbound allies toward Heimdall and Kamorr. Swords in hand, four were the gaunt reptilian warriors their quarries had already encountered. The fifth wore a voluminous brown hooded robe. Despite the need to keep up with the others, this one managed to run along with head bowed, and that combined with the cowl concealed the face inside.

Seemingly undaunted, Heimdall shook out his whip and, when his foes had nearly closed the distance, charged to meet them. The winged woman struck at him, but he leaped aside and made an attack of his own. The lash caught the lead snake-man across the face and dropped him. Heimdall tossed his whip into his off hand, stooped, grabbed the fallen warrior's sword, and advanced on into the midst of the others, where, Kamorr realized, the winged woman would have more difficulty wielding her weapon without fear of hitting one of her own allies.

It was all going well so far, but Heimdall was still facing superior numbers, and Kamorr told himself that, weak and hurting or not, he couldn't just keep lying here and leave his friend to fight alone. Gritting his teeth in a snarl of effort, he clambered to his feet.

As he did so, he noticed the robed figure standing apart from the melee in which Heimdall was embroiled. The figure likewise noticed him standing up and pulled the hood back from her head. She, too, had hissing, coiling serpents where an ordinary woman had hair, but there was no sign of batlike wings, nor, he judged, room for folded ones under her garment. Maybe, he thought, she was the same sort of creature as the whip-women, but crippled. Then he met her stare and realized she was a different manner of threat entirely.

Paralysis and a cold, heavy numbness flowed through his body. It might almost have inspired relief after all the pain if his friend – and all Asgard – hadn't needed him. As it was, he strained to move but accomplished nothing. Then the numbness reached his eyes and ears and robbed him of sight and hearing. I'm dying, he thought, and then his mind, too, was extinguished.

Happily, though, the extinction didn't prove to be permanent. First, simple, muddled consciousness returned, then Kamorr's senses, and finally mobility, not that he could move to much purpose. He and Heimdall were chained side by side to a wall. The fetters were of some unfamiliar metal, golden in hue, while the chamber was made of black stone. Kamorr inferred that he and his friend were now prisoners somewhere in the cluster of dark buildings they'd sought to avoid. A single torch in a sconce slightly relieved what would otherwise have been impenetrable gloom, although the light of the flames seemed dim and subdued like the colors of the flowers in the fields.

Before him, though not so close that a fettered prisoner could stretch out his arm and touch her, stood a black-haired woman in a gray gown. She held the rod in her left hand aloft in a stance that Kamorr had sometimes seen warlocks use when working magic. Green phosphorescence seethed at the core of the crystal on the end of the wand or cane, further evidence that arcane power was at play.

After another moment, seemingly satisfied with the results of her work, she lowered the rod and regarded both prisoners. "You are to be judged," she said. "Be ready." Then she turned and walked toward the doorway in the opposite wall.

Kamorr realized that if he'd understood her, she must possess the Allspeak like an Asgardian. Meanwhile, Heimdall called after her: "Wait! We need to know more! At least tell us who you are!"

Without pausing or looking back, the black-haired woman disappeared through the opening. Heimdall's mouth twisted in frustration.

"I take it," Kamorr said, his old aches waking once more, "you lost the fight."

Heimdall hesitated. "Not exactly."

Kamorr cocked his head. It sent a twinge through his neck. "What does that mean?"

"I *might* have beaten them despite the odds. I had an idea of how to go about it. But then the one creature turned you to stone."

The Blackhammer blinked. "Is that what happened to me?"

"Yes, and afterward, the woman with wings said there was only one way to reverse the effect of Medusa's petrifying gaze. If I surrendered, she'd see to it you received the remedy. If I fought on, you'd be a lifeless statue forever. So, I surrendered."

Kamorr scowled. "Well, you shouldn't have! I've told you, there's too much at stake! You should have fought your way clear and left me behind!"

"That's not what you would have done in my place."

"Yes, it is," the dwarf said, although, his flare of anger cooling, he realized he doubted it.

"Well, anyway, I hoped our captors would prove as good as their word, and once they restored you – as that woman just did – we could escape together." Heimdall extended one of his arms to display the yellowish manacle locked around his wrist. "Can you open these?"

Kamorr snorted. "You realize there's a reason the other Blackhammers had me scrubbing pots and pushing barrows around? I don't have the knack for forging or tinkering. So no, without tools, not a hope."

"And if I ever had anything you could use, I left it back in the world of the living, or somebody took it from me when I was captured the first time. That leaves brute force. Let's see what that can do."

Heimdall rose, turned, and gripped the golden chain

securing his right wrist in both hands. Then he dragged on it with all his might, feet braced and leaning back as though playing tug of war.

Kamorr held his breath in hope. Asgardians were prodigiously strong. Still, neither the chain nor the stone to which it attached yielded, and even when he bestirred his aching body and added what was left of his own strength to the effort, the result remained the same.

At last, Heimdall let go of the clinking chain, glanced at the palms and fingers he'd rubbed raw, and wiped them on his tunic. "Apparently," he said, breathing heavily, "we do have to wait to be judged. Whatever that entails."

Kamorr lowered himself stiffly back onto the floor. "In that case," he answered, "I'll go on with my story. You might as well know all of it, and there isn't that much more to tell."

Fourteen
The Descent, Part Two

Heimdall planted himself in front of a fellow with receding graying hair, a frequent tippler's ruddy, blotchy features, and a pudgy belly bulging out the front of his tunic. "A word, if you please," the Asgardian said.

As he more or less expected, the dead man tried to step around him and continue ceaselessly wandering the fields of pink, yellow, and white flowers. Kamorr, however, positioned himself behind Heimdall to once again block the way.

The spirit blinked and didn't try to go around the pair who'd blocked him a second time. His dazed mind was focusing and realizing the strangers meant to prevent him from trudging any further until Heimdall had his *word*.

"We're looking for a cyclops named Orien," Heimdall said. "A one-eyed giant." The fellow before him probably knew what a cyclops was, but it was better to be sure. "He died a few days ago." There was no sun to mark the passage of time in the enormous cavern, but maybe the estimate would convey something to the man he was questioning.

Heimdall was ready for the spirit to disappoint him just like the first dozen souls he'd asked. But instead, the pudgy man nodded. "Yes," he said, his voice dull and sleepy, "the cyclops. I watched Lord Pluto and some of his guards drive him over the edge to fall into Tartarus. The giant kept saying he'd done nothing to deserve it, but no one heeded him."

That, Heimdall thought, was quite in accord with his opinion of the death god's character. He felt a mixture of disgust at the injustice and brutality and excitement that he might finally be close to finding the object of his search.

"What's Tartarus?" he asked, although he suspected he could guess.

The spirit confirmed he was right: "The pit in the center of everything."

"And Orien was driven over the edge? Could he have survived the fall?"

The dead man's eyes narrowed. He seemed puzzled that Heimdall had asked about something that every resident of the underworld presumably already knew. Still, though his voice was now more wakeful, he provided the answer readily enough: "If you lived and died in the land of the living, you can't die a second time in the land of the dead. Well, you can, but it doesn't last. After a while, you rise again."

"So, what would have happened to Orien once that happened?"

"Lord Pluto has more guards at the bottom. They would have chained the cyclops or confined him somehow."

"Thank you!" Heimdall stepped aside. "We're grateful for your help, and we've held you here long enough."

"Have you seen Eulalia?" the spirit asked. "My little girl?

Her mother took her away when she thought I was drinking too much."

"No," Heimdall said, feeling a twinge of pity. "I'm sorry."

It was only then that the dead man walked onward. Within a couple of paces, his steps slowed and his shoulders slumped. Heimdall judged he was slipping back into his stupor. Maybe he'd even forget the strangers who'd approached him and, if the Fates were kind, Eulalia, too.

Kamorr recalled his companion's thoughts to their own business. "I could only understand your half of that," the Blackhammer said, "but I take it the cyclops is at the bottom of the big hole?"

"Evidently so," Heimdall replied.

"Then let's see if you can spot him down there."

They made their way toward the chasm's edge. Long before they arrived, Heimdall heard anguished screams and sobbing, snapping bones and tearing flesh, clattering chains, snapping whips, and crackling fires. He inferred he and Kamorr were nearing a place of punishment for those who bore the particular disfavor of their gods. Now that his pang of excitement had cooled, it seemed a place to be wary of, and his first glance over the edge confirmed it was as bad as he'd imagined.

Some of the prisoners were giants, some, the size of humans. Some were enduring the various agonies of the torture chamber while others experienced a more whimsical sort of cruelty. Women sought to fill jugs and carry the contents to fill a bath, but the water spilled out from cracks in the vessels. A man struggled to weave a rope from straw, but a donkey ate the cord as fast as he produced it.

Heimdall scowled in disgust. He was aware that much of

Niffleheim, where Odin's less worthy worshippers ended up, was freezing cold, and existence was unpleasant for those who languished there. But there was a considered gloating viciousness at work here that the All-Father and even Hela, Goddess of Death, seldom displayed.

He took a breath and reminded himself he wasn't here to remake the place. Though he was a trusted agent of the court of Asgard, the structure of the cosmos as experienced by unfamiliar pantheons was beyond him. He needed to concentrate on his own errand – finding and questioning Orien while avoiding those who would seek to hinder him. A challenge to be sure, especially here where everything was strange, but he told himself that he and Kamorr had done all right so far. And would continue to do so as long as they kept their nerve and exercised their wits.

He peered about, and despite the gloom and clouds of smoke, the countless tableaus of torment and the guardian creatures prowling among them, eventually he spotted the object of his search. He pointed. "There. Do you see?"

"No," Kamorr replied, "but I'll take your word for it that you do. Can we reach him, do you think?"

"Yes. There are trails down into the pit that nobody's guarding."

The Blackhammer grinned. "Because nobody's expecting us. To them, it's just another boring moment in forever."

"Right, and once we're down there, if we're careful, we should be able to avoid notice as we make our way. Pluto's warriors and watch-beasts are all more interested in keeping an eye on their particular charges than looking out for intruders."

"I believe that. Who'd go down there who didn't have to?"

Once they reached the floor of the pit, they still had to take a winding course and move stealthily to pass unobserved, and Heimdall experienced one jolt of dismay when he was certain a prisoner had caught a glimpse of them anyway. But she, a woman with two open wounds on her back where it looked like wings had been torn away, resumed her weeping without giving the trespassers away, and her guard was oblivious to their presence.

The mutilated prisoner seemed one more proof of the consummate cruelty at work in Tartarus. Heimdall decided he wasn't surprised that Odin had concealed the fact that he was apparently on peaceful terms with gods capable of such things until it became necessary to reveal it. He was, however, surprised that the All-Father was even trying to get along with such beings, although, on further reflection, maybe that was naïve of him. He'd seen ample evidence that Odin could be merciless and vicious in his own right.

Eventually the intruders peeked over the crest of a rise and spied Orien at the bottom of the declivity below. Unlike the other prisoners here, the cyclops wasn't enduring any obvious torture beyond being wrapped in and weighed down with a huge golden chain. Heimdall doubted that even such a giant was capable of squirming free, but one of the gaunt, scaly-limbed warriors stood close by to discourage any such attempt.

"If you distract the guard," Heimdall said, "I can attack them from behind."

Kamorr smiled. "At the moment, you're unarmed. I think that if you distract the snake-man, I might do better attacking him from behind. I've trained at empty-handed combat, and if

I don't manage to subdue the guard fast, you can rush in and help me."

It would feel odd to Heimdall, seasoned warrior that he was, to hang back while someone else took the lead in a fight. But the Blackhammer seemed confident his idea was better, and there was no doubt that dwarves, all dwarves, were a hardy breed. "All right," the Asgardian said, "we'll do it your way."

Heimdall crept some distance away and then stood up. "Hello," he called as he started down the slope toward Orien and the guard. "I hope you can help me. I'm lost. How do I get back to the fields of flowers?"

For a moment, apparently nonplussed, the guard simply stared with crimson eyes. Then he drew his sword and gave a warning hiss.

Heimdall wished he were still carrying Hofund, the Gjallarhorn, or, failing that, any weapon. But he continued his approach as though unaware of the potential danger. "Is that a cyclops?" he asked, nodding toward Orien. "I've never seen one before."

The guard glided on toward the intruder with blade at the ready. Even though he was walking on two legs, there was something of the sinuous, almost hypnotic slither of the serpent in the way he advanced. By now, though, Kamorr was creeping up behind him, and the dwarf likewise stalked his prey with a silent, menacing grace.

Heimdall widened his eyes, raised his hands, and backed up a couple paces. He had to, else the snake-man would have come within striking distance. He tried to look like he'd belatedly recognized the threat but still imagined he could talk his way out of it.

"Hold on," he said. "I told you, I'm just trying to find my way back to where I belong."

The guard held his sword poised to thrust, and Heimdall was likewise ready to twist aside. He never had to, though. Kamorr sprang in, kicked the creature's back leg out from under him, snatched hold of his sword belt, and threw him on his back. The snake-man needed an instant to recover, and the Blackhammer didn't give it to him. He yanked the guard's crested helmet off, exposing hairless, scarlet-eyed features that were half human, half reptile, and bashed the serpent-man unconscious with one hammering blow to the center of the forehead.

Heimdall smiled. "That was well done."

"Just because I'm no good with a battle-axe and armor doesn't mean I can't fight." Kamorr hesitated. "Although it might have been a different story if the snake-man heard me coming." The momentary confidence his success inspired seemed to be fading back into humility or self-doubt.

Heimdall was about to say that he had no doubt the outcome would be the same, but before he could get the words out, the Blackhammer took the sword from the fallen guard's hand and tossed it to him. He caught it by the hilt.

"Take this at least for the moment," Kamorr said. "You question the cyclops while I go back to the top of the rise and keep watch. I wouldn't be able to understand what he says, anyway." The Blackhammer cast about, picked up a couple of stones suitable for throwing or bashing, and headed up the slope.

When Heimdall turned to face the giant, Orien was straining red-faced in a futile effort to break the chain while inching backward as fast as his bonds permitted. After a moment, the Asgardian realized what had so alarmed the cyclops and felt pity to see such a colossus brought so low.

"The sword isn't for you," he said. "I just want to talk and help you if I can."

Orien still looked afraid. "I know you! You're Captain Heimdall from the diggings in the northlands."

"That's right, and I mean you no harm." Heimdall wondered what he could say to convince the one-eyed colossus. "Do you understand you were poisoned?"

"Yes," the cyclops snarled, dread giving way to a flash of anger. "Because *you* poisoned me! You, or one of your kind!"

"No!" Heimdall said. "Why would we?"

"To keep me from reporting what I discovered to my master. But you were too late! I already told Lord Pluto!"

Heimdall still didn't understand, but maybe he was beginning to, enough to make him feel a chill despite the warmth of the smoky eye-stinging air. "What did you discover?"

"That you all lied about the purpose of your Rainbow Bridge, just as my gods suspected all along. I couldn't tell exactly what it will really do. I'm not that learned or powerful. But I could feel the evil inside the work."

"I swear on my honor, on Draupnir and Thrudstok, on my mother's life that my people don't intend for Bifrost to be anything other than what we told you it is to be. If someone else is perverting the work, it isn't us." Maybe it was Amora, conspiring with the frost giants again just as Uschi suspected. Except no, that hypothesis no longer fit the facts.

Orien turned his head and spat. "Your oaths mean nothing to me."

"Please," Heimdall said, "just think it through. You detected something amiss and reported it to Lord Pluto."

"Because Lord Hephaestus wasn't in camp, and I thought one of the gods should know without delay."

"And what was your reward for doing your duty?"

The giant's single eye blinked. "Are you talking about when you or one of your people poisoned me?"

"None of my folk murdered you," Heimdall said, now confident it was so. "If you'd already confided in Lord Pluto, we would no longer have a reason even if we were as wicked as you imagine."

"You would if the poisoner didn't know I already talked to him!"

Heimdall hesitated an instant to consider the point. "Well, that's true, theoretically. But how would an Asgardian or Blackhammer ill-wisher know of your discovery in the first place? And if he was keeping such close track of you as to learn of it, would he not then also know you'd already reported to Pluto? There's a far likelier alternative. Your death god wished to silence you to keep you from reporting to Hephaestus when your master returned. But when I said *reward*, I wasn't referring to the poisoning. I was talking about after. When Pluto had his warriors drive you into the pit and chain you up even though your service should surely have earned you kinder treatment. Why would the god imprison you here unless it was to make certain you didn't speak to anyone who could and would take action even after you were dead?"

Orien's face creased as he pondered what he'd heard. Finally, he said, "You're saying Lord Pluto himself is subverting the work."

"That's exactly what I'm saying."

The giant shook his head. "But that's… No. Just no. He wouldn't do that."

"I realize Pluto is one of your gods and you've ever been a loyal servant of those gods. But, please, put that aside for a moment and think. What do you know of his character? His ambitions? Any past transgressions?"

Orien's features creased in thought. Finally, he frowned and said, "Lord Pluto *would* have been able to put poison in the wineskin. He has a helmet that lets him turn invisible. We cyclopes made it long ago."

Poison the wineskin and hide the remaining hemlock among Kamorr's meager possessions, Heimdall thought. It all hung together.

"Does the guard have the key to the chain?" the Asgardian asked. A massive lock served to keep Orien's bonds tight.

"I don't know," the cyclops said.

"I'll check." Heimdall turned back toward the unconscious snake-man.

An instant later, Ulbrecht, looking as usual like a traveling player costumed to represent the average villager's pointy-bearded, high-collared notion of an evil sorcerer, stepped out of empty air several paces beyond the guard. Violet haze, the visible manifestation of some enchantment, tinged the space in which he stood.

Heimdall stared in astonishment. Ulbrecht was the last person he would have expected to encounter in the depths of Tartarus.

"There you are," the sorcerer growled. "What do you mean, leaving without consulting me and coming here of all places?

You know the All-Father didn't want us to learn anything we didn't have to about the stranger gods!"

"What I've learned," Heimdall replied, feeling a flash of anger at the scolding, "is something we urgently needed to know. Lord Pluto is twisting your work to his own purposes. This is Orien, the murdered cyclops." He gestured toward the chained giant. "He discovered what Pluto is up to and the god poisoned him to stop him revealing what he knew."

Ulbrecht sighed and shook his head. "Ridiculous. Bifrost is *my* great work. No one, not even a god, could subvert the effort without my discerning it."

"We don't know Pluto's powers," Heimdall said, trying to control his temper and sound reasonable. Surely he could convince Ulbrecht if the warlock would only hear him out. "We can't assume—" He heard rushing footsteps at his back and, startled once again, spun around.

Like Ulbrecht before them, figures were emerging from empty air. First out charged a dozen more reptilian guards. Behind them strode Pluto himself, battle-axe ready in one hand, a round black shield engraved with a skull on the opposite arm.

Retreating, Heimdall backed toward the Asgardian mage. "You see now?" he cried. "Help me!"

"I'm afraid that won't be possible," replied the man behind him. With each syllable, his voice altered, changing from the phlegmy, crotchety tones with which Heimdall was familiar to something silky and amused.

Heimdall glanced over his shoulder. To his horror, Ulbrecht was gone. In his place at the center of the purplish light stood a figure whose now-beardless face was corpse-blue on the right side and night-black on the left. His garments recapitulated the division. His tunic was black on the right, red on the left, with a similarly halved many-pointed star emblem in the center of the chest. His hair was long and white, and his ears pointed. Instead of a sorcerer's staff, he held a broadsword in his hand.

He was Malekith the Accursed, Lord of the Wild Hunt, king of Svartalfheim, and sworn enemy of Asgard. Heimdall had never before laid eyes on him, but he'd heard enough tales of the dark elf monarch's singular features, cruelty, and treachery to recognize him.

Maybe Malekith had revealed his true self because he hoped Heimdall would falter in dismay and be all the easier to overcome, but if so, he'd mistaken his man. Though amazed and aghast, the Asgardian shook off his stupefaction, bellowed a battle cry, and rushed the dark elf, sword raised for a killing cut to the head.

Malekith laughed, and the blade rang as it rebounded from the violet haze. Maybe Hofund could have breached the shielding enchantment, but this lesser weapon couldn't.

Footsteps were still pounding closer behind Heimdall, and he had to turn again lest his other foes kill him from behind. He cut down one, then another, noticed Kamorr hadn't revealed himself by joining the fray and, after he thought about it for an instant, was glad. The dwarf had sense enough to realize he could do nothing against so many, one a sorcerer and another a god. Better to remain alive and free now and hope to help Heimdall later. Although it seemed optimistic to imagine Heimdall would have a *later*.

He thrust his sword into the T-shaped opening in a guard's casque, the snake-man dropped, and Pluto stepped up to take the fallen warrior's place. The death god swung his battle-axe and Heimdall ducked it. He riposted with a slash to the neck and Pluto caught it on the black shield.

An instant later, something slammed Heimdall in the back, and, thrown off balance, he lurched forward into the shield. Reptilian guards grabbed him by the arms before he could recover his equilibrium or shake off the shock. One of them pulled the sword from his hand.

Malekith circled back into view of the now-immobilized Asgardian. He still held his off hand raised with a last few crimson sparks winking out of existence on his fingers. Perhaps his vanity demanded that Heimdall recognize whose sorcery had dealt the decisive blow.

"Where's the real Ulbrecht?" Heimdall gritted. He was truly afraid now, but wouldn't give the dark elf the satisfaction of showing it.

Malekith looked surprised at the question. "Murdered, obviously."

Heimdall felt a surge of rage. He and Ulbrecht hadn't been close, but they'd fought the Jotuns together, and he'd considered the mage a friend. "Why?"

The dark elf grinned. "Because when I learned of Bifrost, I understood the potential. If I corrupted the original design, it could be the weapon that destroys all Asgard and so leave other Realms under Odin's protection vulnerable to conquest."

"How is that possible?" Heimdall replied. "The mages at the camp are powerful, but surely not powerful enough to create something capable of that much devastation."

Malekith smiled. "Oh, suffice it to say, there's a way. But I couldn't create my own version of Bifrost without all those subordinate warlocks and dwarf miners Ulbrecht was recruiting – for all their cunning, my subjects don't possess the full range of skills required for the task – or, to be honest, access to his original plans. So, he had to go, and I had to take his place. Afterward, Hephaestus and Pluto showed up to complicate matters, but fortunately, after the latter discovered what was happening, I was able to persuade him where his interests truly lay."

Heimdall turned his head to speak to Pluto. "Across the Nine Realms, Malekith is infamous for his treachery. Whatever he's promised you, you shouldn't trust him."

The death god grinned. "I'm willing to trust him when there's no conflict between his goal and mine. He's out to destroy Asgard so that he can conquer other worlds under its protection, and what are Asgard and those other worlds to me? I'd never even heard of them until the ruler of my pantheon sent me here. My objective is to attract new worshippers among the humans of Earth. Killing your deities will leave those who followed them in need of a new god, and since I'll be anticipating that, I'll be ready to obtain them. Which will be of no consequence to Malekith."

The dark elf nodded. "Exactly so."

Heimdall felt a pang of disappointment at having his feeble hope crushed, for it seemed plain he wouldn't be able to persuade Pluto. "And after throwing in with Malekith," he said heavily, "when Orien discovered something was amiss, you poisoned him and imprisoned his spirit here."

The cyclops roared and thrashed impotently in his chain. The death god, the dark elf king, and even the surviving snake-man guards all ignored him.

"My ally" – Malekith nodded in Pluto's direction – "thought those precautions sufficient. I, however, believe in leaving nothing to chance, and I put a spell on this little area that would alert me if a newcomer ventured here, whereupon I could summon help to the site. And now we see my caution was well-founded. I commend you, captain, for penetrating to a part of the truth if, sadly, not quite enough of–"

"You talk too much," Pluto growled. From his tone, perhaps the implication that Malekith was shrewder than he was had annoyed him. "Time to end this." He raised his axe. Heimdall strained against his captors' grips but couldn't break free.

"Stop!" the dark elf snapped.

"Why?" Pluto asked.

"Do we know for certain what will happen if you kill him?"

Pluto frowned as he thought about it. "I don't recall a living person ever dying in my kingdom before. I suppose that when he does, his spirit will be here with us, and then we can imprison him as we have the cyclops."

Malekith shook his head like a tutor with a dull-witted pupil. "Remember, even if you're right that it would happen to a follower of your pantheon, Heimdall's not one. He's not even a mortal. He's one of the king of Asgard's warriors. What if, instead of here, his ghost materializes at the entrance of your kingdom, and then instead of docilely filing in with all the other spirits, he makes his way back to the Nine Realms to report? Worse, what if you kill him and he's whisked back there instantly? Even if he lands in the realm of our death goddess, he could trek to her fortress, and she could meddle in our scheme if she sees fit."

"Then we'll imprison him down here *without* killing him."

Malekith fingered a lock of his snowy hair. "I wish I were certain that would hold him."

"It will hold him long enough. You told me Bifrost's nearly done, and when it is, Asgard and its gods will perish."

"It is. Still, he proved himself a resourceful fellow to even get this far."

By now, Heimdall had gleaned he was unlikely to be slain on the spot, and the realization stirred him to a mocking jest, for after all, what did he have to lose by a show of defiance?

"Plainly," he said, "you fear me, and you should. Happily for you, I'm willing to compromise. You let Orien and me go and abandon your scheme, and I won't tell anyone what you intended."

Malekith laughed. Pluto gave his captive an ugly sneer of a smile.

"Oh, you won't tell anyone," the death god said. "I have a way to guarantee it to even King Malekith's satisfaction. And while you're fettered down here, I'll provide something to keep you occupied. Your reward for being *a resourceful fellow.*"

He brandished the axe, and, now that he was looking for it with the sight of Mimir, Heimdall saw the shimmer in the air as arcane power opened a portal. He struggled as the guards marched him toward it, but he still couldn't break free.

FIFTEEN

MIDGARD & SVARTALFHEIM:
TWO DAYS UNTIL BIFROST

Malekith sat behind Ulbrecht's cluttered worktable, eyes
narrowed in contemplation and the fingertips of his two hands
pressed together. He considered involving the Jotuns or fire
giants in the next phase of his scheme but quickly decided
neither would be practical. He enjoyed an alliance with neither
at the moment, and it would take too long to convince them to
assist him.

Once he'd had Amora blamed for the cave-in, he'd hoped
to see her either slain on the spot or arrested and hauled off to
Asgard. In his judgment, either outcome would have allayed
any fears or suspicions in the camp and enabled everyone
to work together to finish building Bifrost. Whereupon the
Rainbow Bridge would destroy Asgard, kill Odin and his kin,
and clear the way for new dark elf wars of conquest across the
Nine Realms.

Instead, however, the enchantress had escaped. Malekith

doubted she'd resurface anytime soon or that anyone would believe her protestations of innocence if she did. After all, nobody had before. Still, it seemed a prudent idea to do even more to "prove" she'd been determined to prevent Ulbrecht's great work from coming to fruition.

Since Malekith couldn't use Jotuns or fire giants, he needed to select a tribe of his own people that was strong, but not too strong. The tribe should also live in sufficient isolation that no one would notice what had happened to it until it was too late to determine the reason why. Malekith was confident in his mastery of his domain, but where was the profit in stirring up unnecessary unrest on the eve of a realms-spanning campaign of conquest?

Ideally, the tribe should likewise be one ruled by a sorceress, reasonably powerful but not too bright. Fortunately, Svartalfheim had many extended family groups scattered through its dense forests and deep, echoing caverns, and it didn't take long to think of one that met all three of his requirements.

He rose, murmured an incantation, and swept his hand down as though smearing paint on a surface. Three paces away, in one corner of the pavilion, a subtle rippling distortion shimmered into being, manifesting from top to bottom to mimic his gesture. In a moment, it became a doorway from this world to his own.

Malekith stepped through, and the portal blinked out of existence behind him. Now he stood in a forest, predominantly spruce and pine but with the occasional gray alder or downy birch. At first glance, it was little different than the mountain forests surrounding the Asgardians' encampment. The conifers even gave it the same sharp smell. But the shadows on the needle-strewn ground were deeper, and if one looked up through the branches to find a patch of sky, it was a darker shade of blue.

Malekith made his way parallel to the incline of the mountainside until he encountered the trail. He had no doubt the Rabid Wolf Tribe had mantraps and sentries positioned throughout the forest, but the path seemed the easiest way to avoid the former and make the acquaintance of the latter. He hiked up it with the sword he'd turned into a staff, softly thumping the ground with every other step.

Before long, four sentries exploded from their hiding places beyond the sides of the trail. They'd waited until he'd advanced far enough to put him between one pair in front and the other behind, so there was nowhere to run. Two had blue skin, one pink like an Asgardian, and one orange. The orange one stood a head taller than the others and was as thick-built and brawny as a troll.

Malekith swept out his arms and spoke a word of power. Force blasted forth from his location in all directions. It stripped the leaves from brush, scarred the bark of tree trunks, and bashed the charging dark elves off their feet.

As the four gaped up at him, stunned and bloodied, he abandoned the guise of Ulbrecht and resumed his true appearance. He could have done so immediately upon arrival in his own kingdom, of course. But he enjoyed making a dramatic entrance, and it was never a bad idea to flummox the rabble and remind them who was in control.

One of the would-be ambushers scrambled to assume the proper attitude of kneeling abasement, and, reminded of the protocol, the rest frantically followed suit. Malekith let them grovel for a moment, then bade them rise and accompany him as a sort of rough-and-ready honor guard as he continued on his way.

The Rabid Wolf Tribe made its home in a limestone cavern complex. As Malekith came in sight of the dark elves working in front of the arched entrance into the mountainside, they too goggled for an instant and then hastened to kneel. When a little boy was slow to do so, his mother grabbed him by the shoulder and jerked him down into the proper attitude. Meanwhile, their king ordered the hulking orange-skinned warrior to run ahead and announce him to Lady Gro, the mistress of the tribe.

Lady Gro's hall was a spacious chamber lit by a bluish phosphorescence she'd presumably conjured into the air. A natural unevenness in the floor provided a sort of dais, and a wooden throne perched atop it. She had better sense than to be sitting on the seat when Malekith entered, though, or to occupy the dais at all. She dropped to her knees before him like the lowliest of his subjects.

She was as he remembered her, a frame knotted with muscle but no taller than the average Asgardian woman, a broad, flat nose and a low forehead, and a number of amulets and other witchy trinkets dangling about her person. He gave her leave to rise and, when she raised eyes the color of clotted blood, met her uncertain gaze with a smile.

"Rejoice, my lady," he said. "I've come to honor you and the Rabid Wolf Tribe."

Gro's expression reflected her confusion, and small wonder. She couldn't think of anything she or her inbred relations had done to deserve being singled out any more than he could. "To honor us, Your Majesty?"

"For your exceptional loyalty," he said. As far as he was concerned, one would have to search far and wide to find a dark elf who was loyal as Asgardians understood the word, but it was a convenient term for service provided out of fear or hope of reward.

"Yes, Your Majesty," Gro said. "We *are* loyal!" Malekith could tell she still didn't understand but had decided to go along.

"In the forests of Midgard," he said, "a small group of Asgardians have a hunting camp. I've decided to wipe them out to remind Odin and his people to fear our kind, and I've chosen the Rabid Wolf Tribe to be my warriors in the battle." It was a genuine honor as dark elves reckoned such things, even if it might not be the one Gro was hoping for.

"Thank you, Majesty." She hesitated. "You'll transport us to Midgard?"

"Of course."

"Then I'll muster the fighters at once."

"Bring everyone, even the children. This will be an easy victory and a good way to give the younglings their first taste of war." More to the point, they wouldn't still be in Svartalfheim afterward to tell of their elders' departure.

"As you command, Your Majesty." Gro turned to give orders to the burly, orange-skinned warrior still standing ready to receive them.

"A moment," Malekith said. "I wish to reward you for your assistance." He slid a gold ring set with an emerald off his finger. "Wear this always. It will shield you from harm and augment your mystical power."

She dropped to her knees once more to receive the talisman. "I will, Your Majesty! Thank you!"

It didn't take long to assemble the entire tribe in front of the cave mouth. Even the smallest children clutched weapons, for that was the dark elf way, and a good thing, too. The Asgardians would see them as combatants and treat them as such.

With a casual sweep of his broadsword, Malekith produced another magical doorway, this one wide enough for several dark elves to pass through at a time. "When you arrive," he told Gro, "you'll be due west of the camp. You may catch a glimpse of the fjord at your backs. Head in the opposite direction, toward the rising sun, and you'll come upon the foe."

Gro frowned for an instant. Then she remembered whom she was addressing and changed her expression. "Aren't you going to be there to lead us to the battleground?"

"I'll be with you soon," Malekith told her. "I simply have to attend to something else first, something that will make our triumph even easier. Off you go, now."

When the entire tribe had disappeared through the gate, he closed it and opened a smaller one. He stepped through that one back into Ulbrecht's tent in Midgard and cloaked himself once more in the appearance of the Asgardian mage.

He then took a deep breath and assumed an agitated demeanor appropriate to his disguise and the occasion. With that done, he bolted out of the pavilion and started shouting.

"Attackers are coming! From the west! I've seen it with my Art!"

The call triggered a flurry of activity. The scurrying Asgardians and dwarves reminded Malekith of ants when something broke open the nest. A warrior dashed in the direction of Captain Uschi's tent, and the long-legged Valkyrie soon came striding up.

With Heimdall absent, Uschi was responsible for managing the defense. Malekith assumed she was up to the job. She'd better be. Stripped of his very memory, her friend was chained like a dog in Tartarus and would never return.

"What else can you tell me?" she asked without preamble. From her brusqueness, it was clear she was calm but intent on preparing her warriors for battle as quickly and effectively as possible. Malekith wondered if, underneath it all, she wasn't actually looking forward to the fight. It would be a straightforward task and one she'd performed successfully many times before, as opposed to the less familiar duties that came with managing the camp in the wake of Heimdall's departure.

"Not much," Malekith replied. "Some enchantment clouds my vision. We're lucky I was able to divine as much as I have."

"Do the attackers know about the diggings?"

He paused as though considering. "It doesn't appear so. They're all coming straight toward the camp."

Uschi smiled a fierce smile. "The miners in the western tunnels are already at their work. If we get word to them, they'll turn out to take the enemy on the flanks. Don't worry, Master Ulbrecht. We warriors will protect you and your work."

Malekith shifted his grip on his staff. "We'll *all* protect the work. I'll be fighting alongside you."

"Are you sure?" The Valkyrie no doubt knew Ulbrecht had fought in the siege of Asgard, but of late, she'd grown accustomed to regarding him as a bookish savant who thought only of the prodigious arcane task of creating Bifrost and rarely left his tent. That was necessary if he was to perform the complex magic required to bend Bifrost to his will, but it also had the benefit of limiting her opportunities to see through his disguise.

"Yes," Malekith said. "As there's magic on their side, you'll need magic to counter it."

It was at that point that Pluto and Hephaestus came hurrying up. It pleased Malekith to see that the former had rousted out his fellow god as instructed.

"We and our followers will help, too," said the god of smiths, a sword in one hand and a blacksmith's hammer in the other.

Malekith feigned surprise. "I… wouldn't have expected that."

"We haven't forgotten the poisoning," Hephaestus said. "But there's no evidence anyone left in camp was responsible or that you who remain are doing anything other than what you said you'd do. So, yes, of course we'll fight. We're guests in this camp, and the camp is under attack."

"Then thank you," Malekith said.

"We need to move," Uschi said.

They all did, but Malekith and Pluto lagged a pace behind the others, where they could exchange a quick glance of satisfaction that so far, everything was going according to plan.

Gro lingered where she and the entire Rabid Wolf Tribe had emerged from Svartalfheim into Midgard. She was waiting to see if King Malekith would reappear. He might. Given his ability to travel swiftly from place to place and even from one world to another, *I'll be with you soon* could mean very soon indeed.

A bit of time passed, however, and the monarch with the divided features *didn't* reappear. Meanwhile, her kin were watching her expectantly. In Malekith's absence, they were waiting for her to lead them into battle, just as the king had more or less indicated she should.

Time, she decided, to do exactly that. It was only a small contingent of Asgardians, and she and the other dark elves would take them by surprise. Moreover, should the outcome ever seem in doubt, she had her witchcraft to bring to bear, her power newly enhanced by the gold and emerald ring Malekith had given her. So far, it wasn't making her feel any different, but no doubt the augmentation would become apparent when she started casting spells.

She instructed the archers to skulk up in advance of their fellows. They'd soften up the camp with a rain of arrows. Then the rest of the tribe would charge to kill any foe who yet survived. With luck, the remaining shocked Asgardians would still be fumbling for their weapons and armor when the swordsmen of the Rabid Wolf Tribe rushed in among them. But just in case some enemies were ready to fight, she'd make sure her deadliest melee fighters, the ones who, with their hulking frames might almost be mistaken for trolls, were in the forefront of the charge.

She explained to her kin how they were to proceed. After that, she took another squint at the bright sun rising before her and a glance at the blue water visible through the pines behind, just to make doubly sure of her orientation. Then she started the tribe stalking through the forest.

The woods grew quiet as they made their way. A woodpecker ceased its knocking, and two deer bounded away from the dark elves' path. Meanwhile, eager for a first glimpse of the hunting camp, Gro kept peering ahead.

She didn't find what she was looking for. Instead… was that one of her own bowmen collapsing with an arrow jutting from his shoulder? To her dismay, she saw that it was, and now another fell. The rest scrambled behind tree trunks.

Gro hadn't expected a hunting camp to have pickets out. She certainly hadn't expected a whole line of skirmishers loosing arrows at her own advance, and she didn't understand why such a thing should be. But surely, she told herself, magic would eliminate the bowmen.

She needed to pick them out where they'd taken cover in order to aim her spells. As she struggled to do so despite the glare, she realized that, clever strategist though he was, Malekith had her force attacking with the rising sun in its eyes and uphill to boot. There must be a reason for that, one that would become apparent when he reappeared to help the tribe to that *easy victory*. She hoped it would be soon.

She found one enemy archer, then another, and another. She drew breath to recite an incantation, but the words caught in her throat. Were the trees themselves moving?

No, it wasn't that. Silhouetted by the sunlight behind them, five one-eyed giants were advancing, their shoulders snapping the branches off pines and spruces as they strode along. They gripped crude clubs they appeared to have made in haste, by uprooting other trees and stripping away the foliage, and when they marched past the Asgardian archers without pausing, it was obvious whose side they were on.

Gro had never even heard of such creatures before, let alone seen them. But, she told herself, straining to quell her fear, they were giants, albeit one-eyed ones, and her people knew how to fight giants. They'd battled alongside the armies of Jotunheim and Muspelheim on occasion, but it was more common for Svartalfheim to wage war against any and all other Realms.

"Swordsmen!" she shouted. "Hamstring the giants from behind! Archers, blind them when you have a shot at their eyes!"

For her part, she'd fell the huge attackers with sorcery. As she summoned her mystical strength, she waited again for some stirring to reveal Malekith's ring was aiding her. She still felt nothing. She tried to believe that was all right. Some sort of attunement must still be in process, for surely Malekith could have no motive for sending some of his own subjects out to lose a fight with the hated Asgardians. And while she waited for the magic of the ring to come to life, her own powers, hard-won through decades of study and practice, would be enough.

Standing at the rear of her force, where her howling, scrambling, slashing and stabbing kinsmen distanced her from the long sweeping mauls of the giants, she raised her hands above her head and chanted an incantation that sent shadows swirling like a cyclone around her body. As the spell neared its end, the tatters of darkness started buzzing, and on the final word, they separated into scores of flies the length of her index finger. The insects flew at the nearest giant and lit on his enormous body. They flitted away when he swiped and swatted at them, but returned to bite him anew as soon as he turned his attention to their fellows. Roaring, flailing impotently, he staggered out of the fight into a stand of nearby spruces.

Gro grinned and readied herself to cast the same spell on another giant. It was only then she noticed a man advancing in the wake of the one-eyed creatures. He appeared an insignificant threat compared to the behemoths. Yet the swings of the hammer in one hand and the cuts and thrusts of the sword in the other, both weapons quickly disposing of any dark elf who crossed his path, showed she shouldn't underestimate him.

Still, the giants first, then the stranger with the hammer and sword. She repeated the first few words of the incantation she'd used before, and then a jolt made her fumble over the words and botch the spell. Her gaze drawn by a lingering trace of hostile magic drifting in the air, she looked up the mountainside to where the enemy skirmishers were stationed. Standing in more or less the same line, but disdaining the cover the Asgardian archers were using, stood a burly figure whose dark armor and round shield were graven with skulls and other morbid imagery. The trail of power ended at the head of the battle-axe he was holding.

She snarled the initial words of a curse that should have driven him berserk and made him attack those closest to him, namely, the enemy bowmen. He, however, chopped the air with his axe, and a second jolt knocked her reeling and spoiled the enchantment before she could complete it.

Gro tried several more times to hurl destructive magic at the figure in black armor only to have repeated chops from the battle-axe rattle her bones and disrupt the castings. She didn't understand why he hadn't yet actually tried to strike her down. Perhaps it was a show of contempt.

If so, she'd make him regret it! Because the other portion of the fight was going better than her part. Many dark elves lay pulped and dead on the slope, but the one-eyed giants were finally in retreat. Their skins bristling with arrows, gashed feet leaving bloody prints, using the crude clubs as canes, they plainly realized that if they stood and battled any longer, the Rabid Wolf Tribe would bring them down.

With that obstacle gone, Gro was sure her warriors could overwhelm a handful of Asgardian bowmen, the man with the hammer and sword, and even the magic-wielder in black armor by simple force of arms. She was about to scream the order to charge when someone among the enemy did so instead.

Additional warriors – most Asgardians but some dwarves as well – burst out of the trees behind the archers. In the forefront raced a lanky brown-haired woman with a sword of fire in her hand. Both the man in black armor and his comrade with the leg braces joined the charge as it pounded along.

It's still all right, Gro told herself, resisting true panic for the first time. We can still defeat them. Dark elves can overcome any foe, and anyway, Malekith said he'd help us!

She ordered her warriors to form a shield wall. Scrambling, some of them did, albeit it was too short and had gaps in it, and then, bellowing battle cries, the two forces crashed together. Swords slashed and spears thrust, the weapons spattering gore as they plunged into vulnerable flesh and then pulled back for another stroke.

It was by now obvious the tribe had attacked something more formidable than a mere hunting camp, but for the next few moments, it looked to Gro as if she and her kin might still prevail. Then new war cries rang out. More dwarves were rushing out of the trees to attack the dark elves on both sides.

The Rabid Wolf Tribe, she realized, had done something even more perilous than unwittingly attacking a formidable force. She'd actually walked her kindred into a trap.

Only some of the dwarves driving in on the flanks wore mail and bore shields, spears, war hammers, and battle-axes. The rest were fighting with picks and shovels, but that provided scant reason for hope. They swung the tools with both skill and ferocity, and her kin fell whenever the makeshift weapons struck home. Even glancing or grazing blows they might have otherwise weathered sufficed to fell them, because iron was poison to a dark elf.

Making the situation even more desperate, the dwarves had mages, too. On the left flank, a warlock who, to judge from his wispy beard, was scarcely older than a boy, swept a wand this way and that. Controlled by the motions, a floating sword slashed at more of Gro's people. On the right flank, a matronly-looking female dwarf munched on a hunk of bread. The enchantment she was casting thereby made dark elves stagger and double over, vomiting worms and blood.

"Malekith!" Gro shouted. "Your Majesty! Where are you?"

The ruler of Svartalfheim still didn't appear. With more of her kin dropping by the moment, the attack-turned-defense crumbling, she wanted to run but reckoned she had nowhere to go. The portal to her own world had closed after the tribe passed through, and she'd never mastered the magic to open another.

Accordingly, in mingled rage and despair, she held her ground and cried out to any fell spirit that might heed her, vowing eternal servitude after death if the entity would only lend her power here and now. Something answered. She felt the surge of new strength she'd sought in vain from the ring. She oriented on the dwarf witch with the bread, and then, raised to make the words audible despite the shouts and screams, the clashing of blades on shields and armor, a female voice said, "You should have stayed away!"

Gro turned. The long-legged woman with the flaming sword was advancing on her. Fine. Let *her* be the first to feel her foe's newly bolstered might. The dark elf witch no longer had any hope of victory or even survival. It was clear the Rabid Wolf Tribe was on the brink of extermination, and that included its mistress. But she'd avenge them all before she fell.

Snarling words of power, she thrust her hands out at the oncoming Asgardian. An icy wind blasted into being before her fingertips, a miniature gale that coated the ground beneath it in frost and by right should freeze its target to death in moments. Said target cried out in shock, leaned into the wind to avoid being blown backward, and held her broadsword before her. The corona of the flame surrounding the blade burned brighter as it pitted its heat against the chill of the spell.

Gro was impressed that so far, the Asgardian was still alive and on her feet. The sword plainly contained powerful magic. But not as potent as that she now commanded. She shouted words to strength her spell, and then some opposing force dampened her witchcraft entirely. The conjured wind died. Confused, she looked around.

An Asgardian sorcerer had taken up a position several paces away. Though his people lived for millennia if conflict or accident didn't cut their spans short, over time, a few came to resemble elderly humans, and, wizened, gray-bearded, and gaunt, he was one of them. He wore a voluminous, star-bedizened, high-collared cloak of the sort that a certain type of warlock often chose to proclaim their calling.

Judging from his unruffled appearance, he'd either swung

wide to avoid the battle or used magic to travel down the mountainside without needing to defend himself from Gro's warriors. Either way, he was now staring intently at her, his forehead creased with effort, and she could feel his power smothering her own like layers of cold, soaked blankets weighing it down.

Still shivering from the now-extinguished wind, the warrior glanced at the sorcerer and said, "Thank you." She then returned her gaze to Gro. "It's over, Amora. Surrender, tell your followers to lay down their arms, and you can still survive."

Amora? Gro had heard of the cunning enchantress, but it was insane that anyone should mistake her for that Asgardian lady... unless...

She still didn't understand how or why everything had happened the way it did. But what if she'd never felt the gold and emerald ring adding to her strength because it actually bore an enchantment that did something else entirely? What if it had allowed the tribe to see her as she truly was but caused others to see her as Amora?

If so, she might survive the battle after all. The Asgardians would surely want to question Gro once they understood that their great foe Malekith had for some mysterious reason of his own disguised her as the enchantress and sent the Rabid Wolf Tribe out to die. And now that there was a chance of it, she realized she very much wanted to live, even as a prisoner, even with the rest of her people slain.

She took hold of the ring and tried to slip it off. The band tightened around her finger like a constricting serpent, cutting into her flesh and holding itself in place. She twisted and pulled with all her strength. The ring still wouldn't come off.

Then pain stabbed through her chest, and she realized the Asgardian sorcerer was using his magic to rip her heart asunder. As a phantom, she flew up from her body, out of the sunny morning, and into the frigid darkness that was Ginnungagap, the primordial abyss that existed before all else. Where she found the entity with whom she'd struck her reckless bargain waiting to claim her.

Uschi had sprung forward with sword upraised when it became plain the enchantress didn't intend to surrender. Ulbrecht's magic, however, was even faster than she was, with the result that Amora lay stricken and motionless on the ground, a bloody froth smearing her mouth and chin.

The Valkyrie turned, making sure no other foe was moving in to menace Ulbrecht or her. None was. The fight was effectively over although a last few dark elves were battling to the end.

As there was no more work for the Brightblade to do, Uschi returned her attention to the fallen Amora. "Is she dead?"

"Yes," Ulbrecht said. "I had to do it. She was trying to unleash whatever magic is stored inside that ring."

"I saw," the Valkyrie said. "That's why I was moving to cut her down. Odin would have preferred that a noblewoman of his court, even a treacherous one, be taken alive. But she forced our hands."

Uschi had long mistrusted and disliked the enchantress. She might even have despised her for the conniving traitor she was. Still, she felt an unexpected pang of sadness that the witch had thrown away her life when there'd been no need for it.

It was a kind of glum frustration that extended to the few surviving dark elves because they weren't giving up and crying for quarter, either. Watching the dwarves and Asgardians slay them, she said, "It's almost like they believe against all reason that something will still happen to turn the fight around."

Ulbrecht shrugged. "Or else it's simply dark elf savagery."

"Maybe." Uschi turned back toward Amora's body. "I expect you'll want that ring."

"Don't touch it!" the sorcerer snapped.

The Valkyrie stopped mid-reach. "Why not?"

"Don't touch anything on her person," Ulbrecht said. "For all we know, there's some sort of death curse waiting for anyone who does. Stand back and let me purify the remains."

She did as he'd bade her, and the mage hurled a stream of roaring yellow fire from the head of his upraised staff to bathe Amora's corpse in flame. Uschi backed further away from the sudden leaping blaze. The Brightblade burned hot too, but that heat never troubled the rightful wielder.

In just a few moments, Ulbrecht's sorcery reduced the fallen enchantress to a blackened husk that in no way resembled the golden-haired beauty of Odin's court. Truly, it could have been anyone lying there. The warlock then swept his staff downward. With a rumble, the ground opened under the body, whereupon it dropped into the hole in a shower of ash and embers. A final shift of the rod closed the earth once more.

"That should keep us all safe for the time being," Ulbrecht said. "I'll retrieve the ring and any other talismans she was carrying when I have a chance. For now, though, I want to address all our friends who fought so bravely today. After we've tended the wounded and caught our breaths, of course."

"I'll see to it," Uschi said. It also seemed unfortunate, even strange to her that Ulbrecht had disposed of the body of a lady of Asgard, even a traitor, in such a peremptory fashion. But she supposed the wicked Amora deserved no formal obsequies and that the sorcerer knew best. If there was truly something to be regretted, it was that no one had known the enchantress had formed an alliance with the dark elves, and still, it was unclear why she'd opposed the creation of Bifrost. Maybe the All-Father would turn up an explanation in due course.

As she strode off, she wondered for a moment why Heimdall had been away so long. She hoped he was all right. But considering all the perils and obstacles he'd already overcome while serving as Odin's agent, he likely was, and wouldn't he be chagrined when he learned that his journey had been pointless, and in his absence those who'd stayed behind had solved its problems without him?

The carpenters had knocked the platform together in some haste. Malekith had no doubt it was sturdy even so, but he ascended the steep steps slowly, like a sedentary scholar wary of the structure collapsing beneath him and careful that he might trip. It wouldn't do to bound up with the sure agility of a dark elf who was, among other accomplishments, a skilled swordsman, not while he was wearing the guise of Ulbrecht.

Upon reaching the summit, he gazed out at the assembled Asgardians and Blackhammers, at Pluto, the death god's reptilian warriors, Hephaestus, and the cyclopes. It pleased him to see nearly as many workers as before, and relatively few slings and crutches on display. The mining and other tasks necessary to the completion of Bifrost could proceed as expeditiously as ever.

He was happy, too, to see the smiles on so many faces. The

dolts were full of self-satisfaction at their victory, with never a thought that he'd managed the entire battle to hand them success on a platter.

Best of all, perhaps, dwarves stood clustered around the bandaged feet of cyclopes, and Asgardians within easy striking distance of snake-men, whereas before one group would have taken care to leave space between them and the other. Now that everyone had fought side by side, suspicion had yielded to camaraderie.

Truly, Malekith thought, his little oration might be unnecessary. Yet having come this far, he might as well make it. It would do no harm and ought to keep any of his listeners from backsliding into doubt. He raised his hands for quiet and, once he had it, began to speak.

"Noble friends, thank you for defending our great work today from those who sought to destroy it. I will be forever grateful.

"I say *our* great work because it belongs to each and every one of you no less than myself. I had the original idea, but it has been your skill and care and now your valor that will bring our Rainbow Bridge into being.

"And when I say *each and every one of you*, never doubt that includes the strangers who fought shoulder to shoulder with us builders today. Visitors from afar, you came to us because you had concerns about the true purpose of Bifrost, concerns naturally exacerbated by the murder of poor Orien. But when the attack came, you stood with us and battled like the heroes you are."

That brought a clamor of appreciation from the Asgardians and Blackhammers. When people called up to them, the cyclopes smiled and answered in kind. Pluto's reptilian warriors were more awkward, as if "thank you" and claps on the shoulder were an alien language to them. But at least they didn't hiss, recoil, or snatch for the hilts of their swords.

Malekith raised his hands again, and when the good-natured commotion died down, continued. "Now, about that attack and those concerns. Lord Hephaestus, Lord Pluto, you no doubt realized early on that many among my folk doubted the loyalty and intentions of Amora the Enchantress. We suspected she poisoned Orien and caused a collapse in one of the diggings, and now that she's led an attack on us and tried to kill us all, it's plain we were right about her. So, I ask you, mighty gods: in light of all we now know and have experienced together, do you believe the purpose of Bifrost is simply what I've told you all along?"

"I do," said Pluto, just as Malekith had instructed him to.

"And so do I," Hephaestus called.

The disguised dark elf smiled. "I'm glad. Because the bridge will help riders like brave Uschi there go about their sacred task as choosers of the slain. It will facilitate travel and trade between my master's world and others in our sphere. I hope the day will even come when the kings of our two peoples decide there is no longer reason to limit our contact with one another, and on that day, Bifrost will aid in that communication as well. Do those sound like goals worth striving for?"

The people assembled before him roared in affirmation.

"Good," Malekith said, "because we're close to finishing our task. Another day might do it." He looked to Hephaestus. "Especially if there's a bit less scrutiny of every tiny detail?"

The god of smiths grunted. "We'll continue to oversee the work. It's what our sovereign charged us to do. But we'll bring a … friendlier spirit to the task."

The Asgardians and particularly the Blackhammers cheered again.

After Malekith descended from the platform and the crowd began to disperse, Pluto found him. The two repaired to the dark elf's pavilion, where they could converse without being overheard.

"That went well," the death god said.

"I was rather persuasive, wasn't I?" Malekith opened a leather flask of mead. "Of course, it helped that we gave them plenty of reason to lay their suspicions and hard feelings to rest. And that they're imbeciles."

Pluto grinned. "So they are. Still, I'm a little concerned about what might happen if the true Amora reappears."

"Even if she decides to return here or fly to Odin – both of which I doubt – she's running out of time to do so, especially now that Hephaestus and the cyclopes are no longer inclined to hinder the work. But suppose she does. Given her history of treason, will anyone believe her if she claims she isn't the true enemy? Everyone here saw her commanding the dark elves in the battle."

"Everyone saw her die, too, which could raise questions if she turns up alive."

Malekith waved his hand in a dismissive gesture. "In that case, she cast convincing illusions to deceive her attackers, avoid death, and run away when the battle was manifestly lost. It's exactly the kind of thing she's done before."

"All right. I'm convinced she's no longer a problem. It's just too bad that you had to send so many of your people to die for the sake of the deception."

Malekith shrugged. "That's what pawns and dupes are for, to do as they're told and die if need be."

As he poured the golden liquor into silver cups, he reflected that perhaps it had been reckless to include *dupes* in his comment. But he hadn't quite been able to resist, and he could detect no indication that the stranger deity might suspect the observation also applied to him.

Sixteen

The Underworld:
One Day Until Bifrost

"It was good luck," Kamorr said, "that I was hiding at the top of the rise when Malekith and then Pluto and the snake-men arrived. I kept on hiding, and they kept on not noticing me." He smiled a wry smile. "Not exactly a unique event in my life, and maybe that's all I deserve. I could have rushed down and fought beside you. I knew it at the time."

The chain attached to his wrist rattling, Heimdall laid his hand on the Blackhammer's shoulder. "You did the right thing. You're brave and a skilled fighter. I've seen it. But even together, we couldn't have prevailed against those odds."

"Maybe," Kamorr said. "But look at us now, stuck in this dungeon awaiting *judgment*. How are we any better off?"

Heimdall suspected his friend had a point, but he pushed the despairing thought away. This couldn't be the end after they'd come so far and fought their way through so much. "We're still alive," he said. "We may yet find a way to turn things around."

Kamorr grunted. "Yes. Maybe. In any case, we can't give up, not with the survival of all Asgard depending on us."

"I still don't understand how even a corrupted Bifrost could muster sufficient power to bring that about. But I'm not a warlock. If he thinks there's a way, I believe him."

"So do I. Anyway, before he and Malekith took you away, I heard Pluto say that when he was done with you, you'd end up imprisoned in the pit. So, I snuck around down there until I found you and set you free."

"Yes," Heimdall said, "and afterward, you fought terrible creatures and kept marching onward without complaint even when you were wounded. I never would have gotten this far without such a staunch comrade. So it pains me whenever I hear you speak slightingly of yourself. I wish you'd stop."

Kamorr snorted. "Thanks for that. And maybe it is time I stop saying those things and thinking those thoughts. Anyway, now you have the whole story of how we landed here." He peered at his fellow prisoner. "Doesn't any of it spark your memory?"

Heimdall felt frustrated as well as guilty for disappointing his friend. "No. I'm truly sorry, but no."

The Blackhammer sighed. "I suppose I can tell you other things I know about your life, other stories, but they'll be different. Just tales I've heard, not experiences we lived through together."

Heimdall wondered if there was any point in putting Kamorr to the trouble. Then the door to the prison opened, and eight crimson-eyed reptilian guards entered. One removed the shackles that had been securing the prisoners only to lock new fetters on their wrists and ankles. The others stood poised to respond to any resistance with sword thrusts. Once the new manacles were in place, the snake-men herded them shuffling toward the exit.

"I guess we're headed for *judgment*," Kamorr whispered. "You'll probably have to do the talking. Unless the judge has the Allspeak, I won't even understand him."

Wonderful, Heimdall thought, the one who can't remember is the spokesman. Aloud, he said, "I'll do my best."

"Do you know what you're going to say?"

"The truth, I suppose."

The dwarf frowned. "Is that wise?"

"It definitely is when you can't think of anything else."

The guards eventually marched them into a chamber as shadowy and cheerless as the prison. The echoing stone space was far more ornate, however. A statue of Lord Pluto sneering and brandishing his battle-axe stood on a pedestal, and the bas relief carvings along the walls memorialized what were apparently important moments in the god's existence. But it was the two-level dais like a truncated pyramid and those who occupied it that commanded Heimdall's attention.

On the lower level sat three men with stern expressions. Their features were lined and their beards white, but their frames were still robust. On the shorter upper tier reposed another pair of stone thrones, these unoccupied. One was larger than the other, but both were grander than the chairs below.

The judge in the middle drew breath to speak, and then a woman who appeared to be the one in Kamorr's story, she of the black hair and gray gown, entered the chamber through a doorway at the back. Light glimmered in the green crystal at the end of her rod. Or, Heimdall wondered, was it a scepter? From the way the judges jumped up from their seats to bow to her, and the guards made haste to salute her, the answer might well be yes.

Still, scepter or no, it was clear the judges hadn't been expecting her, and as she claimed the smaller of the two thrones on the upper tier, the judge on Heimdall's left, a fellow with a lantern jaw and a long face even more sour and severe than those of his fellows, asked, "My queen?"

"Yes?" she replied.

"It's just…" He was plainly groping for a tactful way to proceed. "We don't usually see you here. It's more common for King Pluto to oversee our deliberations, though as a general rule, even he–"

"My husband has spent the past several days away from his kingdom," the raven-haired woman answered. "I can only assume something of considerable interest is happening in the land of the living. In his absence, I rule and fulfill my responsibilities as I see fit. I trust you have no objection to my being here."

"Of course not, Your Majesty."

She smiled. "Then please take your seats and proceed as you normally do. Pay no attention to me. I'll speak up if I have something to say."

The judges sat down in their places. Afterward, the middle one said, "Prisoners, some days ago, you invaded this kingdom–"

The queen cleared her throat.

The three judges twisted their heads around. "Yes, Your Majesty?" the one in the center said.

"I think," she said, "it would be appropriate for you to declare who and what you are, so the prisoners will understand what tribunal they face."

"As Your Majesty wishes," the man in the middle said. "I am Minos. On your left, prisoners, is Rhadamanthus, and on your right Aeacus. In life, we were kings and sons of Zeus Panhellionos. Afterward, Pluto appointed us judges of the dead. We have been advised that you two somehow invaded this realm where you, men still living, have no right to be. King Pluto apprehended the taller of you and imprisoned you in Tartarus for your transgression. You then escaped, perhaps with the aid of your smaller comrade, and after that the pair of you resisted all efforts to bring you to heel, offering violence to our lord's agents until a patrol compelled your surrender. Your guilt seems plain beyond all doubt." He glanced at one of his colleagues, then the other, and received grim nods from both. "Accordingly, I sentence–"

"Wait!" Heimdall cried. He felt bombarded and confused by this barrage of strange names and accusations, but knew he had to present some semblance of a defense. "My friend and I did all you said, but there's more to the story. We had good reasons for our *transgressions*. If you are to judge us fairly, you must hear them."

"Nonsense," Rhadamanthus said. "The facts are clear."

Minos frowned, pondering. Of the three, he had the most thoughtful and possibly even kindly face, like someone's esteemed grandfather, and Heimdall hoped he might disagree with his fellow judge. Thus, he was bitterly disappointed when, at length, the magistrate seated in the middle said, "I concur. Therefore, let the prisoners be taken forth–"

"*I'd* like to hear what the trespasser has to say," said the queen. "If only because the intrusion of two such strangers is exceedingly strange."

Minos and Rhadamanthus exchanged glances. The judge in the center of the dais likewise sought to meet the gaze of Aeacus, but the latter, the smallest of the three, with ears that stuck out and slightly diminished the impression of august magisterial dignity, wouldn't meet his colleague's eyes. He seemed to want to stay out of even the most trivial disagreement between his fellow judges and the monarch.

"Your Majesty," Rhadamanthus said, "with all respect, even as we speak, Charon is ferrying the newly dead across the Styx, and the queue grows longer and longer outside. We must use our time wisely lest the numbers get away from us."

The black-haired woman smiled. "To use your own word, nonsense. You have all eternity to clear any backlog, and spirits will enjoy their rewards or suffer their punishments for eternity whether you judge them now or an hour hence. There can be no harm, then, in listening to what the prisoner has to say."

"Yes, Your Majesty," Minos said. He returned his attention to Heimdall. "Give us your tale, then, and be quick about it."

Moments before, Heimdall had wanted nothing more. It had been one last chance to avoid a return to picking up gravel in the depths of Tartarus, to save Kamorr from whatever punishment awaited him, even to prevent, apparently, the annihilation of an entire world. Now, however, a feeling of futility welled up inside him.

How could he tell the story effectively when he still couldn't remember anything from before his torture? And even if, relying on what Kamorr had told him, he managed to provide a coherent account, how could he hope to win his listeners' sympathy when his tale would be, among other things, an indictment of the very god they served?

Still, there was nothing for it but to make the attempt, and he did so as clearly as he could. It wasn't easy, particularly once it became clear the judges knew no more of Asgard than he'd initially known of the pantheon they followed, and he had apparently been ordered not to share the particulars. Still, he persevered.

Eventually, he came to the part where Malekith revealed himself, and then he learned the dark elf and Pluto had conspired against Asgard together. That provoked a furious glare from Rhadamanthus. Minos frowned, and Aeacus fidgeted and once again looked like he wished he were somewhere else. Heimdall inferred that the judge on the left was inclined to reject any accusations leveled against his master out of hand, the one in the middle was troubled but mindful of his obligation to be fair, and the one on the right would have been happy to avoid the whole matter.

As for the queen, Heimdall could tell she was paying close attention to his story, but her impassive expression provided no clue as to how she was reacting to it. Previously, he'd seen some reason for hope that she was on his and Kamorr's side, but if so, she was evidently trying to appear impartial now. Or maybe she always had been, and she'd insisted that Heimdall be allowed to offer his defense simply because her notions of fairness required it.

Heimdall hurried through the last part of the story, which was to say, the only portion he recalled firsthand. If he hadn't managed to impress the judges with what he'd already related – and he could see no indication that he had – a detailed recounting of his and Kamorr's battles to escape the underworld was unlikely to improve the situation.

When he reached the end, Rhadamanthus said, "So. Your story merely confirms what was already clear. You and your companion are enemies of King Pluto."

"Not by choice," Heimdall replied. "But when someone seeks to destroy a man's home, his entire world, what choice does he have but to defend it?" Though he still remembered nothing of Asgard, the prospect of its loss and the death of all its people nonetheless stirred anger inside him.

"But we know nothing of your world," said the lantern-jawed judge. "Not even its name, which you have chosen not to give us. Perhaps your story is a lie, and it doesn't even exist."

Minos frowned. "Your pardon, Rhadamanthus, but you know that's not correct. It's our gift to recognize the truth when we hear it."

"Fine," Rhadamanthus snapped. "In any case, prisoner, we don't *care* about your world. If King Pluto wants it gone, it wouldn't be our place to object even if we thought the idea unwise. Which of course we do not. Do my fellow judges agree?" He sent a hard, challenging stare down the length of the dais.

Aeacus was quick to say he did. Minos took a while longer, but then he too concurred. Afterward, he gazed down at the two prisoners. "We end where we began," he said. "You two trespassed where you were forbidden to come. One of you helped the other escape the punishment our master ordained, and then you resisted those who sought to capture you. Nothing you have said mitigates these offences, and so I will now pass sentence."

Heimdall raised his eyes to the queen on her throne. At the start of the tribunal, she'd seemed sympathetic. Surely, she'd intercede again now!

She didn't speak up, though. She simply looked intently back as though she'd given all the help she was minded to give. As though willing Heimdall to use what she'd already provided.

And maybe, just maybe, there was something. "Stop!" he shouted.

Rhadamanthus sneered. "You already had your chance to speak." Two of the snake-man guards aimed their swords as though anticipating the order to stick Heimdall a time or two to rebuke his impudence.

Ignoring the threat of the blades, Heimdall said, "You three have spoken as well, and I heard you. When Kamorr and I first came before you, you said you were the judges *of the dead*."

"What of it?" Rhadamanthus replied.

"My friend and I are alive. You have no authority over us."

"Preposterous!"

"Actually," the black-haired woman said, "the prisoner raises an interesting point."

Rhadamanthus's long jaw clenched, and it took a moment for him to master his anger sufficiently to respond in something approximating a respectful tone. "Your Majesty, we know the prisoners were forbidden to come here. We know King Pluto decreed punishment for the tall one. Surely, *surely*, there can be no reasonable objection to our lord's loyal servants enforcing what we know to be his will."

The queen shrugged. "But you *can't* know with certainty, good Rhadamanthus, and each of us has his or her proper role in the order my husband has decreed. It's presumptuous to overstep, prudent to await *his* decisions about matters that lie beyond one's proper concerns."

Plainly seeking their support, Rhadamanthus looked to his fellow judges. Minos looked like he might possibly agree but wouldn't say as much unless he hit on a diplomatic way of doing so. Aeacus simply appeared miserably uncomfortable.

After another moment, Minos offered what was apparently the best solution he'd been able to devise. "Your Majesty is wise. We can return the prisoners to their cell for King Pluto to judge when he returns."

The raven-haired woman frowned and cocked her head as though considering the suggestion. At length she said, "That is perhaps unduly harsh when they have yet to be judged guilty of anything. It would be better to release them into my custody."

Rhadamanthus couldn't contain himself. "Your Majesty!"

"You surely don't think they could hurt me," said the queen, "and it's equally impossible for them to escape our kingdom. So, where's the harm?"

Acceding to what he now must regard as an inevitability, Minos said, "I recommend we at least leave the fetters on."

"Why?" the woman with the scepter replied. "As we've just said, they pose no threat to a goddess, and there's no possibility of actual escape. Guards, unchain them." The snake-men did so. "And now, strangers, come with me."

She led Heimdall and Kamorr through murky black marble chambers and out into a walled garden that was the most cheerful, welcoming place the Asgardian had encountered in the underworld. Colors still seemed subtly duller than they would in a land of the living, but brighter than they did elsewhere in the prodigious cavern. Red, white, and purple anemones, lavender five-petaled dianthus, white hellebore, and a rainbow profusion of flowers the Asgardian didn't recognize flourished and suffused the air with their scents as though the sun was somehow making its nurturing power felt despite the ceiling of stone arching high overhead.

Rubbing his wrist where the manacle had chafed it, peering about, Heimdall had a momentary sense of unreality. He and Kamorr had stood awaiting some ghastly punishment, and now, suddenly it seemed, they were here in this pleasant place. He felt tempted to relax and reminded himself he and his friend still had to return to the world from which they'd come and save this Asgard place. If it wasn't too late already.

Kamorr looked around the garden with a wondering appreciation akin to Heimdall's own. Then he gave a hiss of discomfort and swayed on his feet as a pang of pain and weakness once again got the better of him.

"Please, sit," said the queen. "This is my special place. There's no ceremony here."

When Kamorr hiked himself up on a marble bench, Heimdall realized the black-haired goddess must possess the Allspeak, too. "Thank you," said the dwarf. "For this and for saving us back there." He grinned. "Although from what I could understand, you made my friend here work for it."

"That was not by choice," she replied. "My name is Persephone, or Kora if you prefer the one I bore as a goddess of trees and flowers." As if to reinforce the point, sprouts burst from the earth, lengthened, and put forth narrow blue-green leaves. After that, a yellow or white blossom appeared at the top of each and opened into a flower, the entire process completed in a heartbeat.

"I rule here while my husband is away," the goddess continued. "But he will consider what I've done upon his return, and I have some cause to be wary of his displeasure as the judges of the dead are wary of mine. I want to remain on amiable terms with him and not make him regret granting me the authority I possess."

Heimdal scowled. "You have my sympathy for being wed to such a husband."

To his surprise, Persephone frowned at his reaction. "Don't judge him too harshly. He's a good man overall, and I do love him."

"But you saved us from the tribunal," Kamorr said, "and despite what you argued at the time, you must know Pluto would want us chained up back in the pit."

Persephone sighed. "I said he's a good man and I love him. That doesn't mean he has no faults. He resents it that his brother, the king of us all, decreed that he must rule here while putting other gods in charge of pleasanter dominions. At the same time, he's obsessed with making his realm as mighty as it can be. That's why he's taken such pains to ensure that few who come here ever leave. Once in a while, though, he decides even that's not enough for him and embarks on some grandiose scheme to increase his power beyond all reason."

"Which is more or less what Malekith promised him," Heimdall said. "When the gods I serve perish, Pluto will move to attract their former worshipers to himself." Which, as far as he was concerned, meant Persephone's assessment of her husband's character was far too charitable. Anyone who'd help destroy an entire world just to increase his personal power was a monster. But he saw no profit in arguing with this woman who'd proved a benefactor.

"Yes," said the queen of the dead. "I understood his hopes from your testimony before the judges. When my husband hatches such a scheme, I do my best to subvert it, in part because, however much I love him, I have a duty to the ruler of us all. But even more because I want to shield Pluto from what I suspect will otherwise be the dire consequences of his overweening ambition. I try to do this surreptitiously, so as not to provoke a rift between us. By helping you obtain your freedom, I hope to see the plot foiled without me taking any of the blame for its failure."

"You must have been aware of what was afoot even before Heimdall spoke in court," Kamorr said. "That's why you didn't call attention to us when we first came here."

"I suspected something," she said. "Pluto's manner invariably changes when ambition gets the better of him. So, when I spied two of the living sneaking into his domain, I said nothing in the hope you'd come to somehow avert whatever he has in mind."

"You were right," Heimdall said. He smiled. "Well, essentially. We didn't understand nearly as much as we do now. Anyway, now that you've freed us from the tribunal, we can escape your custody, so to speak, while your back is turned, and once we return to the land of the living, I promise we'll do all in our power to ruin Malekith's plan without harming Pluto." Although if the haughty death god had to fall to save Asgard from destruction, he wouldn't shed any tears.

The goddess smiled. "I *hoped* you had a way to get back."

The Asgardian felt nonplussed by that burst of happiness. "Well, yes. It's not so very clever. Make our way to a part of the riverbank distant enough that the huge hound isn't likely to notice us, then swim across so we don't have to convince the ferryman to carry us."

Persephone's glad expression wilted into dismay. "But that won't work! Wherever you approach the river, Cerberus will be there. That's his gift. And even if you could overcome him, you'd need Charon's boat. There are terrible beasts lurking under the water that will tear you to pieces if you try to swim."

Kamorr frowned. "Can't you command the watchdog to let us past and the ferryman to take us?"

"No," said the queen. "I've already explained Pluto is intent on making sure no one leaves his domain without his permission, and in this regard, neither Cerberus nor Charon would obey me. My husband's will and magic forbid them to transport anyone back across the Styx without his personal command. He's woven the imperative into their very natures."

"Curse it!" Heimdall snarled. Not for the first time, he felt the obstacles in his and Kamorr's way were so numerous and difficult that there was no hope of surmounting them in time to save Asgard or indeed at all. He struggled to quash the feeling. "Pardon me, Queen Persephone. Please forgive my outburst. Is there a safe vantage point from which we can view the hound, the ferryman, and the river?"

That vantage point proved to be a hillock at the edge of the cluster of black marble buildings. There, he surveyed the vista before him. Seated cross-legged on the ground, Kamorr waited, his face betraying his growing impatience or maybe the nagging pain of his wounds. Meanwhile, a supernatural influence radiated out from Persephone's sandaled feet. The grass around her took on a richer green.

Heimdall focused most of his attention on the hound. Cerberus stood as tall as a ring fortress's outer wall and was longer from noses to tail than some prosperous family's longhouse. Despite his hugeness, though, the watchdog moved fast as an expert warrior's sword stroke and with a comparable agility, and the Asgardian could detect no hint of a lack of coordination among the three heads such as had allowed him to turn the cat-goat-snake beast's fire against itself.

His final hope came to nothing when Cerberus walked in a circle, trampling the grass, flopped down, and curled up to nap. Two heads closed their eyes and slept, but the third still rose above the others and peered and sniffed about, alert as ever.

With that, once again feeling useless and unworthy of Kamorr's trust, Heimdall said, "I can't see any way to do it."

"Come on!" the Blackhammer said. "We beat the other three-headed thing."

"It was as big as a bear, not a house, and anyway…" Heimdall waved his hand. "It doesn't matter. What does matter is that I don't know how to handle the dog."

"But you're a giant-slayer."

"Maybe I was when I had this magic trumpet and sword you tell me I used to carry."

"Before that, too."

Heimdall grimaced. "I admit, some of my fighting skill has come back, but it's not enough. Maybe if I could recall all those battles you tell me of, all the tactics I used…" He rounded on Persephone. "Your Majesty, do you have any notion of how Lord Pluto wiped away my memories?"

"I might," said the queen. "One of Hades's rivers is the Lethe. Mortals believe its waters erase memory, but that's not entirely true. Downriver, the magic fades, and other streams flow into the Lethe to further dilute its potency. If you drank from it there, you might, for example, forget your father's face but recall your childhood pet. Whereas if you drank from the spring where it emerges from the earth, the power is pure and strong, and you would unquestionably lose *all* memory. Pluto keeps a bit of the spring water bottled and must have forced you to drink."

"Between when Pluto, and the snake-men whisked you out of Tartarus," Kamorr said, "and when they brought you back again."

"If you know about the water," Heimdall said to Persephone, "surely you know how to reverse the effect."

"I know of only one way," the goddess said. "You must drink someone else's blood."

The prospect of that was unappealing, but the Asgardian's distaste was nothing beside the possibility of regaining all he had once been. He grinned and said, "I'm sure I can find someone to help me out. Maybe that wretch Rhadamanthus if I can catch him alone."

Persephone's expression reflected none of his own excitement. She still looked solemn to the point of glumness. "You haven't fully understood. The blood that flows in the veins of the dead won't serve. Neither will the ichor of one such as myself. It must be the blood of a living mortal."

Kamorr gave a harsh little laugh. "And I'm the only one available, aren't I? It figures."

Heimdall looked at Persephone. "Is a drop or two enough?"

She shook her head. "You must drink deeply."

"Then I won't do it. Kamorr's already lost too much blood. This could kill him."

The Blackhammer said, "You've got to do it. The life of everyone in your world depends on it."

"We may already be too late to save the place, and I don't even remember it anyway."

"But you're about to, and you shouldn't worry about me. Not long ago, you were praising my strength and willpower, weren't you? Well, then, I'm hardy enough to live through this."

Heimdall couldn't tell if the dwarf's confidence was justified or mere bravado, but little as he liked what was to come, with his initial reaction passed, he realized there truly wasn't any other choice. "All right," he said. "I'll hold you to that promise."

Kamorr clambered to his feet and looked up at Persephone. "We're going to need something sharp and a cup. My friend's not some filthy draug. He's not going to sink his teeth into my flesh and guzzle."

The black-haired goddess led them back into her garden, where, through some petty exercise of divine magic, a small, sheathed dagger and a golden goblet sat waiting on one of the benches. "The surroundings here may bolster your strength," she told the dwarf.

"Couldn't hurt," Kamorr replied. "Well, let's do this." He hoisted himself onto the bench, drew the knife, and, features clenched against the pain and his instinctive reluctance, gashed his arm. He caught the resulting flow in the cup and proffered it to Heimdall.

"First," the Asgardian said, "we need to stop the bleeding."

"Her Majesty and I will attend to that," Kamorr said, fingers clamped around the wound. "You go ahead and drink."

Suppressing a fresh surge of repugnance, Heimdall raised the warm, coppery draught to his lips and did his best to gulp it down quickly, without tasting it. Afterward, wiping his mouth with the back of his hand, he tried to find something in his head that hadn't been there before. He couldn't.

"It didn't work," he said.

"You just need some more," Kamorr said. The lips moving behind his beard were ashen. "It's just as well Her Majesty and I hadn't gotten around to bandaging the cut yet."

"I'm not taking any more of your blood," Heimdall answered.

The Blackhammer glowered. "Don't make this harder than it needs to be. Give me the goblet and I'll fill it back up. Or I'll just let myself bleed to no purpose. Your choice."

Heimdall started to return the cup. Though he could remember nothing of his life before collecting stones at the bottom of the chasm, he doubted he'd ever done anything he hated more than this.

Then, suddenly, his head swam. He staggered and fumbled his grip on the cup, and he and the goblet fell to the ground together. Kamorr called his name and he tried to answer, but then the dwarf, the goddess, and the garden disappeared, swept away by a torrent of images, sounds, smells, tastes, and sensations.

He and his sister Sif were children growing up in Vanaheim. They and their friends played at being warriors in the woods around the castle. It was cool in the shadows under the deep green boughs. He pored over one of the books that fascinated him even though the other children couldn't understand why he cared to learn about matters less practical than swordplay, archery, or sailing a longship. The scent of old parchment tickled his nose. Beaming, his mother gave him a treat, apple dessert with honey-roasted rye bread warm from the oven. It smelled enticing and tasted even better.

He and Sif had grown to adulthood, if not by much, and were callow new recruits to Asgard's army when Jotunheim invaded. His heart pounded as he and his comrades were about to enter his first ever fight with frost giants, and he wondered if his courage would hold and if he could survive. He and his sister sneaked into the vault, and he gazed in awe at the recumbent All-Father sleeping an unnaturally protracted Odinsleep. He swung his sword at one of the trees the enchantress's magic had animated and felt the jolt as the blade bit into the wood. Belly hollow with hunger, straining to hear any sound that might warn of the approach of hostile creatures, he groped his way through the lightless tunnels of the trolls. Half angry and half afraid, he faced Amora again in her lair in Skrymir's tower and smashed the stolen head of Mimir so she couldn't use its power anymore. He blew the Gjallarhorn and rejoiced when the blaring note shattered one of the ice giants.

In the catacombs beneath an abandoned city, he, Uschi, and a company of Vanir warriors fought the living dead, and the thick stench of putrescent flesh nearly made him puke. He and the Valkyrie feasted with Maarav and the other dignitaries of the Blackhammer clan, and while acutely aware that a single unwary word could expose their masquerade, he nonetheless savored the unexpected spiciness of the unfamiliar dishes set before him. Smelling the smoke and feeling the heat of the trees burning at his back, he held Hofund's point at Lord Frey's throat and felt less triumphant than amazed that he'd bested a true god of Asgard.

These and countless other memories surged back from wherever they'd been sequestered like floodwater exploding from a broken dam. He recalled his family, his friends, his enemies, his romances, his pastimes, centuries of explorations, missions, and battles throughout the Nine Realms. Everything came back, and when the delirious rush abated, he found he was weeping with joy to be restored to himself.

The joy ended abruptly, however, when he recalled his immediate circumstances. Then he bolted up from the ground and looked frantically around in search of Kamorr. Instead of sitting on the bench, the dwarf now lay, one arm wrapped in a bloodstained bandage, amid a patch of peony bushes that Heimdall was all but certain hadn't been there when the return of his memories overwhelmed him. Purple-red, yellow, and white flowers suffused their fragrance into the air around the Blackhammer's body, and to the Asgardian's relief, his friend's chest rose and fell. Kamorr was unconscious but breathing.

Heimdall peered about and found Persephone watching the two of them. "How long has Kamorr been asleep? How long was I?" *Asleep* was an inexact term for what he'd just experienced, but it would do.

"A while," the goddess answered.

"Then is it safe to wake him?"

"I believe so."

Heimdall reached through the peony bushes, took hold of the shoulder of the unwounded arm, and gave Kamorr a gentle shake.

The dwarf's eyes fluttered open, then fixed on his companion. "Fire and forge," he said, "I *did* live through it. In fact, I feel stronger than I have in a while."

"Thank the garden," Persephone said. "It likes you."

Kamorr grinned. "My clan would call that one more proof I don't belong in the mines or the workshop." Waving away the hand Heimdall extended to help him, he climbed to his feet. "And how are you, Asgardian? Did drinking the blood rouse your memory?"

"Yes," Heimdall said. "I'm myself again."

"Then it's time for us to figure out a way out of here."

That took the edge off Heimdall's happiness, for after all, despite the Blackhammer's confidence, it was by no means a certainty that even with all his memories and battle-craft accessible he could devise a means for them to get past Cerberus and onto the ferry. But, frowning, he mulled the problem over for several moments, and then a possible solution came to him. The answer, if indeed it was such, grew from his recollection of the encounter with Amora's witchcraft in the forest in Asgard.

He looked Kamorr up and down. "Are you fit enough for another fight?"

The Blackhammer said, "I can do whatever you need me to do."

"Then that's one part of the plan taken care of." Heimdall turned to Persephone. "Which brings us to you, Your Majesty. You've helped us so much already, and for that, we thank you. But now, assuming your powers are as I believe them to be, we must ask for more." He told her what he and Kamorr would require of her.

By the end, she was shaking her head. "No. I've told you, I don't want to risk having it discovered that I directly opposed my husband's will. I can provide you with weapons and claim you sneaked away when I wasn't looking, but as for the rest, you must find another way."

"There isn't another way," Heimdall said. Not without Hofund, the Gjallarhorn, or Golden Mane. "Look. I never met

Malekith until he murdered and impersonated poor Ulbrecht, and during most of that time, I had no idea who I was really talking to. But all my people know him by reputation, and his deceitfulness and treachery are legendary. I'll wager that whatever he promised Lord Pluto, if the scheme succeeds, only he will profit."

Persephone hesitated. "But you can't know that."

"I admit it, and so I ask you to reflect on something *you* know. The mind of the supreme ruler of all your people. Whatever Pluto in his ambition imagines, what would your overlord think of the destruction of an entire world and everyone in it? Would he be happy that now, perhaps, your pantheon could attract new mortal worshippers, or would he respond to such a monstrous act by throwing your husband into the depths for all time?"

Biting her lower lip, the queen of the dead stood and thought for a time. Nearby plants dropped leaves, apparently in response to her troubled mood. Eventually she asked, "Do you truly think I can play my part without being found out?"

"If you do it the way I suggested," Heimdall replied.

"Then I'll help," Persephone said.

SEVENTEEN

MIDGARD & SVARTALFHEIM: ONE DAY UNTIL BIFROST

Uschi tramped through the benighted forest with the shovel she'd borrowed from the dwarves in one hand and the Brightblade burning to serve as a torch in the other. It was taking longer than expected to find the spot where Ulbrecht's magic had interred the enchantress at the westernmost edge of the battleground. Apparently, the Valkyrie thought sourly, the instinct that drew her sisterhood to valiant spirits newly fallen in war didn't work as well when one was seeking the burned remains of a traitor's corpse.

She supposed it would serve her and her foolishness right if she spent all night out here looking for Amora's body after Ulbrecht had told her to leave it alone. But recent events were nagging at her and stirring formless suspicions just when the rest of the camp seemed convinced the trouble was over.

No reasonable person could doubt Ulbrecht was himself. His appearance and voice were the same as ever, and he was still engaged in the great work he'd conceived and which the All-Father had commanded him to bring into actuality.

Yet she couldn't shake the feeling that since the dark elves attacked, the sorcerer had been behaving differently. He was no coward. He'd fought the frost giants at the siege of Asgard. But he'd stayed on the battlements and cast spells at targets below. He hadn't battled in the thick of the melee like she had. This time, confronting Amora, he'd dared to come within easy reach of the enemy's blades.

The victory oration seemed out of character, too. Where had the somewhat reclusive, antisocial Ulbrecht even found the inclination to give a speech, let alone the eloquence to do it well?

And while Uschi was contemplating people behaving differently from expected, what about Amora? The Valkyrie had no doubt the other woman had been as conniving and self-serving as ever, but why would she collapse the tunnel with magical forces in her distinctive colors and then appear at the scene immediately afterward, thus making everyone assume she was responsible? For that matter, it was difficult to imagine what she might have had to gain by leading an attack on the camp. Moreover, when Uschi and Ulbrecht plainly had the upper hand, why hadn't she surrendered to worm her way back into Odin's favor and scheme again another day? It was panic that made her keep fighting and throw her life away, and however little a person might think of the enchantress, she'd never been one to succumb to that kind of overwhelming fear.

Which all added up to… nothing much. Everyone acted out of character on occasion, and the great work was done. If Uschi had any sense, instead of prowling around in the dark, she'd seek her bed, rise in the morning, and, well-rested, enjoy the noontime celebration when Ulbrecht would bring Bifrost to life for the first time.

Yet here she was, because some amorphous something didn't feel right. Perhaps she had Heimdall's example to thank for that. He was the one who was forever looking for telltale discrepancies, sometimes where none existed. Sometimes they did, though, and while she'd tried to tell herself that her friend and Kamorr were surely all right, their continued absence was adding fuel to her worries.

She'd only been able to think of one way to address those anxieties, and that was by giving Amora's remains a good going over. Because Ulbrecht's frantic command that she not touch the ring and his eagerness to burn and bury the body seemed, in retrospect, another bit of strangeness. Why would the enchantress prepare a death curse if, as seemed likely, she'd expected her dark elf allies to carry the day?

Fortunately, there was still ash from the conflagration to be discovered, and Ulbrecht's splitting and closing of the ground had left its own mark. Thus, eventually, Uschi determined where to dig, only to hesitate for a moment thereafter. The true concern of Valkyries was the spirits of fallen warriors, not corpses. But her station had nonetheless made her mindful of the respect due the resting places of the dead, and the grave of a noblewoman of Asgard, even a traitor, was arguably due more than most. Still, she could think of no other way to address her misgivings, and she'd come too far to shrink from the completion of her self-appointed task.

She stabbed the Brightblade into a bare patch of earth where it wouldn't start a forest fire, and then, by the light of the yellow flames, plunged the spade crunching into the dirt.

Before long, the digging made her sweat, and as the soil from the excavation piled up beside her, she realized that from where she'd been standing previously, she hadn't been able to see how far down the sorcerer had buried Amora. She supposed she'd look ridiculous if the body was hundreds of feet below the surface, and, dirty and disheveled, she was still shoveling doggedly away when morning came.

It didn't come to that, though. The grave was no deeper than an ordinary one, and Asgardian strength soon began to reveal the charred-black corpse. At that point, Uschi dug slower and more carefully to minimize further damage to the remains as she uncovered them.

In due course, the body lay exposed from head to toe, and, regarding it, Uschi wondered why intuition had prompted her to bother. Ulbrecht's conjured blaze had essentially reduced the corpse to a skeleton. What could she possibly learn from what was left?

Well, one thing, maybe. The gold and emerald ring still gleamed on a bony finger. Apparently, it had proved resistant to Ulbrecht's fire.

The mage had warned Uschi that simply touching the ring could mean her death, and she had no real reason to doubt that was the case. But nobody had to touch it for Gulbrand, Bergljot, and Ailpein to examine it. She'd cut off the finger wearing the ornament and carry it to the Blackhammer mages on the head of her shovel.

She raised the spade and thrust it down. The edge severed the ring-wearing digit and the others on that shriveled hand as well. She rolled the one she wanted away from the rest and scooped it up.

As she did, the corpse changed shape. It had been a charred, twisted husk before the alteration, and that was what it remained. Still, there were differences. The shoulders were broader and the bones thicker. The brow of the skull was lower, and in general, the body more closely resembled that of a troll than that of a slender beauty of the court of Asgard.

Uschi had no idea what that might mean. Except... the ring had disguised the true appearance of the body in death. That must mean it had masked the wearer in illusion when she was alive, too. Which meant the real Amora remained alive. Was she still lurking about somewhere plotting further mischief?

Having been so certain of Amora's death, irascible old Ulbrecht might be slow to accept that he'd been mistaken despite what Uschi could now tell him. Thus, she decided to wake the dwarf mages and have them use their magic to look for the enchantress. She picked up the Brightblade, quelled its fire, and sheathed it. She wanted to carry the shovel with both hands to keep a safe distance between the ring and its finger and her, and the moon would suffice to light the way back to camp.

Rising from his chair in the darkened tent – a measure intended to make it look like he'd gone to bed – Malekith noticed that, even though alone, he was moving in the slower, more cautious manner of Ulbrecht. That spoke to his mastery of impersonation while likewise prompting the reflection that it would be nice to discard this disguise once and for all.

He was on the brink. He'd killed the Asgardian sorcerer and

taken his place. Stolen and figured out how to subvert his work, convinced Odin to let him create Bifrost, and overseen the digging and the conjuring, all the while concealing his actual purpose from everyone. The arrival of Pluto and Hephaestus had produced complications, and he hadn't liked having the notoriously shrewd Heimdall poking around either. Yet he'd overcome all obstacles, with the result that the labor was finished, and the camp expected that at noon tomorrow he'd bring the Rainbow Bridge to glorious life.

It wouldn't really be at noon in front of everyone, of course. That would give people a chance to realize what was happening and interfere. He'd do it sooner, but first, a final maelstrom of chaos and bloodshed should keep everyone else too frantic and bewildered to pay any attention to him. With a bit of luck, he might even achieve a massacre that removed all possible opposition from the board.

He shifted back into his own proper form and, with a wave of his hand, opened a gateway to Svartalfheim as he had before. When he stepped through this time, however, it wasn't to a wooded mountainside and the approach to the caverns where some obscure, isolated rabble made their home. He emerged into a courtyard of his own palace with its looming battlements and spires and the stinking, withered remains of notable enemies hanging from gibbets or in bronze cages. A permanent portal, an arch engraved with runes, dominated the center of one wall. Once Malekith passed through, there were only more granite blocks to be seen below the half circle, but when a sorcerer reawakened the magic, the doorway would reveal one of dozens of locations throughout the Nine Realms.

The courtyard was big enough to serve as a parade ground,

and ranks of dark elf warriors stood at attention awaiting his arrival as previously commanded. These weren't untrained barbarians like the Rabid Wolf Tribe but elite, well-equipped fighters from Malekith's royal guard. They should be more than capable of butchering a band of Asgardians, dwarves, and what have you, especially after catching them asleep, but just to be certain, he'd made sure they'd have the advantage of numbers as well.

Their commander, a trollish-looking dark elf with one pointed ear chopped short and his profile scarred and puckered by some old, poorly healed wound, stepped forward and saluted. "All is in readiness," he said.

"You've seen the map I provided," Malekith replied. "You know the locations of the camp and all the tunnels. You're to kill everyone you find there, and anyone who approaches after the initial fighting is through. Is that understood?"

"Yes, Your Majesty!" The officer nodded to one of the mages under his direction. The sorceress, whose left hand had been replaced with an extremity made of crystal or glass, recited a brief incantation, whereupon the stonework inside the arch became an opening to a benighted forest. A cool breeze bearing the scent of conifers wafted through.

The commander pointed with his spear, and the ranks of warriors started marching into the portal. Watching them in their disciplined martial splendor, Malekith thought it rather a pity they were likely as doomed as the Rabid Wolf Tribe that had gone before them. He had no doubt they'd gain the upper hand in the battle to come, but subsequent events would probably put an end to them. Fortunately, formidable as they were, they were only one company of a far larger army, one large enough to conquer six Realms, albeit not all at once. Happily, Jotunheim and Muspelheim would throw in with him once their rulers learned of his initial victories, and then he could turn on each when the time was right.

Still carrying her shovel in both hands, the shaft parallel to the ground, Uschi noticed a shadowy figure moving ahead and to her left. She wondered if it was some mortal of Midgard encroaching on the territory the Asgardians and Blackhammers had temporarily claimed for their own. She and Heimdall had believed that, relying on a combination of the awe winged stallions inspired and gifts of Odin's silver, they'd convinced all such folk to stay away for the duration of the work. But maybe someone hadn't believed the stories others carried back to their village or had succumbed to the temptation to see the otherworldly visitors for him- or herself.

Yes, that was likely who it was. But Uschi was out here wandering in the night because her instincts had whispered something was amiss, and she wasn't going to simply assume the person before her was harmless. She sneaked toward the figure intending to get a better look before the other realized she was here.

Ordinarily, it might well have worked out that way. Though she was a thane in the All-Father's elite flying cavalry, the many confidential missions she'd undertaken at his or Queen Frigga's command, often with Heimdall at her side, had taught her to prowl silently as a housebreaker or assassin.

Generally, though, she wasn't trying to do so while simultaneously balancing a severed finger and its ring on the end of a spade. That robbed her of a measure of her agility, and after a couple steps, she decided she'd do better to lay the tool on the ground. Just as she came to that realization, however, her leather boot brushed the long, trailing branch of a juniper shrub. The low-spreading bush only rustled faintly, but the noise was loud enough to snap the figure's head around in Uschi's direction.

"Halt!" she called. She hoped that even dirty and sweaty from her digging and carrying the stupid shovel, she still looked intimidating.

The stranger leveled a spear and charged her. When his course took him through a shaft of moonlight streaming through a gap in the pine boughs overhead, she saw he was a dark elf warrior.

He was fast and already nearly upon her. Suspecting she didn't have time to draw the Brightblade, she reflexively poised the shovel to serve as her means of defense. That involved tilting it upward, and the bony finger and gold and emerald ring rolled out, tumbled down the shaft, and bumped her right hand before falling off.

She only registered that for an instant and then thrust the discovery to the back of her mind to consider later. It seemed to confirm her suspicions that something was badly amiss, but for now, she had to focus on the duel about to begin.

The dark elf thrust the spear at her torso. She knocked the attack aside with a clank of the spade and thrust the blade at his lead leg. He hopped back far enough to make the stab fall short.

Snarling, he tried another thrust. Despite his speed and facility with the spear, she once again managed to parry and seemingly responded with the same riposte to the knee she'd attempted before. Expecting it, the dark elf shifted just far enough to the side to cause it to miss while remaining in the distance. She jerked the spade up out of the feint and made her true attack, a jab to her adversary's feint.

He saw the real attack coming and was almost fast enough to sidestep that one as well. She'd meant to drive the shovel into his skull but only succeeded in grazing his cheek.

The scrape, however, was enough to make him cry out and stagger. A cut from iron, even a superficial one, was toxic to a dark elf, and that was what the shovel was made of. Her foe's distress gave her an opening to renew the attack and thrust the spade deep into his face as she'd intended before. He dropped with his blue flesh smoking, sizzling, and bubbling around his wounds.

Now that she'd disposed of the dark elf, she could consider further that the ring and severed finger had come into contact with her, yet she'd suffered no ill effects. Surely, surely it was a sign that matters were not as Ulbrecht and everyone else in camp believed them to be, but she felt no wiser when it came to understanding what the actual situation was. In hopes of enlightenment, she drew the Brightblade, woke its fire, and used the yellow light to examine the corpse of her erstwhile foe.

The dark elves who'd attacked the camp before had manifestly been a ragtag bunch of barbarians. Had this one been a survivor of that same assault, one who had, perhaps, fled to save himself when his fellows were fighting to the last, she would have expected him to bear arms and mail and wear garments reflecting a similar lack of sophistication. The spear, lamellar armor, and the clothing beneath, however, were clearly the work of highly skilled craftsmen, maybe even as skilled as the artisans who equipped the Valkyries.

Uschi decided the priority now was determining how many more dark elves might be lurking in the night. The ring and bony finger would have to wait. Reasoning that if touching them once hadn't killed her, a second contact likely wouldn't either, she picked them up and stuck them in her belt pouch. Then she willed away the fire sheathing her broadsword, slid it back into its scabbard, and stalked north, the direction the spearman had come from.

In time, slipping from the cover of one tree trunk to the next, she found her way to a company of dark elves. In the gloom, she couldn't tell how many there were, but she was certain there were more than had attacked the camp before. They had more mages, too, some of whom had conjured floating orbs of dim blue phosphorescence to provide a bit of light. The luminescence just sufficed to reveal the arched magical portal through which they'd emerged and hint at the fortress on the other side.

Uschi surmised that the dark elf she'd fought had been a scout dispatched to spy out the lay of the land and watch for trouble while the company got itself organized. As it was manifestly doing. The leaders were dividing it into groups, one significantly larger than the others. After she counted them, the Valkyrie was sure she understood the broad strokes of the enemy's battle plan. The largest force meant to attack the camp and slaughter the people there in their sleep. The smaller ones each intended to invade one of the tunnels comprising the huge subterranean runes and, presumably, collapse it.

Uschi peered to locate Amora but couldn't find her. Nor could she afford to wait. She had to race back to camp and warn of what was coming. She crept away from the dark elves until reasonably certain they would no longer be able to see or hear her, then started running through the forest.

EIGHTEEN

THE UNDERWORLD:
THE DAY OF BIFROST

A shovel cocked over his shoulder, Kamorr walked across the misty fields where the dead were making their way from the river to the cluster of black marble buildings and where the gigantic hound was presently lying down but surveying his surroundings with all three of his heads. The Blackhammer told himself he had no reason to fear the watchdog yet. He hadn't come dangerously near the water, nor had he done anything else to attract Cerberus's wrathful attention. Still, his mouth was dry, and he couldn't resist taking frequent furtive glances at the beast as he made his way along.

Anyone with sense would be reluctant to do what he was about to attempt, but he supposed his trepidation stemmed in part from concern that he still wasn't fully recovered from his wounds and blood loss. Lying among Queen Persephone's magic flowers had helped more than he would have expected, but maybe not as much as he'd led Heimdall to believe. He assessed himself as he walked along, checking for pain and awkwardness, trying to judge just how strong and capable he truly was.

With a scowl, he made himself stop doing that. He'd be as strong and capable as necessary. Because he'd assured his friend he would be, and the survival of Asgard depended on it.

He reached the spot where, when he and Heimdall had first arrived in the underworld, they'd noticed Cerberus pawing at the ground like an ordinary dog that had buried a bone. Once there, he waited for the ferryman to bring his boat and its cargo of dead souls to the near shore. Heimdall had conjectured, and Persephone deemed it likely, that Charon, bored with the tedium of his eternal task, would halt his labors long enough to watch a spectacle if one were provided. The trick, then, was to serve it up when the boat was accessible.

The ferryman brought the craft adjacent to the riverbank and pointed at the black buildings with his oar. His passengers began to disembark, and Kamorr realized the moment had come. He poised the spade and began to dig.

The maker had sized the tool for someone the size of the typical Asgardian or inhabitant of Midgard, not a dwarf, and that made the shoveling awkward. Still, he managed to gouge out scoops of earth, which he then flung high over his shoulder in the hope that would make it easier to attract Cerberus's notice.

Nonetheless, the gigantic watchdog wasn't moving. Maybe Heimdall had been wrong, and the beast didn't care what Kamorr was doing. Or maybe, whether the Blackhammer was tossing dirt high or not, he was simply too small to capture Cerberus's attention, or anyway, to capture it in time. It would be worse than useless to draw it when the ferry was already back in the middle of the river.

As the last few dead souls climbed out of the boat in their somnambulistic way, Kamorr started to sing as he dug, an old Blackhammer mining song. The result wasn't notably melodious, but he didn't care about being in tune. He only wanted to roar out the work song at maximum volume.

At last Cerberus turned his three heads toward Kamorr. The creature stared for a moment, then leaped up and charged toward the dwarf. Kamorr dropped the shovel and fled parallel to the course of the river. As he did so, he was grimly aware that a dwarf's legs couldn't keep him ahead of a beast with limbs long as pillars for more than a few heartbeats. But he'd done what needed doing and now could only depend on Heimdall and Persephone to save him.

Standing at the edge of the cluster of black buildings with Queen Persephone at his side, Heimdall gazed out at the field, the river, and all they contained – Cerberus, Kamorr, the dead trudging to face judgment, Charon's ferry floating by the shore – and imagined all the different things that could go wrong to wreck his plan. It had seemed feasible when he initially conceived it, but now it felt too complicated. Uschi, or Sif, for that matter, would have told him it was too clever by half.

One concern was the gear he now carried, the javelin in his hand, the large round wooden shield made of layered bronze, wood, and leather on the opposite arm, and the curved sword called a *kopis* sheathed at his side. He'd asked for a two-handed sword only to have Persephone tell him there was none to be had. Apparently neither her fellow gods nor their servants and worshippers had ever conceived of such a weapon.

He could fight with the arms he carried, no doubt about that. But maybe not as well as with the kind of sword that had, ever since his father first started teaching him how to fight, always been his weapon of choice.

Taking slow, deep breaths, Heimdall told himself he was just going to have to cope. Or anyway, that was the hope. The last few passengers were coming off the ferry and Cerberus still hadn't moved. If the triple-headed hound didn't actually care about the buried bone – or whatever – and this plan failed, the Asgardian would have to try to come up with another. He couldn't imagine what it would be. Something even unlikelier, he supposed.

Then Kamorr started singing. With the gifts of Mimir, Heimdall could hear the sound as though his distant friend were standing right beside him. He hoped the watchdog heard as well.

And Cerberus did. The beast finally sprang to his feet and raced in Kamorr's direction. While hitherto, the dead filing across the fields toward judgment had looked like sleepwalkers, they now demonstrated sufficient awareness to avoid being trampled or knocked flying by the paws of such a colossal creature. They scattered and cleared a path for the angry beast.

As Heimdall sprinted in pursuit, it was apparent that he, unaided, had no hope of catching up with Cerberus before the watchdog closed on the fleeing Kamorr, and it occurred to him that here was one more thing that could go wrong with the plan. What if, at the last moment, Persephone balked because she decided that she shouldn't interfere with her husband's scheme after all?

That didn't happen, though. Prompted by the goddess's power, strands of grass grown thick as vines sprang up from the earth and whipped tight around one of Cerberus's hind legs just above the foot; Persephone was keeping her bindings low to the ground to make it less likely the judges of the dead or any other onlooker would spot them. The triple-headed hound lurched off balance and fell.

As, hind leg still held, Cerberus clambered awkwardly up again, Heimdall stopped running and cocked back the javelin.

He couldn't kill Cerberus. Not permanently, anyway. Persephone had explained that, if slain, the hound would rise again like any other inhabitant of the kingdom of the dead. But Heimdall had to at least incapacitate the beast long enough to clear his path to the river. Vines alone wouldn't do the job.

His preternatural hearing enabled him to identify the exact point in the beast's body where the heart was beating, and with luck, Asgardian strength would enable him to plunge a missile into the organ despite the layers of muscle in the way. He threw the spear.

As he did, Cerberus, with all the strength and quickness Heimdall had noticed previously, tore himself free of Persephone's binding. The motion shifted the watchdog's body, and Heimdall heard a *crack* as the javelin impacted a rib. Afterward, its flight arrested, it dangled drooping and bouncing from the creature's chest. Heimdall had inflicted a wound, but not the devastating one he'd intended. As Cerberus spun toward him, it was clear that all he'd truly accomplished was to divert the beast's attention from Kamorr to himself.

As he looked up at the three pairs of glaring eyes, the three sets of slavering jaws with their rows of long, bared fangs, his trepidations fell away just when a less seasoned warrior might have succumbed to outright terror. It was past time to fret about Charon's reaction upon beholding the confrontation, the lack of a two-handed sword, or anything else. It was simply him against Cerberus now, and happily, he was fully himself again, a giant-slayer who'd defeated any number of monsters in his time. He snatched out the curved sword and shouted, "Come on, then!"

Cerberus obliged, heads low and jaws gaping to bite. He dodged to the side and slashed at the nose of the head on his right. The sword bit deep and drew blood, but that didn't arrest the watchdog's momentum. Some part of the creature's body – he didn't even see which – slammed into him and knocked him sprawling. Before he could spring back up from his supine position, the jaws of the right-side head plunged down at him.

There wasn't time to do anything but interpose his shield. Fangs closed on the edges, and the armor started to crack and buckle. Hoping the punishment would prompt the beast to let go, Heimdall hacked at Cerberus's muzzle.

Instead, the enormous watchdog maintained the pressure and raised his head high into the air, carrying Heimdall with it. The middle head snapped at his dangling legs. The creature's own anatomy made it difficult for it to catch one, but even so, it was only a matter of time before it would nip a limb off.

Heimdall left off slashing at parts of the jaws within easy reach and stretched out his arm to attack one of the eyes behind the muzzle. The point of the sword fell short by the length of his little finger, but the thrust must have startled Cerberus. The beast whipped his head and flung him through the air.

He slammed down on the ground hard enough to snap a mortal's bones. As it was, the impact half-stunned him, and he was slow in scrambling to his feet. Cerberus lunged and would have closed before he managed it except that a second binding of long, thick grass coiled tight around the watchdog's foreleg, and it cost the beast a moment to tear free.

Panting, Heimdall took a fresh grip on the handle of his splintered half-ruined shield and considered what to try next.

After running for a time, Kamorr dared to look back. Cerberus wasn't chasing him anymore. The three-headed watchdog was fighting Heimdall, so the first part of the plan was working. Now it was up to him to handle the next bit.

He turned and ran toward the river, then beside it, his looping course carrying him toward the ferry. To his relief, the high-prowed boat was still floating by the shore, and Charon had stepped onto dry land to watch the battle. Even the dead he'd just transported across the water, all of whom had finished disembarking, were standing and peering.

Kamorr tried to keep the spirits between Charon and him as he made his approach. Maybe the cover, his stature, and the ferryman's attention on the fight would enable him to close unnoticed and make a sneak attack.

Alas, no. Charon heard him when he was still a dozen strides away and jerked around to face him.

At that moment, the unkempt, white-bearded ferryman could have ruined the plan beyond saving by simply stepping back aboard his craft and pushing it out beyond reach into the river. But apparently his disposition was too choleric for that, or else he didn't see how an assailant Kamorr's size could pose a threat. He poised his long oar to serve as a makeshift weapon.

Kamorr kept rushing in. Charon swept the oar in a horizontal arc low enough to swish the blades of grass beneath it. The dwarf sprang over the wooden blade. He was almost close enough to make an attack of his own.

But the ferryman sprang back with a nimbleness the Blackhammer hadn't expected and opened the distance once again. The oar whirled back in a backhand blow, and this time, caught by surprise, Kamorr failed to avoid it. The attack bashed him and sent him staggering to the side. He struggled to recover his balance and might have managed it except that the grass was slippery beneath his feet. As it was, he ran out of solid ground, tumbled off the riverbank, and splashed down in the water.

Kamorr had taught himself to swim, another quality that set him apart from the average Blackhammer. Despite the shock of the blow he'd just endured, he floundered into an upright treading-water position. As his head broke the surface, however, he heard a stirring in the water behind him and recalled Persephone's warning that the river was full of terrible beasts eager to gobble him up.

Fast as he could, he stroked and kicked for the shore, that, luckily, was only a few yards away. He scrambled onto the muddy slope without ever actually seeing the creatures pursuing him. But fearful imagination painted a vivid picture of enormous jaws that nearly caught him as they gaped and gnashed.

He half-expected Charon to strike at him again the moment

he regained the shore, but happily, that didn't happen. Maybe the ferryman in his ragged rust-colored tunic imagined his first blow sufficient, or that the river beasts would account for Kamorr. At any rate, the Blackhammer had a precious moment to assume a fighting stance before Charon snarled and came at him again, shoving aside a dead soul in the process. The spirits he'd just transported were now dividing their attention between the dwarf's fight with the oarsman and Heimdall's more distant one with Cerberus, but their dull expressions betrayed no inclination to participate in either.

As his foe advanced, Kamorr reminded himself of all the fighting tactics and tricks painstaking practice had taught him. Use your size. If your opponent underestimates you, good. Get in close where it's awkward for him to attack but easy for you. Superior strength means nothing once you put the foe off balance.

Easing forward, Kamorr feigned a limp as he closed the distance. The ferryman's lips twisted in a sort of satisfied, contemptuous sneer at this apparent indication that he'd hurt his assailant after all. He swung the oar.

Ducking and lunging put Kamorr safely inside the path of the wooden blade, the shaft whizzing by above his head. Now that he was the one caught by surprise, Charon belatedly hopped back and repeatedly jabbed the oar straight down at the enemy at his feet, but to no avail. The Blackhammer dodged the strikes and, as the ferryman lifted his weapon for another attempt, saw an opening. He bellowed and lashed out at his opponent's knobby knee with a side thrust kick.

The attack connected, and Charon stumbled. Kamorr swept the foot that was at that moment supporting his adversary's weight, and the ferryman fell headlong. The dwarf threw himself onto Charon's shoulders and dug his fingers into the sides of his neck to apply a blood choke.

Charon let go of the oar, floundered to his knees, and tore at Kamorr's hands in an effort to break his grip. He couldn't do it, though, and after what felt like a long time but might have only been a few heartbeats, he fell unconscious.

Breathing heavily, Kamorr surveyed the nearby dead just in case they'd finally decided to join in the fight and take the ferryman's side. They hadn't. Their faces were dazed and empty as before. The Blackhammer then glanced in the direction of the boat. It was still here, *accessible*, the bow drawn up on the edge of the bank to keep the craft from drifting away.

He stood up and shouted across the fields to where Heimdall was fighting. "The ferryman's out! I've got the boat! Come on!"

Though Heimdall was intent on his own battle, the gifts of Mimir enabled him to register Kamorr's call, and for an instant, he smiled a wry smile.

It was all well and good for the Blackhammer to exhort him to *come on*, but he couldn't just break away. Cerberus would catch him and rip him apart from behind if he turned and ran. His only real chance was to kill or incapacitate the enormous three-headed beast.

Even though he'd told her to be careful and not let any of the other inhabitants of the black buildings see what she was doing, he wished Persephone wasn't so stingy with her long-distance magical attacks. More grassy bindings snaking up around Cerberus's legs might have helped him considerably.

But after aiding him a time or two early on, she'd mostly stood, watched, and let the combat play out as it would.

Apparently, she trusted Heimdall's prowess to carry the day. If so, it was time to justify her faith, before the beast finally bit him to pieces or some hostile person noticed Kamorr had captured the ferry and moved to reverse the situation.

Heimdall shifted a half-step to the right and then dodged back to the left. Undeceived by a trick that had fooled him before, Cerberus pivoted and followed the true circling movement toward his flank. One enormous head plunged down, jaws spread wide to bite. Heimdall leaped aside. The attack still brushed his shield, and even a graze was forceful enough to further damage the crumpled, splintered armor. What was left of the outermost bronze layer tore mostly away and hung dangling.

Heimdall struck back, and his sword cut deep. Cerberus snatched his head up with another gash in his muzzle. Both the side heads were dripping blood while the middle one was relatively unscathed because the Asgardian had consistently tried to position himself where all three heads couldn't snap at him at once.

That tactic had thus far kept him alive, but it hadn't deterred Cerberus's aggression, and now that the watchdog was figuring it out, it was unlikely to work even as well as it had hitherto. He needed to try something else.

His shield was all but useless now. As Cerberus turned to put his adversary squarely in front of him again, Heimdall released the handle, jerked his arm free of the strap, and caught the shield by the rim. He flung it spinning to the side, and the hound's heads reflexively turned to track the flight. Instantly, he charged.

He was running straight at Cerberus on a path that would allow the creature to bring all three heads to bear. But over the course of the fight, he'd trained his foe to expect him to do the opposite, and that, or the distraction of the thrown shield, kept the watchdog from attacking for a critical moment. The heads did hurtle down, one after another after another, but he was already past them if only barely. He raced on under the watchdog's body.

He knew he had only an instant before Cerberus would leap away, uncovering him and making his desperate maneuver useless. He bellowed "Asgard" and struck at the beast's foreleg like a woodsman chopping a tree.

He sensed immediately that the first cut hadn't been sufficient, and now the enormous watchdog was starting to spring away. All but certain the action was too slow, futile, he pulled his sword back for another attack, and then, at last, another green grass binding spiraled up and caught Cerberus by the other foreleg. Tripping, the creature spilled off balance.

Heimdall cut and, amid a spray of arterial blood, deepened the wound previously inflicted to become the crippling injury he'd intended. Cerberus yowled and snatched the bloody foreleg high into the air.

That gave Heimdall time to dash to the other foreleg and attack that one. This time, he was luckier. A single sword stroke cut deep enough into the limb to bring Cerberus toppling forward. The Asgardian sprinted out from under him in time to keep the huge creature from slamming down on top of him.

Even now, Cerberus wasn't done. Furious, the huge creature flopped and crawled in an effort to bring Heimdall within reach of one or another pair of his gnashing, frothing jaws.

Realizing he now had another chance to attack the three-headed hound in some vital place, Heimdall reminded himself that his purpose wasn't to slay Cerberus but to clear a path to the boat before Medusa, vulture-hags, or some other servants of Pluto emerged from the black buildings to stop him.

He bolted toward the river. Leaving a trail of blood on the ground, Cerberus wormed after him but couldn't keep up.

When Heimdall reached the boat, he glanced back to see the watchdog clambering to his feet. Apparently, Cerberus recovered from wounds as fast as an Asgardian.

A track in the mud revealed where Charon usually dragged the ferry partway up onto the shore. Only the very tip of the vessel was now on solid ground, however. Heimdall realized Kamorr had shoved the boat most of the way back into the water to expedite their departure, even if only by an instant.

Kamorr thrust the oar into his hands. "I'll wager you know boats better than I do!" said the Blackhammer. "You take over!"

Fumbling in his haste, Heimdall laid his curved bloody sword on the deck and pushed off the riverbank with the oar. Just as the bow scraped off the shore and the boat floated free, Cerberus came bounding up. The three heads glared and snarled, but he didn't wade into the water after the ferry or bite at the fugitives who were still within reach. Recalling what Persephone had told him and Kamorr, Heimdall decided the beast must indeed be constrained by imperatives Pluto had imposed, and the death god had charged him with mauling those who tried to escape the underworld by reaching the river, not with menacing anyone who was already traversing it.

Heimdall decided he'd better continue doing exactly that,

before some chance wavelet bumped the boat back against the shore and made Kamorr and him valid targets once more. He plied the oar with the skill of someone whose life had often placed him aboard longships and other vessels and soon left the riverbank well behind.

In time, he looked back. Just because Cerberus wouldn't bother fugitives on the river, didn't mean winged women with whips or somebody else wouldn't. But so far, no such pursuers had appeared, and the boat had nearly reached the opposite shore.

With the sight of Mimir, he spotted Persephone still watching from the edge of the cluster of black stone buildings. The light at the heart of the green crystal at the end of her scepter glimmered. He wished he could give her a bow or salute, but didn't. A show of gratitude might reveal her complicity in the escape.

"That actually worked," Kamorr said. He grinned. "Of course, I had the hard part. You just had to deal with a dog."

Heimdall chuckled. "Just so you know, your singing is awful."

They reached the shore. The Asgardian dropped the oar, retrieved his sword, and he and Kamorr shoved their way through the crowd of blank-faced dead who were docilely waiting for the ferry to take them across. The pair then raced up the tunnel, past other spirits shuffling down.

Some of the entities in the niches along the walls took it upon themselves to jump out and try to bar the way. With escape finally at hand, however, Heimdall fought savagely. He refused to believe one of these lesser beings could stop him where Cerberus had failed.

He was right. A creature gaunt as a skeleton evidently meant to embody Hunger, a yawning man with drooping eyelids whose presence threatened to plunge him into slumber before he shook off the influence, and even the personification of War all fell to his blade. Then the mouth of the cavern, the arch framing a piece of the starry night sky of Midgard, appeared ahead.

Nineteen

Midgard:
the Day of Bifrost

When Malekith began the incantation, the wavering flame of a single soapstone lamp had illuminated the interior of Ulbrecht's tent. Now the magic was writing phosphorescent crimson runes on the air, but still, he doubted the increased light would attract attention. Here in the time between midnight and dawn, everyone was asleep but a couple of sentries, and they were posted around the periphery of the camp. His pavilion was in the center.

Thus, he expected to finish the sorcery and depart before the new dark elf attack, after which, anyone who survived the initial onslaught should be too busy to look for him. It was accordingly a surprise when he heard a woman's voice crying the call to arms and the noises of the camp springing to life in response.

Moments later, Captain Uschi burst through the tent flap. Malekith supposed he shouldn't be entirely surprised to see her. With her comrade Heimdall chained in Tartarus, she'd seemed the person most likely to prove a last-minute hindrance to his plans. Still, *most likely* hadn't felt especially likely at all.

"Good," she said, a bit out of breath from shouting and rushing about, "you're already awake."

"I was too excited to sleep," he replied, "so I was amusing myself." The Valkyrie was no witch and wouldn't recognize the floating red runes as anything more than a diversion. "What's this about another attack?"

"A second company of dark elves is on its way," Uschi said. "More numerous, better armed, and better disciplined than the first. Many will attack the camp, but there are also smaller groups that I believe will strike at the rune diggings."

He suspected she knew that because she'd seen it for herself. He wondered what in the name of all that was fell and tainted she'd been doing roaming the forest in the middle of the night. But he didn't ask. Rather, he said what the real Ulbrecht might well have said in his place:

"I don't understand why the dark elves are back when Lady Amora's dead."

"She might not be. I thought that, right before you killed her, she wasn't acting like herself, so I dug up her grave. I don't believe that's her body. I cut the magic ring from its hand, and afterward, the corpse looked different."

So *that* explained what Uschi was doing prowling around in the dark. He hadn't expected her to question his version of events, and, now that it was too late, wondered if he should have arranged for her destruction or imprisonment alongside Heimdall. Irked as he was, the temptation to smite her now with a bolt of magic was strong. But the prudent course was once again to react as Ulbrecht would have reacted.

"Did you see the enchantress?" he asked.

The Valkyrie shook her head. "No. I couldn't spy for long. I had to race back here to warn of what was coming. I *did* see a number of dark elf warlocks and witches. I'm glad we'll have your magic to counter theirs."

Naturally, she expected him to be in the forefront because the person she believed to be Ulbrecht had played such an active part in the previous battle. Well, it had served a purpose at the time and should provide no real difficulty now. Malekith merely had to persuade her that it was reasonable for him to linger in the pavilion rather than leaving in her company forthwith.

"Of course," he said. "You go organize the warriors to fight. I'll prepare some spells and join you presently. In advance of the dark elves' arrival, I have no doubt."

"Should I have the other mages report to you?" Uschi asked.

"No. I'm sure each is already making ready in his or her own way. A group ritual isn't possible in the time remaining."

"All right, then." Uschi turned and strode out of the tent.

Malekith took a deep breath and let it out slowly. This unexpected development had disconcerted him, but truly, the plan was still on track. It had amused him to imagine the Asgardians and dwarves butchered like pigs, without a proper chance to arm and defend themselves, but a pitched battle would serve his purposes just as well. The commotion would still provide cover for him to absent himself before anyone else came looking for him.

Or so he imagined. He faced the glowing runes anew and

resumed whispering sibilant words of power. New symbols shimmered into being, a whiff of decay suffused the air, and then someone else brushed through the tent flap. Hearing the sound, he turned to find Pluto.

If the death god had been asleep like the rest of the camp, he must have awakened when Uschi first started shouting and armed himself in haste. Because he was fully equipped for battle now, his breastplate strapped on his burly frame and his battle-axe in his fist. He gave Malekith a glower that fairly reeked of suspicion.

This second intrusion might pose a genuine problem. Pluto was far closer to understanding the complete truth of things than Uschi was, and unlike the Valkyrie, he commanded magic. It wasn't sorcery exactly as practiced in the various worlds perched on the branches of Yggdrasil, but still, who was to say the stranger god couldn't glean something of the meaning of the runes Malekith had written on the air?

Malekith made what he hoped looked like a casual little sidestep. In reality, he was trying to obscure Pluto's view of the luminous glyphs as much as possible. "I've been expecting you," he said.

"I don't doubt it," Pluto said. "The camp's in an uproar because more dark elves are about to attack. What's the point of *that*?"

What indeed, considering that the death god had been expecting the two of them to depart a peaceful camp together a bit later in the morning? Malekith produced an explanation he hoped would serve.

"To be honest, my lord, not every ruler controls his dominions as completely as you control your kingdom of the dead."

"Meaning what?" Pluto growled. "Spit it out!"

"Svartalfheim has its share of traitors who would like nothing better than to dethrone me and usurp my place. It appears one of them is attacking me here, away from my fortress and army and, theoretically, vulnerable."

"What does this mean for the plan?"

"Well," Malekith said, "obviously, the excavations and, to be blunt, my person, must be protected, or Bifrost will never come into existence. After we defeat the attacking force – an effort I trust you and the blacksmith god will support – we two will inconspicuously take our leave while the rest of the camp is recovering from the battle."

Pluto's brow creased as he mulled over what Malekith had told him. At length, he said, "You never mentioned having rebels before."

Malekith shrugged. "It had nothing to do with the business at hand, and what king cares to disclose that his mastery of his chattels is less than absolute?"

"This doesn't smell right."

Malekith manufactured a disappointed expression on Ulbrecht's counterfeited face. "I hoped we were past this. You know my objective. Bifrost will destroy Asgard and its people. That will open the way for me to conquer others of the Nine Realms. Meanwhile, the death of the All-Father and his kin will likewise make it possible for your pantheon to find new worshippers here in the northlands of Earth. You, in particular, will benefit because you'll be ready to seize the opportunity. Thus, our interests coincide, and it would make no sense for me to play you false."

Pluto kept scowling. Plainly, he was torn between the wish to believe and what his instincts were suggesting.

A clamor of war cries roared outside. At a distance, other voices answered in kind. A first volley of arrows thrummed in flight.

"The battle's starting," Malekith said. "Fight or sit it out as you prefer. I'll be out to fight as soon as I prepare the proper magic."

Pluto was a death god, and, as Malekith had hoped, the imminence of a considerable amount of death exerted a pull. The stranger deity wanted to witness it and cause a fair amount of it himself.

He growled, "You'd better not be lying," and tramped out of the tent. Without, apparently, ever questioning how the alleged rebels knew how to find their king disguised as an Asgardian here in the human world.

Malekith sighed with relief, returned to his conjuring, and his whispering evoked the final red shining runes without further interruption. A glimmering portal appeared before him, and he stepped through.

He didn't look around to verify that the gate then curdled from existence, or that the floating runes on the other side did the same. He was confident the magic had ended itself as instructed.

Uschi strode through the camp giving orders, shouting them when warriors were too muddled with the sudden awakening to obey swiftly. As she did, she noticed the sky above the mountains to the east had gone from black to gray. Dawn was on its way. Assuming that she and her comrades withstood the initial onslaught, they would at least have light to fight by thereafter.

In due course, her circuit brought her to the burrows of the Blackhammers. Dwarf warriors were pouring out of the entrances, in some cases still adjusting their coats of mail or the shields on their arms. She was glad to see that none looked afraid to face a numerically superior force of dark elves. To the contrary. They appeared eager for a fight.

In the midst of the frantic preparations, Gulbrand, Bergljot, and Ailpein stood facing each other in a little circle. The mages were murmuring in unison, and a silvery flickering swirled around them. Something about that tugged at Uschi's mind. It seemed like it ought to signify something beyond the obvious, but she sensed a form looming above her, and the thought slipped away before she could grasp it.

She looked around expecting to see a cyclops, perhaps one bearing a message from Hephaestus. Instead, it was Avalanche swooping overhead. A groom who'd apparently understood the intelligence and devotion of Valkyrie steeds had saddled the winged stallion and turned him loose to find his rider. Dwarves cleared a space for the white horse to set down.

Avalanche whickered, then eyed her as though expecting her to mount up immediately. But it would be a bad idea to take to the air when scores of arrows were arcing back and forth. She told the stallion, "Soon," and made her way on to the Blackhammer mages, who were just finishing their little ceremony. Avalanche folded his rustling wings and plodded after her.

Blackhammer warriors were raising their shields over their heads, and the barriers clattered as enemy arrows showered down against them. Gulbrand made a brusque, impatient-looking gesture, and what was evidently a protective dome of bluish light arced over him and the other dwarf mages as well. Uschi was grateful he'd made it high and wide enough to accommodate her and Avalanche, too, albeit only barely.

"Where's Ulbrecht?" Bergljot asked.

"He was preparing spells in his tent. He's probably out by now." Uschi looked to where the Asgardian archers were shooting, and their fellows were forming a shield wall. She could see a couple of Ulbrecht's subordinate mages, but not him. Maybe that didn't mean anything, though. The way everyone was rushing around, it would be easy to miss him in the midst of the commotion. At any rate, with the battle beginning, there was no time to think about the matter now.

An arrow stabbed into the ground. It had plunged down just a finger length beyond the edge of the dome of light and accordingly a mere finger length from Ailpein's foot. He pulled it out of the earth, whispered to it, and tossed it into the air. It streaked away over the heads of his fellow Blackhammers to, Uschi suspected, seek the dark elf bowman who'd shot it originally.

Looking pleased with himself, the boyish warlock said, "We heard you shouting to rouse the camp. What else do we need to know?"

"That force you see yonder isn't the only band of dark elves," Uschi said. "Other warriors are headed for the tunnel runes. To destroy them, I assume."

Bergljot pursed her lips and shook her head in a way that reminded Uschi momentarily of her mother. "I still don't see the point of any of this."

The Valkyrie shrugged. "I suppose anything bad for Asgard is good for Svartalfheim. At any rate, it's happening."

Ailpein scowled. "And all the Blackhammers sleep here in camp. There's no one to protect the diggings."

"Even so," Gulbrand said, "the tunnels won't be easy to collapse. That's the best work of dwarf miners buttressed by strong enchantments. We three have time to lead our own bands of warriors and retake the excavations."

"If you do that," Uschi replied, "will there be enough Blackhammers left here to defend the camp?"

"There will have to be," said the mage with the dye-streaked beard and shaven tattooed scalp. "We'll organize our fighters. You go see to your Asgardians."

"Can you leave the magic dome in place for Avalanche to shelter under?" The stallion might be safer still back in the paddock well away from the arrows, but she wanted him ready to hand when the moment arrived to fight on horseback.

Bergljot smiled. "Of course, dear. We wouldn't let such a wonderful steed come to harm."

Her shield poised above her head, feeling the jolts whenever a falling arrow banged against it, Uschi hurried back to her own people. Everything seemed in order except there was still no sign of Ulbrecht, although all the lesser Asgardian mages had joined the fight. A sorceress concluded an incantation on a rising note with a screamed word of command, pointed a staff intricately carved from a single long bone, and sent a stream of seething, ragged shadow hurtling at the massed dark elves. The darkness faded away before reaching the enemy, however, evidently quelled by counter-magic.

Uschi looked around to determine if there was any additional order she could usefully give, and it was then that Pluto, Hephaestus, and their followers came to join the battle line, the five surviving cyclopes towering over the gods and snake-man warriors. It pleased the Valkyrie to see that this time, the one-eyed giants had armed themselves properly, with bronze crested helms, breastplates, greaves, and long-handled war hammers. After the previous battle, the god of artificers must have fetched the proper martial equipment just in case there was another.

"My lords," Uschi said. "The dark elves outnumber us. They'll try to envelop our flanks, but they won't be able to if you and your people anchor them. I suggest Lord Hephaestus and three cyclopes on the right and Lord Pluto, two cyclopes, and his bodyguards on the left."

Hephaestus gave a curt nod to indicate that was fine. Pluto, however, sneered and asked, "Who are you to give orders to us?"

"Captain Heimdall has gone away on a mission. In his absence, Master Ulbrecht has put me in charge of military matters."

"And who is Ulbrecht to dictate to gods?"

"If you have a better battle plan," Uschi said, "let's hear it."

The death god hesitated, and that gave Hephaestus the chance to jump in. "He doesn't. He's just asserting his dignity, but, uncle, there isn't time for that. The fight has begun, Captain Uschi's plan is sound, and you'll have plenty of foes to kill if you position yourself as she suggests."

Pluto grunted. "If you say so." He and his contingent stalked in one direction, the cyclopes taking care not to step on any smaller allies who were still scurrying about, and the god of smiths and the other one-eyed giants headed in the other.

Shortly after that, the rain of arrows abated. The bowmen on both sides had likely run short of shafts to loose, and now the battle was entering its next phase.

The dark elf force advanced, and not in the wild, undisciplined manner of the previous battle. The attackers had a shield wall of their own six ranks thick, well-armored fighters in the first three, spearmen behind. Uschi was keenly aware that the defenders' wall consisted of only four.

The sides shouted insults back and forth as the distance between them narrowed. The mages hidden behind their warrior comrades hurled magic that more often than not splashed harmlessly against the other side's mystical defenses. Occasionally, though, such an attack scored, and warriors in the front ranks fell writhing and shrieking or simply dropped dead or insensible. Then their fellows pushed up to fill the gap.

Uschi was one of them, stepping over the dead, shoving and squirming her way through those she commanded to claim a place in the forefront. By no means was this her preferred kind of fighting. She would rather have been mounted on Avalanche harrying frost giants or trolls from the air. But now that the time for giving orders was through, a Valkyrie thane's place was battling at the head of her troops.

She unsheathed the Brightblade. In another sort of combat, she would have set it blazing nonstop to daunt the enemy, but she didn't want to alarm or burn the comrades standing close to either side. She'd invoke the fire briefly, judiciously, when it would do the most good.

With a roar of war cries from both sides, the shield walls crashed together. Suddenly, the heaving, shoving press was such that it wasn't easy to wield a broadsword, even an enchanted one, to good effect. Maybe, Uschi thought, she should have opted for a short sword or dagger, but it was too late now. She and the Brightblade would just have to do the best they could.

At first, instead of attacking the foe directly in front of her, she cut and thrust at those on the left and right as canny shield wall tactics suggested. She willed her sword to burst into flame at the moment the weapon scored, or when continued contact with a dark elf's shield might set the armor alight, and then snuffed the fire when she pulled the Brightblade back for another action.

That all worked for a while. She felled three of the enemy, but then an orange-skinned foeman burly as a troll but nimble as a cat trampled a fallen comrade to confront her. Bellowing wordless hatred, swinging a war hammer, the creature attacked so savagely that she had to contend with him herself.

She caught the dark elf's first blow on her shield. The impact sent her off balance, and despite the ongoing roar of the battle, she heard a *crack* as the armor's planking began to split. She slashed at her foe, but he too defended with his shield, and the flash of yellow fire she willed into being hurt him no more than the blade.

Uschi barely glimpsed a long spear stabbing low through the front ranks of the dark elves to take her in the lead leg. A sweep of the Brightblade knocked the lance aside, but at the same moment the creature with the war hammer lunged forward, grinding his shield against hers. He didn't seem to care about any danger to himself as long as he could push her back and so make a breach in the shield wall for his fellows to exploit. She reckoned she understood why. Such a breach often resulted in victory for the side that created it.

The Valkyrie braced herself and shoved back. Still, she could feel she was about to give way. She was strong, but the trollish dark elf was stronger, and with their bodies jammed together, she couldn't cut or thrust and score a lethal or crippling attack.

But, teeth gritted with the strain, she *could* push the broad, flat base of her sword into proximity with her adversary's face. She did so and set the Brightblade aflame. He howled, lurched backward, and in that vulnerable moment, the Asgardian warrior on her right stabbed him in the ribs and felled him.

Uschi fought on, the dark elves attacked and attacked, and, with the advent of dawn, the sky brightened in the east. She no longer had time to think about how any of her comrades other than those to her immediate right and left were faring, or if the three Blackhammer mages were succeeding in protecting the subterranean runes. Her world contracted to killing the next foe, and the one after that.

Or at least it did until she caught voices at her back exclaiming in excitement. Fighters on both sides risked taking their eyes off their opponents for an instant to glance upward, and she did the same. The largest, brightest rainbow she'd ever seen was arching across the sky.

Uschi laughed in fierce delight, for now, she believed, she understood why Ulbrecht had lingered in his tent. He'd been awakening Bifrost. She didn't know precisely how the bridge between worlds was supposed to work. The sorcerer had said he'd demonstrate once it came to life. But no doubt he'd used it to travel to Asgard and would return with reinforcements momentarily. Maybe Thor with his hammer and lightning, or a company of her own Valkyrie sisters swooping out of the sky.

As she battled on, however, no such allies appeared. Instead, a wavering ran through the wooded mountainsides to the north, as if she were viewing them through a haze of heated air.

Was Bifrost causing the wavering? Was it supposed to? She truly had no idea, but her momentary excitement gave way to a pang of trepidation.

TWENTY

MIDGARD:
THE DAY OF BIFROST

Heimdall and Kamorr hurried past the spirits coalescing from nothingness to vapor to the semblance of living men, women, and children at the mouth of the passage that led to the underworld. The dead here paid the fugitives no more attention than those encountered in the tunnel.

Fearing pursuit, the pair nonetheless kept rushing as they clambered away from the low ground outside the cave entrance up the rocky slope beyond. It wasn't until they reached the woodlands, and there was still no sign of anyone or anything chasing them, that they slowed down to catch their breath.

"Can you find our proper clothes and your gear in the dark?" Kamorr asked.

Heimdall smiled. "Yes. It isn't all that dark to me."

As he led the Blackhammer on through the dregs of the night, and the eastern sky began to brighten, he was grateful anew for the sight of Mimir that allowed him to find his way, and grateful again when he and the dwarf located their possessions undisturbed in the brush where they'd stashed them. They made haste to discard the tattered, filthy, bloodstained remains of the chitons and sandals they'd bought in the nearby town and don their own familiar tunics, trousers, and boots in their place.

Heimdall had rejoiced when his memory returned. He felt something of the sort again when he had on his mail, Hofund sheathed on his back and the Gjallarhorn hanging at his side. He raised the trumpet to his lips and blew a blaring note. Almost immediately, Golden Mane swooped down from the sky, furled his black-feathered wings, and landed before him.

Now, Heimdall thought, *I'm truly, fully myself again. A thane of Asgard as before.*

Another thought followed immediately, however, and the new one was like a dash of ice water: *assuming Asgard still exists. That Kamorr and I didn't return from the land of the dead too late to save it.*

He tried to draw reassurance from the peaceful scene around him, the oaks, firs, and other trees whose names he didn't know, the hooting of an owl and the rustling passage of some small animal through the undergrowth, the mingled scents of verdure and the nearby sea borne on a cool breeze. Surely the Realm Eternal couldn't perish without the devastation being felt in Midgard.

But then again, maybe it could, particularly in a part of the human world where gods other than the Aesir and Vanir held sway. Who could say when such a calamity had never happened before?

Moreover, even if Asgard still endured for the moment, Malekith might be commencing its destruction even now, when Heimdall and Kamorr were still more than a thousand miles away.

The Blackhammer's thoughts must have been running parallel to Heimdall's, or else he gleaned what his friend was thinking from the play of expressions on his face. "We need to get back fast," he said.

"You're right." Heimdall pulled Golden Mane's tack out of the brush and saddled the stallion as quickly as he could.

Once they were in the air with the dwarf clinging behind him, he urged the Valkyrie horse to fly north with every iota of his supernatural speed. Black pinions beating, legs galloping for all that there was only empty air beneath his hooves, Golden Mane responded eagerly, and forests, rivers, and the occasional thatch-roofed mortal settlement flashed past below.

For a time, the stallion's rapid progress was a comfort. Then, however, the biggest, most vivid rainbow Heimdall had ever seen arched across the sky ahead. Despite its beauty, he felt a surge of fear, for he had no doubt this was Bifrost, Malekith's world-destroying weapon, coming to life.

"There's still time!" Kamorr shouted. "Surely it can't destroy Asgard all in an instant!"

I hope you're right, Heimdall thought. He kicked back with his heels to exhort Golden Mane to fly even faster, and somehow the stallion managed to do so. Not fast enough, however, to reach the Asgardian camp before the world around them began to waver, flicker, and change.

Ahead, wisps of cirrus cloud gave way to empty blue sky only to return moments later. The sun rising in the east jumped a hand's breadth higher in the sky and then dropped back to its former position.

The land far below manifested similar instabilities. Patches of forest blurred and presented new patterns of trees. A broad, winding river vanished and reappeared. A farmer's field of barley briefly became the overgrown environs of the entrance to a troll warren with skulls heaped outside the entrance to proclaim the tribe's prowess and warn trespassers away.

"I don't understand what's happening!" Kamorr called.

"It means," Heimdall replied, "things are even worse than we feared!" Beyond that, explanation would have to wait. He was too intent on riding as well as ever in his life to help Golden Mane travel as fast as possible.

Finally, he spied the mountaintop where one of the southern rune diggings lay. To his surprised dismay, dark elves had taken possession of the excavation and were defending it against the Blackhammers trying to fight their way in. Once upon a time, he'd believed the foes of Asgard wanted to destroy the tunnels. Now that he understood that Malekith was the current enemy and what his intentions were, he assumed the dark elves meant to protect them while the Rainbow Bridge did its evil work, although the dwarves might not understand the situation that way. Ironically, they might slay the occupiers only to take on the task of protecting the diggings themselves.

Heimdall also noted the battle had come to a momentary lull. Probably while everyone took in the changes Bifrost was producing.

"It looks like Malekith summoned his warriors!" Kamorr shouted once he too could see what was happening. "We should help retake the digging!"

But Heimdall had already considered that and decided against it. "We need to go to the camp," he replied. "Find out the overall situation. Then we'll come back here if that seems best."

In another moment, peering ahead, he realized that if his companion was keen to fight, he was at least taking him from the site of a smaller battle to a bigger one. A company of dark elves had assaulted the camp from the north. Thus far, the skill and valor of the defenders had offset the numerical superiority of the attackers, although the moans of the wounded and the corpses stretched on the ground, including that of an enormous, armored cyclops, demonstrated resistance had come at a cost.

Here, too, the fight had reached a hiatus when the dark elves fell back, perhaps to assess the transitory changes happening to the sky and the landscapes in the distance. Evidently, they'd decided the alterations wouldn't hurt them, or else their hatred of Asgardians and dwarves or fear of displeasing their king was such that they'd decided to keep fighting anyway, because they were reassembling their shield wall for another onslaught.

Uschi had observed the same thing. When Heimdall spied her, she was shouting orders to her own warriors and making sure they were ready to resume the fight. She scowled when he set Golden Mane down in front of her, the stallion trembling and lathered from his exertions.

For his part, he was delighted to find her still alive, well, and commanding what was thus far a successful defense. Dire as the present situation was, if they were fighting side by side, maybe they could avert calamity as they had so many times before.

"It no longer matters who killed Orien," she said. "As you can see, we've got real trouble now."

"More than you know, I imagine." Heimdall waited while Kamorr jumped down from his perch, then swung himself out of the saddle after him. "Where's Ulbrecht?"

"Gone to Asgard for reinforcements, I think."

"I very much doubt it. Where are Ailpein, Bergljot, and Gulbrand?" He could see other sorcerers and sorceresses defending the camp, but the dwarf mages were the ones he knew and trusted best.

"Gone to some of the underground runes," the Valkyrie answered, "to keep the dark elves from destroying them."

Heimdall felt a twinge of annoyance that he hadn't spotted a Blackhammer witch or warlock when he sighted the satellite battle to the south. But even the vision of Mimir couldn't register every detail when a fellow was streaking past high overhead.

"The Blackhammers do need to retake the diggings," he said. "But to destroy them themselves, not preserve them. Bifrost–"

"You!" someone exclaimed.

Heimdall spun around to behold Pluto. Apparently, the stranger god had come tramping up to confer with Uschi and, with people rushing this way and that, hadn't spotted the two who'd escaped Tartarus until he was only a few strides away.

The sight of Pluto brought a surge of anger. The rational part of Heimdall warned that one should be wary of attacking any deity, particularly a death god, but at that moment, he refused to heed it. He'd bested Frey and the Lurking Unknown, hadn't he? He pulled Hofund from its scabbard and came on guard. Pluto lifted his axe and did the same.

Uschi scrambled between the two would-be combatants, snatched out the Brightblade, and set it ablaze as a further deterrent to violence. "What's the matter with you two?" she cried. "We're all on the same side!"

"No, we're not," Heimdall said. "Pluto is in league with Malekith. Who murdered the real Ulbrecht and has been impersonating him all along."

"It's true," Kamorr said. "We learned it when we traveled to Pluto's kingdom. And it explains why, all of a sudden, we're up to our necks in dark elves."

"Preposterous!" the death god said. "I've been fighting to protect the camp!" He hefted his battle-axe to display the blood still smearing the blade.

"Maybe you thought you had to," Heimdall said, "to mask your treachery. But it doesn't matter. I heard what you and Malekith said while you were imprisoning me and stripping me of my memory."

"I *did* imprison you. Because you trespassed where you were forbidden to go." Pluto gave Uschi a look apparently intended to be apologetic, although it looked unnatural on his arrogant countenance. "I didn't mention it lest I stir up additional friction between our two groups. But as for the rest… Captain Heimdall admits something addled his mind. It has him believing he recalls something that never happened."

Uschi pivoted and sidestepped so that both the Brightblade and Hofund pointed squarely at the stranger god. "I know Heimdall well, and he doesn't sound much more ridiculous than usual. Which is to say, I believe him."

Though his appearance didn't alter in a way that even the sight of Mimir could define, Pluto nonetheless seemed to become denser, more truly present, than anything around him. Apparently undaunted by the two swords threatening him, Kamorr slipping around behind him, or the fact that none of his snake-man bodyguards was in the immediate vicinity, the death god was raising his powers for a fight.

"Surrender," Uschi said. "Or don't. It's three against one, and Heimdall and I have bested foes as powerful as you."

The Valkyrie might even be right about that, but Heimdall decided that in her anger, she'd lost sight of something that he, his initial flare of rage cooling, now realized. If a fight broke out, the snake-men, Hephaestus, and his cyclopes might well rush to Pluto's aid, and the defense of the camp would shatter into chaos. And even if, somehow, it didn't, with Bifrost arching across the sky, he and his friends might not have time to fight Pluto.

To everyone's manifest surprise, he lowered Hofund so it was no longer threatening the death god. "Captain Uschi is right, Lord Pluto. You shouldn't fight us. Not because you fear us – it's plain that you don't – but because it would be contrary to your own interests."

Pluto sneered. "What pathetic nonsense. Malekith said that if I helped him keep his intent secret while he created and corrupted Bifrost, it would destroy your world. And there it is up in the sky, commencing its work even now."

"I don't doubt it," Heimdall said. "But in Tartarus, you told me that from your point of view, the point of destroying my world with its gods was so that more humans of Earth, bereft of their former deities, would turn to your pantheon in general and you in particular. But that won't work out for you if Asgard and Earth, the worlds at the two ends of Bifrost, perish together."

Pluto's eyes widened in uncertainty, and then he mustered a sneer. "That's not happening!"

"Of course it is," Heimdall said. "Just look around you. You can already see inconstancy bubbling up in the mountains and sky on every side. Ever since Malekith told me of his plans, I've been wondering how even all the mages and deities assembled here could create something strong enough to destroy an entire world. But it was never a matter of raw force. Ulbrecht – the real one – intended Bifrost to serve as a bridge between Realms, and so it is, except that Malekith's version is doing more. It's drawing our world and this one together, superimposing one on the other. That's why, at certain moments, we glimpse a bit of Asgard instead of the reality we're standing in. And when the two truly come together, well, the sages I've listened to and whose treatises I've read are all of the opinion that two things can't occupy the same space at the same time."

"Apparently," said Kamorr, "Malekith is willing to destroy this world to get rid of Asgard. Makes sense. He'll still have other Realms of the World Tree to conquer. But those new worshippers you're looking for will be in short supply. In fact, good luck finding any humans after Midgard dies."

"I don't believe you!" Pluto cried.

"No?" Heimdall asked. "I think you're starting to, but if not, consider this. Why weren't you at Malekith's side when he summoned the Rainbow Bridge into being? Didn't he tell you that you would be?"

Pluto hesitated. "With rebel dark elves attacking, he wanted me to aid in the defense of the camp."

"Trust me," Heimdall said. "If Svartalfheim currently had any rebel lords worth the name, I'd know. It's my business to. The attackers are his own loyal troops meant to create a diversion while he, undisturbed, brings Bifrost to life. Ideally, I'm sure, the attack is meant to slaughter anyone who might otherwise interfere at the last moment, including you."

The death god spat. "It would take more than a gaggle of dark elves to kill me."

"But could they delay you until the Earth itself ceased to be?" Uschi asked. "Could you survive if you were here when it happened?"

"I wonder if even your land of the dead would endure," Kamorr said. "It's kind of hooked to this realm, being inside that big cave. And if it dies, would you survive even if you fled back to your place of power?"

"In short," Heimdall said, "Malekith's plan seems well devised to ensure that once Asgard and Earth are gone, he won't have to deal with a disappointed Pluto showing up to trouble him thereafter."

Pluto frowned as if all he'd just heard, together with any suspicions he might have entertained hitherto, might finally be overwhelming his wish to believe the lies the dark elf king had told him. "I left Malekith in his tent," he said.

"So did I," Uschi replied. "He said he'd be out momentarily to fight alongside the rest of us. But I haven't seen him. Have you?"

"No." The death god turned and headed into one of the alleyways running between rows of tents toward the center of the camp. "Let's find out what he has to say for himself."

Heimdall, Uschi, and Kamorr fell in behind Pluto. "So, this son of a sow is our friend now?" the Blackhammer asked.

"I wouldn't go that far," Heimdall replied. "Still, it's only a matter of time before Asgard and Midgard converge and annihilate each other. If we're going to stop it, we should take all the help we can get."

"It's good to see you," said Uschi to her fellow Asgardian. She sighed. "And not just because we're friends. I thought I could manage here in your absence, but everything's gone to the brink of ruin."

"Don't blame yourself," Heimdall said. "Malekith gulled us all every step of the way."

"I suppose. He even fooled me here at the end, when he told me there wasn't time for him and the other mages to join together in a ritual, and then I saw proof it wasn't so. All I can say in my defense is that Lady Amora made a good scapegoat. That's more or less who I believed the enemy was right until you showed up to tell me otherwise."

"Yet despite all the misdirection, you succeeded in defending the camp against the dark elves. There wouldn't be any hope of turning things around if Kamorr and I had returned to find it overrun."

Uschi flashed a crooked smile. "Thanks for saying that. I hope your hope involves me running Malekith through with the Brightblade and cooking his guts from the inside out."

"We're about to find out," Heimdall said.

Arriving at Malekith's pavilion, Pluto ripped aside the flap hanging in front of the entrance. Though the interior was shadowy, it was nonetheless obvious that no one was inside. The death god cursed.

"I take it," Heimdall said, advancing to peer beside the deity, "that Malekith is controlling Bifrost from some other location where no one is likely to intervene."

"He hinted he was going to," Pluto growled. "As your friend guessed, he also told me he was going to take me with him when the time came."

"But you're a god," Heimdall said. "With your powers, you can take us there now even if it means a jump between worlds. As I imagine it will. Malekith wouldn't want to be inside this one when it stops existing."

Pluto scowled. "I'd have to know where he's gone. The thrice-cursed knave never told me."

"And you never insisted on seeing," Kamorr said. "You really are a fool."

Hitherto, Pluto had rarely even glanced down to acknowledge the Blackhammer's presence, but now he glared and hefted his axe. "How dare you speak to me that way?"

"We haven't got time for this!" Uschi snapped. "Malekith probably ran home to his royal palace in Svartalfheim. I understand that your worlds and ours only overlap here on Midgard, Lord Pluto, but still, maybe you can find it if Heimdall and I point the way."

"But what if he's not there?" Heimdall said. "I wouldn't be if I was as wily and cautious as he's been all along, devising one deception after another to balk my enemies. I'd go somewhere less obvious and let anyone trying to avert what's coming get bogged down in a useless fight with my castle guards for the brief time remaining."

"Then where do you think he's gone?" Kamorr asked.

"That's what we have to find out." Heimdall waved his two-handed sword to indicate the litter of parchments on the trestle table. "Maybe there's a clue here. Or somewhere in this tent."

Uschi gave a curt nod. "I just hope I'll know it if I see it."

"No," Heimdall said. "We need you to perform another task. We may be able to stop Bifrost a different way. Find Ailpein, Gulbrand, or Bergljot and explain that they and their warriors have things backwards. The dark elves are actually fighting to protect the underground runes, and our side needs to destroy them."

As Uschi ran back toward the spot where Avalanche stood waiting, she spied the warriors preparing for the resumption of the battle, and she realized Heimdall had been mistaken. There weren't two jobs that needed doing. There were three. Even if she were willing to let the Asgardians and Blackhammers flounder for want of a leader, her fellow thane, Kamorr, and Pluto couldn't search the tent if dark elves breached the defense, rampaged through the camp, and interrupted.

She cast about for some seasoned fighter to whom she could pass the role of commander. To her relief, it only took a moment to spot burly, red-bearded Bjorn, bleeding from a cut on the arm but not deigning to notice it. She told him he was in charge until she returned, ignored his question in response, and dashed on.

When she spied Avalanche, the white Valkyrie steed raised his head, stepped out from under the dome of blue light, and unfurled his wings with a snap. He evidently realized she meant to ride him into battle at last and was eager to proceed.

Uschi swung herself into the saddle. "Maybe I should have left you in command," she said to the stallion, "but since I didn't, let's fly."

A few strides sufficed to bring Avalanche from standing still to a full-on gallop while people scattered to clear a path for him. Once he was up to speed, he beat his wings, and the tip of one brushed a tent and toppled it. The white stallion soared into the air.

Uschi's immediate concern was that she and the steed had thus made themselves tempting targets for dark elf bowmen, but no arrows hurtled her way. Maybe the enemy was conserving the few shafts they had left, or, intent on their preparations for a second assault on the camp, were slow to react to anyone, even a Valkyrie who was departing the scene.

Avalanche carried her high above the ground. That provided an even better view of the ripples of distortion blurring the sky, mountains, and the fjord to the west, but Uschi did her best to ignore the disquieting spectacle and scrutinize the sites of the rune diggings.

Though she lacked Heimdall's preternaturally keen eyesight, she could make out where dwarves and dark elves were fighting. There were three such battles underway, no doubt because the three Blackhammer mages had each led a force to start retaking the excavations.

From her vantage point, it didn't appear that any of the Blackhammer groups were faring better than the other two. So she couldn't choose a first destination on that basis.

She knew, however, that the miners and mages had begun work first on the northeastern excavation, and if warlocks and witches read and wrote runes from right to left like ordinary folk, that was the first symbol in the colossal incantation of earth and rock they'd created. One of the battles was unfolding there, and maybe the Blackhammer mages had targeted that symbol because it was of particular importance to the existence of Bifrost. With no better information or insights to guide her, Uschi tugged on the reins and turned Avalanche in that direction.

She intended to set down behind the Blackhammer battle line, an arc of warriors curving around the tunnel entrance, so she could seek out whichever dwarf mage was in command here and apprise him or her of the true importance of the fight without immediately being in the thick of it herself. But she was still high above the ground when swirls of darkness seethed into being in a patch of the morning sky. In a matter of moments, they coalesced into the form of a dragon, or rather, the shadow of one. The murky apparition turned its wedge-shaped silhouette of a head in her direction and spat something that might have been flame if flame ate light instead of emitting it.

Apparently, a dark elf sorcerer sheltering in the tunnel mouth was shrewder than those attacking the camp, or maybe he was simply more alarmed by the sight of a Valkyrie and her horse approaching. Either way, he'd conjured this horror to keep her out of the battle, and she and Avalanche would have to fight their way through it before they could carry tidings to the Blackhammers on the ground.

Uschi drew the Brightblade and woke its fire. Avalanche veered in flight and dodged the burst of dark dragon breath. Though the stallion avoided the attack, for a moment, its mere proximity made the Valkyrie feel dizzy and sick.

The shouts, screams, and clash of weapons on shields and armor revealed the battle for the camp had resumed. Meanwhile, inside Malekith's pavilion, Heimdall, Kamorr, and Pluto ransacked the dark elf's possessions for any clue to his current whereabouts. Judging from his scowl, the death god was growing more and more frustrated as the search progressed. Without even trying to lift the lid of a chest, he stamped on it, smashed it to pieces, and raked through the garments inside with his axe. "Nothing!" he snarled.

"Here, either," Kamorr said. Malekith had slept on a cot, and after looking under the mattress, the Blackhammer had shredded it and the pillow with a knife. He now stood in a litter of straw, scraps of animal skin, and feathers, with more flecks of down drifting in the air around him.

"Nor here," Heimdall said, abandoning his perusal of the scattered parchments on the trestle table. Many pertained to arcane matters, but, so far as he could tell, none revealed where Malekith had intended to go or held the secret of quelling Bifrost before it completed its realms-destroying work.

"Then let's go to the royal castle in Svartalfheim," Kamorr said. "I know you don't think Malekith's there, Heimdall, but he might be, and one chance in a thousand is better than none."

"Or," Pluto said, "we could try to capture one of the dark elf leaders and see if he knows where his king has gone. Or do what Uschi's doing and try to destroy the mystic symbols underground."

"Not yet," Heimdall said. Both his companions had proposed courses seemingly more promising than a continuation of the search. Still, he couldn't shake the feeling that only such a continuation afforded any hope of saving Asgard and Midgard.

He'd already used the eyesight of Mimir to examine Malekith's parchments despite the scant illumination in the tent and to check various objects for hidden compartments. But he hadn't employed it during every instant nor directed it absolutely everywhere.

He closed his eyes, took a deep breath, let it out slowly, and tried to sharpen his senses to the utmost. When he felt ready, he peered around the pavilion, and something appeared that he hadn't noticed before.

Even to his eyes, they were scarcely more visible than smears of clear water on transparent glass, but lines of floating runes defined a door-sized rectangle in one part of the tent. They lacked the shimmer he generally saw when viewing magic, but he suspected they were the remains of a spell that had already served its purpose.

Even as he beheld them, the symbols grew fainter still, either because Malekith had intended them to erase themselves utterly or simply because it was their nature to do so. Heimdall flipped one of the parchments on the worktable over to the blank side, grabbed a quill, dipped it in ink, and copied furiously.

"What are you doing?" Pluto growled. He might be a god, but evidently he couldn't see the runes.

"Quiet," Heimdall said. "I have to concentrate."

Pluto hefted his battle-axe. "Be careful how you speak to me."

"Shut up," Kamorr said. "I don't understand, either, but he's doing something important."

The stranger god rounded on the dwarf. "You deserve even less forbearance than he does."

Heimdall finished his transcription just as the symbols faded away entirely. "Enough!" he cried. "Kamorr was right. This *is* important. I saw the… ghosts, I suppose, of the runes Malekith used to open a portal to wherever he's gone."

"And if one of us recites the incantation," Kamorr said, "we might be able to follow."

Pluto seemed torn between hope and the continuing desire to strike down two people he deemed insolent before the world ended. "Are you sure about this?" he asked.

"No," Heimdall said, "but I'm sure it's our best chance."

"Read the spell out loud, then."

Preparing to do so, the Asgardian skimmed the text. Before, he'd been too intent on reproducing each rune before it disappeared to contemplate the entire incantation, but now he realized some of the characters combined to spell out seeming gibberish. These words, he suspected, were the names of demons or other arcane powers with which he was unfamiliar.

Heimdall knew he was no sorcerer. He simply lacked the knack. But maybe, with the writing to guide him, he could manage this one incantation. Maybe the Allspeak would make the names of the demons come out correctly despite his ignorance, compelling the spirits to answer to his need. He'd heard of such magic before, rune spells written out so any Asgardian could use them, and if that was the case here, he could save the precious time that would otherwise be required to fetch a friendly witch or warlock from the midst of the battle raging at the edge of camp.

He recited the incantation and, as he neared the end, poised himself to drop the parchment and seize Hofund or the Gjallarhorn to deal with any sentinel who might be waiting on the other side of the gate. Standing to either side of him, Kamorr raised his hands and Pluto drew a gleam of power from his axe as they readied themselves to do the same. But when the spell was through, and over the course of several heartbeats, nothing happened, it became plain no portal was going to appear.

"I'll try again," Heimdall said. He repeated the spell, only this time speaking the name of each of the runes that made up what seemed to be nonsense words individually. Unfortunately, to no more effect than before.

"You're not a mage," Pluto said. "I am. I'll open the way."

"If you can," Heimdall said, "by all means, do it." He proffered the parchment. "Do you want this?"

Pluto sneered and waved the offering away. "I'm a god, idiot. I can remember what I heard just moments ago."

When he repeated Heimdall's first attempt at the incantation, it was evident he could. No doorway opened, however. The stranger god spat and tried the Asgardian's second version of the spell. That didn't work either.

"What are we doing wrong?" Kamorr asked.

Heimdall had no idea. He was only certain they needed to follow Malekith before time ran out.

Twenty-One

Alfheim, Midgard, & Elsewhere:
the Day of Bifrost

The revels had entered their third day with no end in sight, and Amora's mansion was full of light elves, some she recognized and others who'd tagged along with invited guests or were simply party crashers. A pair of spice elves refilled their crystal goblets from one of Alfheim's champagne springs. The quality was exceptional, which was why the enchantress had opted to build the house around the source. Glowing moon elves and sea elves with inconspicuous gill slits in the sides of their necks danced a running dance while a band played a lively tune on horn, flute, panpipe, and drum. Out in one of the many gardens, an elf of the vale had her unicorn doing tricks while a groundskeeper eyed the creature suspiciously. He seemed worried the horned steed would paw up a flowerbed or relieve itself on the grass.

At first, Amora had delighted in the celebration with its abundant pleasures as much as any of the attendees, but pure sensual gratification had begun to pale sooner than expected. Wishing everyone would go home, she extricated herself from a circle of chattering sycophants eager to curry favor with the light elf aristocrat they believed her to be and walked to a part of the house she'd kept the revelers out of. She said, "Close," and the enchanted door swung shut behind her. Suddenly, it was quiet, and she breathed a sigh of relief. Now that no one was looking, she allowed the illusory disguise that enabled her to pass for a light elf to dissolve.

She knew why the celebration had lost its allure. Despite herself, she was too curious about what was happening back in the camp on Midgard. Perhaps the scoundrel who'd truly caused the tunnel to collapse had been unmasked. Or maybe Ulbrecht's great work was failing without her participation. Either would be satisfying in its way.

Her steps clicking on the marble floor, she made her way deeper into the private precincts of the palatial country house and in due course came to the chambers where she kept a miscellany of pentacles painstakingly laid out on the floor, ritual staves, athames, and chalices, and other occult paraphernalia.

A pool of water superficially like a bath occupied the center of the floor in one small chamber. She'd stolen the liquid from Urdarbrunnr, the Well of Fate, one of the three fountains nourishing the roots of Yggdrasil, and it churned and flickered green and gold as she paced nearer. The water sensed her presence and knew she wished to make use of it.

Amora dropped to one knee at the edge of the pool and swished her fingertips in the frigid water. "Show me Midgard," she said. "Show me the northlands and the camp where I worked on Bifrost until the wretches turned on me."

The water swirled, the colors glowed brighter, and then the incidental manifestations of witchcraft subsided. The liquid grew still, the shining faded, and now she was looking down through what might have been an open window on the vista she'd told the scrying pool to show her.

First, she noticed a brilliant rainbow arching across the sky and frowned with pique that cranky old Ulbrecht and his crew had completed Bifrost without her help. Immediately thereafter, though, she caught her breath in surprise as mountains in the distance momentarily changed form, and even the clouds in the sky displayed a similar inconstancy. The Rainbow Bridge shouldn't be causing *that*.

Wondering exactly what *that* portended, she next spotted the battles raging here and there. Uschi on her Valkyrie horse was contending with the shadow of a dragon in the sky. Below her and elsewhere, Asgardians, dwarves, and towering cyclopes were fighting dark elves. One of the enemy sorcerers had likely bartered for a drake's shadow or simply wrested it away by force.

Dark elves meant Malekith. He must be the one who'd somehow perverted Ulbrecht's design, and once she realized that, she, with her deep knowledge of wizardry, understood why the peaks and clouds were wavering. Vicious, ambitious tyrant that he was, Malekith had Bifrost drawing two Realms into the same space, where they'd annihilate one another. He was willing to kill everyone on Midgard if that would eradicate Odin and his people as well and open the way for Svartalfheim to wage wars of conquest on the remaining worlds without the All-Father, Thor, or some other busybody interfering. She admired the ruthless audacity of the plan but was also shocked that her homeland and all its people were about to perish.

Amora assumed there were those in camp who might also understand and take exception to the plan. She waved her hand from side to side and up and down, and the view afforded by the pool altered in response to her gestures.

It wasn't difficult to find Hephaestus. Together with a couple of the towering one-eyed giants, the god of artificers was anchoring one end of the defenders' shield wall. Dolt! Though respecting the deity's knowledge of his craft, she'd never deemed him keen-witted overall, and here was the proof. He evidently didn't understand it ultimately didn't matter who won the battle for the camp. Bifrost was going to kill victors and vanquished alike.

She shifted her spying to the interior of Ulbrecht's pavilion. Here, Pluto, Heimdall, and the Blackhammer the Asgardian had exonerated – Kamorr, that was the name – were at least trying to accomplish something that might matter in the long run. First Heimdall and then the death god recited versions of an incantation intended to open a portal. Her guess was that it would be a door to wherever Malekith currently was, which might allow them to stop the worlds-destroying magic short of its conclusion.

Unfortunately, their own attempt at sorcery wasn't working. Despite dogged repetitions of two versions of the spell, no gateway appeared.

Amora smirked at their ever-increasing desperation. This serves them all right, she thought, for accusing me and trying to kill me when, all along, I was only performing the service Odin required of me.

In fact, destruction would serve all Asgard right. The Realm Eternal had never treated her as her manifest superiority deserved. Rather, she'd endured disappointment after disappointment, humiliation after humiliation. Karnilla had ended her tutelage in witchcraft prematurely, before Amora could learn the Norn Queen's final secrets. Odin had never asked her to be his wife or even raised her up to rule a portion of his kingdom as she saw fit. Who could blame her, then, for trying to win that prize for herself by aiding Skrymir when he and his frost giants invaded? Afterward, when the Asgardians won, the so-called god of wisdom should have recognized that the fault for her disloyalty lay with him and sought to make amends. Instead, he'd proclaimed her a traitor and banished her for a hundred years.

And yet...

The other folk in the camp hadn't *all* been ready to assume the worst of her. Even Uschi, who disliked her, had intervened more than once to rescue her from those seeking to put an end to her. True, Amora's tenure at the diggings had finished with the other woman threatening her with her flaming sword, but now that her temper had cooled, she admitted to herself that might not have been entirely the Valkyrie's fault. By then, matters were thoroughly out of hand.

Which, surely, was Malekith's fault. He must have made Amora appear responsible for the cave-in to divert attention from his own machinations. She resented being made his pawn, resented, too, that it was he and not she on the verge of bringing Asgard to heel.

Not that subjugation per se was what the king of Svartalfheim had in mind. Amora had often schemed to steal the Realm Eternal's magical secrets, enhance her standing in Odin's court, even to seize a piece of the All-Father's lands to be her queendom, but she'd never wanted to destroy the place.

Though her detractors thought her heartless, she truly was fond of certain scenes and even people, and she was far from certain that, with Asgard erased, Yggdrasil's remaining worlds with dark elf armies on the march would provide a congenial haven for a surviving Aesir witch.

Besides, Midgard was about to perish too, with all its additional lives. That just seemed a waste, and to her own surprise, Amora realized she felt a bit of compassion for all the poor mortals as well.

Still, she thought, it's late in the game to stop Malekith, and I'm safe where I am. If I were prudent, I'd stay here. Then she smiled, rose, and murmured the enchantment to open a shimmering doorway in empty air.

Kamorr felt a crawling sensation on the exposed skin on the nape of his neck. He turned to see the glimmering rectangle that had appeared behind him, Heimdall, and Pluto.

For an instant, he believed the incantation the death god was reciting for the fourth time had finally opened the portal to Malekith's bolt hole. The gate just hadn't appeared where they all expected it to. Then blond Amora in her garb of yellow-trimmed green sauntered through, whereupon the doorway vanished. "Would you like some help?" she asked.

Heimdall and Pluto had turned around as well. Predictably, the stranger deity glowered and snarled, "You!"

"Yes," Heimdall said, "Lady Amora. Who, remember, whatever her past transgressions, is *not* responsible for our current problems. Lady, Malekith of the dark elves–"

"I understand what's happening," the enchantress said, "at least the essentials. Malekith is in the process of destroying

Asgard and Midgard, and you need to open the door to wherever he's locked himself away to have any hope of stopping him." She held out her hand. "Let me see the incantation, and I'll do that for you."

Heimdall handed her the parchment, and she pored over the characters for a time while the sounds of the ongoing battle howled and crashed from the edge of camp. At length, Pluto snarled, "Well?"

Amora sighed. "You're not an especially patient person, are you, death god?"

"I have mystical strength and knowledge and the Allspeak too. I could have been trying the spell again instead of just standing here watching you read."

"And it would have done no more good than before," the blonde woman said. "In our kind of magic, runes have esoteric meanings as well as the common ones used to spell out words. In this incantation, the characters that might be taken to denote unfamiliar names are meant to be recited individually. You were on the right track there, Captain Heimdall."

"Then why didn't the magic work?" Pluto asked, and though Kamorr disliked the stranger god's abrasive manner, he might have posed the same question himself.

"Because it's not enough simply to recite the runes or even to possess the knack for sorcery," Amora said. "The mage must focus his or her will on the arcane meanings the creator of the spell intended, and in this instance, some of those meanings are peculiar to the dark elf style of sorcery. Fortunately, I've made a study of it."

"Then if you're ready," Heimdall said, "work the magic. There can't be much time left."

"As you wish." Amora murmured words of power, and glowing red runes, presumably the same symbols Heimdall had copied down, began appearing in the air. Starting from top to bottom, the lines of characters gradually defined a rectangle the size and shape of a doorway. When they filled it in all the way to the ground, the shape became a portal in truth, another luminous vacancy like the one the enchantress had come through.

Heimdall and Pluto strode through with greatsword and battle-axe at the ready. Kamorr raised his hands into a fighting position and started to do the same, then registered that Amora looked in no hurry to accompany him.

"Aren't you coming?" he asked.

She raised an eyebrow. "You don't think I've done enough?"

"I suppose," he said. "I just thought you might want to get even with Malekith face to face. I do. And if we *don't* stop him, I wouldn't want to be here when the two worlds smash together."

"Well," she said, "when you put it that way. Lead on, dwarf. I'll follow."

They emerged on a square stone platform behind Heimdall and Pluto, and the portal blinked out of existence. Looking about, Kamorr discerned that the platform appeared to be floating unsupported in a void.

Though gloomy, the void wasn't entirely without light. On every side towered a shining diagram-like structure with imperfect ovals like chipped, lumpy dishes perched on lines radiating from the long vertical axis at the center. The structures glowed brightly enough to turn what would otherwise have been utter darkness to twilight.

For a moment, Kamorr didn't understand what he was

looking at. Then he perceived the structures were moving in unison. Each was dipping a line to bring one of the ovals lower while lifting the round attached to another. In due course, the shapes would come together.

The structures, then, must be abstract representations of Yggdrasil and reflections of the deadly sorcery in progress. Judging from the proximity of the two rounds representing Asgard and Midgard, Heimdall had been right that he and his companions were running out of time to stop the magic short of its realms-destroying culmination.

As seemingly unsupported as the platform, steep stone stairs ran up from the side of it to a landing. From that second platform, three sets of steps climbed in different directions to still more landings, which gave rise to still more staircases. In total, it all made a labyrinthine tangle suspended overhead.

Pluto took a step toward the bottom staircase, then thought better of it. Sneering as though to show contempt for Malekith's attempt to flummox anyone who managed to pursue him this far, he turned, chopped with his battle-axe in the direction of one of the luminous abstractions representing the World Tree, and hurled a flare of power from the blade. By all appearances, the death god's weapon could hurl blasts of force as devastating as the bursts of flame Heimdall could throw from the sword Hofund, but, to Kamorr's disappointment, the attack passed through its target without damaging it.

"It wouldn't have mattered anyway," Amora said. "Those illusions are incidental to the magic. To stop it, we need to confront Malekith, who, I infer, is at the top of the maze of staircases."

"I imagine so," Heimdall said, gazing upward, "although

I can't see him or anything at the top. The way the staircases crisscross again and again is blocking my view."

"No matter," Amora said. "I can shift us to the top even if I can't see it." She recited three words in her lilting soprano voice and twirled her hand in the air. She and her companions remained where they were.

"Well?" Pluto spat.

"Apparently," the enchantress said, looking annoyed, "that particular magic doesn't work here. Bifrost is a recent development, but Malekith must have long ago begun creating this place to be his ultimate refuge. It's a little bubble of space outside any of the Nine Realms where he got to make the rules."

"Then it's the stairs," Heimdall said. His grim tone made it plain he begrudged the time it would take to climb them.

"I hope not," Amora said. She whispered another brief incantation and floated up a finger-length above the platform. "It appears Malekith didn't take away my ability to fly. Which means I can soar to his level without bothering with the steps, take him by surprise, and turn him into something harmless yet unpleasant."

Blonde hair swinging around her shoulders, she turned and flew off the platform and upward in a trajectory plainly intended to raise her alongside the tangled stairways. Heimdall shouted, "Wait!" and lunged with his hand outstretched to hold her back, but she was already beyond the edge of the floating square of stone before he could.

The reason for Heimdall's alarm became clear immediately thereafter. The space below Amora had seemed empty before, a bottomless nothingness extending down and down to infinity, but Kamorr's friend with his preternatural eyesight must have seen a preliminary stirring of magic, and now the enchantment manifested. Gray as the sea on a sunless day, seemingly as numerous as blades of grass in a meadow, scaly tentacles shot up from the emptiness. One whipped around the flyer's ankle, a second pinned an arm to her side, and a third wrapped around her throat. In an instant, they dragged her below the level of the platform, maybe to be chewed to bits and devoured by whatever colossal creature had snared her.

Heimdall, Pluto, and Kamorr rushed to the edge of the stone. Heimdall hurled flame from his two-handed sword at the mass of writhing tentacles below. Pluto threw another blast of force from his axe.

Neither attack landed particularly near Amora, maybe because Heimdall and Pluto were leery of hurting her and because they assumed all the tentacles were part of a single creature, and hurting any part of it would be beneficial. Unfortunately, though, their initial efforts didn't prompt the arm gripping the enchantress to let her go.

Lacking any such means of attacking at range, Kamorr screwed up his courage and dived off the edge. He was, after all, the one who'd encouraged Amora to come through the portal. By his reckoning, that made him responsible for her, and anyway, this tactic had worked for Heimdall back in Tartarus, hadn't it?

Happily, so many arms had twisted up from below to menace Amora that he had little trouble catching hold of one of them. Less happily, it wasn't one of the ones gripping his companion, and the end of it was curling around to grab him. Body dangling, he swung himself to another tentacle before it could.

Meanwhile, more bursts of flame and concussive force exploded around him. It was plain they were hurting the creature. Heimdall's sword was burning patches of the tentacles black, making them stink of charred flesh. The death god's axe blasted hide and muscle away, sometimes close enough that the spatter splashed Kamorr as he made his way along. But clearly, the creature still wasn't hurt sorely enough to relinquish its prey.

With a grunt of effort, Kamorr swung himself onto the tentacle clutching Amora by the throat, heaved himself on top of it as if it were a donkey, and crawled down it until he reached the enchantress herself. As he did, he felt sorely ill-prepared for what would come next. His victories in Tartarus had left him convinced that he truly did know how to fight and fight well, but he was accustomed to doing so with a solid surface under his feet. This was going to be different.

He punched and pounded the tentacle. His hands were callused and tough, but the scaly hide scratched, scraped, and bloodied them even so. Amora squeezed the tentacle with her free hand, and her fingers flickered green and gold with whatever witchcraft she was invoking, but neither her effort nor Kamorr's loosened the creature's grip on her neck. Her face was red, her lips swollen, and she reminded him of combatants on the verge of being choked unconscious on the mat.

"Turn your head!" he shouted. "You'll be able to breathe!" He hoped. The tentacle wasn't like the jointed arm of a man, which perforce compressed a person's windpipe imperfectly. It was more like a noose. Still, maybe there was a chance.

With an effort, the enchantress twisted her head to the left, and as the Blackhammer had hoped, the tentacle's hold on her neck wasn't absolute lethal perfection. She sucked in a breath and croaked an incantation.

The words of power increased the strength of the magic she was already working. Her fist closed, crushing the tentacle she was gripping. Some of the gray flesh oozed out around and between her fingers. What remained in her grasp could be little thicker than a length of string. She jerked her arm and broke it in two.

The tentacle flailed, carrying Kamorr away from her. As the distance widened, she used the same magic to tear the ends off the other arms that had her in their grips.

At that point, something, maybe what the enchantress was doing, maybe the continuing blasts of yellow flame and raw force from overhead, maybe all of it together, must have convinced the creature to retreat. Waving, the tentacles retracted, or the thing to which they were attached fled downward, and the floating stone square overhead, and the Asgardian and stranger god peering over the side, looked smaller by the moment.

Borne helplessly into the depths, Kamorr couldn't know exactly what awaited him, but assumed it would be death in one form or another. He hoped it would be fast, took a deep breath and resolved to meet it like a proper Blackhammer no matter what, and then, to his surprise, instead of flying directly back to safety, Amora swooped to him, gripped him by the forearms, and bore him off the twisting, truncated tentacle and upward.

As they landed on the platform, he took stock of her. She stood favoring the leg the creature had grasped, and bruises were already coming up on her neck. She had pinpoint red spots in her left eye, the right one was completely bloodshot, and when she spoke, her previously melodious voice was a rasp:

"You didn't think I'd come after you, did you?"

Evidently, while he'd been taking stock of her, she'd done the same to him. Feeling sheepish, he said, "To be honest, no, I didn't."

Amora snorted. "I always pay my debts, Blackhammer." She looked up. "And it's past time to pay one of a different sort."

"Are you still up to it?" Heimdall asked. He sounded winded. Maybe calling on Hofund's magic many times in quick succession took a toll on his stamina.

"I'd better be, hadn't I?" she replied. "With Asgard about to die and Midgard with it."

Kamorr peered warily over the side of the platform. The gulf below looked empty once again. "Can you fly to the top now? Maybe take the rest of us with you?"

"I wouldn't advise it," Heimdall said. "The magic that summoned or birthed the tentacle-thing is still there waiting to make another the moment anyone ventures off the platform or the stairs."

"Then we take the stairs!" Pluto snarled. "Come on, before we run out of time!"

The steps were wide enough for him and Heimdall to run up them side by side. Rather than put weight on her injured ankle, Amora flew after them with her feet above the stonework. Bringing up the rear, Kamorr exerted himself to the utmost to keep up with his companions. Given the urgency of their task, he couldn't ask them to slow down, nor was he willing to be left behind lest they need him once again.

But after several flights, it was Heimdall who said, "Stop! We have to double back."

"Why?" Pluto asked.

"Because if we stay on this path, the next set of stairs will collapse under our feet. I can see the hairline cracks."

"Why didn't you see them before?" the death god said.

"I already told you. Even I can't see a thing if something else is blocking the view, and the crisscrossing of the various staircases is accomplishing that nicely. And before you ask, I don't think Lady Amora can safely fly over that section of steps without putting her weight on them. There's an enchantment seething there along with the cracks."

"Then we go back and find another way," Kamorr said. He turned and descended, and his companions followed. When they reached a landing where a different staircase also ascended, Pluto and Heimdall took the lead again.

They climbed another four flights. Until the Asgardian warrior said, "We've strayed onto another false path. We need to go back down to the last landing."

"There isn't time for this!" Pluto brandished his battle-axe at one of the floating representations of the World Tree, where the rounds representing Asgard and Midgard were inexorably converging.

"You're right," Heimdall said. He bowed his head, his brow creased, and his gray eyes narrowed. It was an expression Kamorr had come to recognize. His friend was trying to come up with a solution to their predicament.

After a moment, the Asgardian warrior raised his head. "When my steed and I were flying over the camp," he said, "I spotted a small roof made of mystical force. It was shielding

Uschi's horse from arrows arcing down from overhead. Lady Amora, Lord Pluto, can either of you conjure something similar?"

"Of course," the god and the sorceress said as one.

"Good," Heimdall said. "We're going back to the last landing. Once we get there, layer the shields one on top of the other and make them as strong as you can. They need to ward off something heavier than arrows."

The floating roof Pluto produced scarcely glowed at all. The levitation notwithstanding, it looked heavy, a dark gray creation that reminded Kamorr of the rocky landscapes of Tartarus. When the enchantress's witchcraft produced an emerald shimmer on top of it, the combination seemed as incongruous as a coating of honey on an anvil.

The four companions all sheltered under the layered mystical barrier. Still hovering a finger length above the platform, Amora asked, "What now?"

"Now," Heimdall said, "I suggest you all cover your ears." When they'd done so, he raised the Gjallarhorn to his mouth and blew a long, blaring note. Though Kamorr's hands presumably kept out some of the noise, what came through was still stunningly loud, a howl that rendered thought impossible and his cry of pain inaudible.

But as far as the Blackhammer could tell, though the trumpet's call staggered Amora and Pluto as well, nothing else happened. The death god glowered at Heimdall and jabbered something Kamorr couldn't hear. In the aftermath of the blare, he couldn't hear anything and suspected the sorceress and Pluto had fallen prey to the same temporary deafness.

Heimdall ignored whatever Pluto was shouting at him. The

Asgardian took a deep breath and sounded the Gjallarhorn again.

This time, peering out from under the conjured shelter, Kamorr gleaned something of what Heimdall had in mind. Sections of the tangle of staircases – those that would collapse if an intruder sought to negotiate them, presumably – shivered in response to the vibrations but remained in place.

Until Heimdall sounded the Gjallarhorn a third time. At which point, the false stairs shattered.

Chunks of stone, some as long as a mining cart, plummeted into the bottomless gulf below. Some smashed to bits against the layered protection magic had created. One especially large fragment clipped the edge of the landing on its way down, whereupon the platform tilted. Kamorr flailed as he tried to recover his balance and *not* reel over the brink into the sea of tentacles that the destruction of the traps had brought forth.

Then, however, the landing righted itself. Malekith had apparently created the true ascent to his aerie to endure. The rain of broken stone ended, and the tentacles, evidently sensing there was no prey to clutch after all, vanished as abruptly as they'd appeared.

Amora and Pluto let their magical creation dissolve. Both, even the god, slumped as though maintaining the protection through the repeated impacts had been a strain.

Heimdall pointed upward. Following the gesture, Kamorr realized the destruction wrought by the Gjallarhorn had simplified the vista above him considerably. With all the gaps now present in the maze of staircases, even a fellow lacking the gifts of Mimir could make out the platform at the top and the proper way to climb to it. As yet, he could only see the flat, featureless underside of the final slab of stone, but surely, he and his companions would find Malekith on the upper face of it.

They charged up the switchbacking stairs with Heimdall and Pluto once more in the lead. Kamorr could still hear nothing but a ringing in his ears. Imagination had to supply the sounds of the frantic ascent. The pounding of racing footsteps. The panting of labored respiration. Maybe rasping words of power as the enchantress forced them out despite the damage to her voice.

She might well be preparing a spell because only two more flights of stairs separated them from the access to Malekith's aerie. We're going to get him, Kamorr thought. We're going to stop him in spite of everything he could do.

Then, with a pang of fear, he saw that Malekith, who'd layered defense on defense to ensure no one could interrupt him here, had yet another trick to play.

One moment, the stairs above were empty. The next, the Hounds of the Hunter, savage creatures that Malekith, as Lord of the Wild Hunt, commanded, were hurtling down the steps to rend the folk ascending. The hounds were pony-sized wolf-like beasts with shaggy coats of gray and white and blazing yellow eyes. The whine in Kamorr's ears had faded enough for him to make out the maddened baying of the ones in the rear. The ones in the front ranks were too intent on taking down their prey to make a comparable noise.

Heimdall threw flame from Hofund, and Pluto chopped the air with his axe to cast a blast of force. The flame burned hounds to blackened, sizzling lumps while the force smashed them flat, but the swift slaughter of the lupine brutes in the lead in no way deterred the packmates rushing behind them. Clambering over the remains of their fellows, they sprang at the Asgardian warrior and the death god with fanged jaws open wide to bite, and it was surely only the duo's exceptional strength and pure determination that kept the momentum of the charge from knocking them back down the steps.

Now that the hounds had closed the distance, Heimdall and Pluto slashed and hacked at them. Levitating high enough that she had a clear shot over their shoulders, Amora hurled blazes of green and yellow magic at the creatures further back. And gradually, the trio gained ground. Despite the relentless fury and seemingly endless supply of the beasts, the intruders forced their way up another step and then another after that, slowly ascending even after the bodies of the hounds they'd already killed made the warriors' footing treacherous.

It was an extraordinary feat of arms. But because the stairs afforded no room for Kamorr to fight, he was in the back and could look around. Thus, he could see what his companions, who were of necessity focused on the leaping, lunging hounds with their daggerlike teeth and snapping, slavering jaws, possibly hadn't discerned.

On the various representations of Yggdrasil, the ovals representing Asgard and Midgard were nearly touching. His comrades might indeed be capable of slaughtering all the creatures blocking the way, but it was plain they couldn't do so in time.

Twenty-Two

Midgard & Malekith's Aerie:
the Day of Bifrost

The black dragon spat another stream of cold, murky quasi-flame. If it truly was a dragon. In the time Uschi had been fighting it, she noticed an inconstancy to its appearance. Sometimes it was dark and opaque as tar, at other moments, a pale, misty gray. Sometimes it seemed to possess height, length, and width like any normal being or object, yet occasionally, it looked flat as a parchment cutout.

Whatever it was, she was certain it would be a bad idea to let its spew wash over her and Avalanche. Sickness and weakness might well be the least of it. Fortunately, the winged stallion had survived combat with all manner of foes. Without her needing to prompt him, he raised one pinion, dipped the other, and veered out of the way of the attack.

That was good as far as it went, but avoiding harm wasn't the same as disposing of the drake, and she needed to do that to reach the Blackhammers on the ground. Vivid and beautiful,

Bifrost still arched across the sky, distant landscapes and cloudscapes were still wavering from one form to another, and it was anybody's guess how much time Midgard and Asgard had left before the two worlds smashed together.

She'd studied her adversary while she and Avalanche circled and dodged to keep away from it. As best she could determine, it couldn't spit and then immediately do so again. There was a lag while more venom accumulated in its throat.

It *had* just spewed dark fire at her, so now was the time to close with it. The Brightblade blazing in her hand, she urged Avalanche toward it, and, white wings beating, the Valkyrie steed charged their huge foe as fearlessly as he'd charged frost giants, trolls, and other enemies during their centuries-long partnership.

Lashing its own batlike wings, the drake turned to face them head on and flew to meet them. The immense jaws gaped wide enough to engulf rider and stallion together. Even up close, the dragon's form was so murky that Uschi had trouble discerning the fangs as long as swords from the dim blur that was the rest of it, but she was certain they were there.

When she and her foe were nearly within reach of one another, she flicked the reins. Avalanche's wings swept down, and he rose higher like a common horse galloping up a hillside. Though the dragon tried to compensate, as her study of it had likewise revealed, it wasn't as nimble in flight as the stallion was. It jerked up its head and snapped, but the bite fell short of Avalanche's churning legs.

Steed and rider swooped and hurtled down the length of the dragon's spine, where it couldn't bring its fangs and claws to bear. Avalanche flew low enough for Uschi to lean out of the saddle and cut repeatedly with her flaming broadsword, low enough that, though his pinions still beat, he was more galloping than flying, his hooves hammering the creature's body.

By the time they reached the root of the dragon's tail, the creature was twisting around to confront them. Avalanche wrenched himself around at the same moment and kept himself and the Valkyrie in a position where they could attack but their foe couldn't easily strike back. They started another charge down the creature's back and Uschi slashed at it as furiously as before, all the time hoping she was truly hurting the drake. The Brightblade was meeting solidity, but once again, the all-but-featureless darkness made it impossible to tell if the wounds were bleeding or even remained once she lifted the sword away for another cut.

She was halfway down the dragon's back when it rolled over. The maneuver caught her by surprise, and she and Avalanche barely dodged a gigantic wing that would otherwise have pulped flesh and broken bone.

Now that the dragon was belly up, it could bring its talons to bear. Lost in the smear of murk until it almost reached the target, a foot raked to rip Uschi and her steed to pieces. She didn't see the attack until it was too late. Avalanche did, however, and evaded without her prompting.

Then the drake was plummeting earthward. Apparently, even it, shadowy abomination that it was, couldn't fly upside down. It likely intended to right itself and soar to meet its foes again, and Uschi doubted the maneuver that had put it in a vulnerable attitude would work a second time.

So, with time running out for two worlds, there really wasn't any choice. The Valkyrie urged Avalanche to dive after the drake.

They had to dodge another claw swipe on the way in, but then they were in proximity to the drake's belly, where its feet couldn't readily bend around to reach them. Avalanche battered with his hooves, Uschi hacked, and this time the attacks seemed to be having more of an effect. The huge body jerked as though the creature was feeling pain.

Not incapacitating pain, however. Uschi sensed something looming above her. When she looked up, the dragon had twisted its wedge-shaped head around to regard her. The top of the long neck swelled with the gulping motion that meant the creature was about to spit.

She urged Avalanche forward to the spot where the dragon *might* carry its heart if it even had one and if its murky smear of a body and the frenzy of the moment allowed her to judge accurately. Leaning as far to the side as she could, she thrust in the Brightblade as deep as it would go.

The wound caught fire, the blaze spreading as rapidly as though the dragon were made of parchment in truth. The creature then spewed its own dark version of flame, but it was convulsing, its neck whipping back and forth, and the spray came nowhere near the intended targets.

The fire rapidly consuming the drake's form was a different matter. Uschi and her mount were impervious to the flames of the Brightblade itself, but conflagrations the sword kindled were nonetheless a danger. Avalanche lashed his wings and lifted away.

Which was to say, he distanced himself from the burning form of the dragon. He was still falling, the momentum built up in the last several moments impelling him along, and the ground was coming up fast. Uschi held her breath until the stallion managed to level off and swoop along no higher than the roof of a longhouse.

Under less exigent circumstances, she might have slumped and collected herself for a panting breath or two. As it was, she immediately urged Avalanche onward to set down among the Blackhammers assaulting the rune tunnels. "Where's the mage?" she shouted, jumping down from the saddle.

"Over here!" a tenor voice replied. She turned and spotted Ailpein several strides away.

As she rushed up to him, the youthful-looking warlock said, "Thanks for destroying the shadow dragon. I wasn't looking forward to–"

"Shut up!" Uschi snapped. "Listen! You have to destroy the rune!"

Ailpein stared up at her in a confused way that made her want to slap him. "The dark elves want to destroy it. We're fighting to retake it before they can."

"No!" Uschi said. "The dark elves seized it to protect it! Because Malekith has subverted Bifrost to a vile purpose! You must have noticed what's going on!" She swung the Brightblade to indicate the melting, wavering peaks and the changes in the sky above, where only the arch of the Rainbow Bridge held steady.

"Well… yes. I meant to look into it after we defeated the dark elves."

"You're seeing it because Bifrost is pulling Midgard and Asgard together! When they meet, they'll destroy each other!"

The dwarf frowned. "How do you know this?"

"There isn't time to explain! Just trust me!"

"All right," Ailpein said. "I will."

Maybe, the Valkyrie thought fleetingly, he remembered how she protected him and the other dwarf mages when they were vulnerable in their trance, and that helped to win him over.

She belatedly noticed Ailpein had been fighting with a small hammer in his hand. Judging from its modest size and the ripples of gleaming that kept running through the head, it was an implement of magic, not a conventional weapon, and now, with a flick of his wrist, he tossed it into the air, where it vanished. At once, an ivory wand appeared to take its place, and the warlock caught it deftly.

"This tool is good for moving things around," he said. "Let's hope it's good enough to collapse those tunnels."

He pointed the wand at the tunnel mouth behind the ranks of dark elves on the far side of the battlefield. He took a deep breath and chanted rhyming words.

The incantation eventually came to its end, whereupon Ailpein went back to the beginning. In due course, the spell repeated again, while Uschi felt impatient and taut as a bowstring.

Then the Blackhammer cried out and reeled. Uschi grabbed him to keep him from falling. "What's wrong?" she asked.

Ailpein sucked in a breath. "The enchantments we put in place ourselves were fighting against me, and now a dark elf mage is, too."

"Can you still destroy the rune?" the Valkyrie asked.

Ailpein smiled and at that moment, his boyish features and wispy beard notwithstanding, looked as fierce and resolute as any of the Blackhammer warriors on the battle line. "Watch."

He aimed the wand again and resumed his chanting. For a time, nothing else happened except that sweat beaded his furrowed brow. Then dust puffed from the distant tunnel mouth a moment before the entrance caved in, with a grinding and growling of dislodged earth. A shivering in the ground under Uschi's boots suggested the collapse encompassed more than just what she'd been able to see. The dark elves arrayed outside the former excavation cried out to see the site they'd been defending obliterated and any comrades who'd been inside abruptly buried. Blackhammers who didn't realize their objective had changed cursed and exclaimed as well.

Turning, Uschi looked up and around. No more mirages were coming and going to alter the shapes of neighboring peaks. Fading and dwindling, Bifrost was no brighter than the ordinary sort of rainbow.

"You did it!" she said to Ailpein.

Then, as if to mock her jubilant words, Bifrost waxed vivid once again. A new wavering distortion stretched a mountain taller.

"The runes were necessary to create the magic," the dwarf sorcerer said, "but once it was unleashed, it was so powerful that the destruction of a single symbol wouldn't be enough to stop it. We slowed it down, but that's all."

"So what now?" Uschi asked.

"We find Gulbrand and Bergljot and collapse more tunnels," Ailpein answered. "I don't know what else to try."

"Right. Avalanche will carry us." She whistled, and the winged steed trotted up to her. She swung herself into the saddle and then pulled the Blackhammer up to sit behind her.

As she did, it was clear to her that the warlock was correct.

Save for what they were attempting, there was nothing else to do. But the sick, hollow feeling in her gut told her they didn't have enough time remaining to destroy even one more subterranean rune. If Midgard and Asgard could yet be saved, it was now up to Heimdall and his companions.

Heimdall cut, and Hofund sent the head of the hound above him tumbling away from its body. One of the greatsword's powers was to lend extra force to his blows, and he was using that power freely despite the toll it took on him. He and his companions had to reach Malekith's aerie as swiftly as possible. Despite the frenzy of the battle on the stairs, he'd managed to take an occasional quick glance at the looming representations of Yggdrasil, and it seemed to him that for some reason, the convergence of Asgard and Midgard had paused for a time. But now it had resumed.

Beside him, Pluto bellowed, struck, and his battle-axe split the skull of the hound he was facing. A greenish flare of Amora's power burned over the heads of the two warriors and smashed the next snarling, snapping lupine beasts backward. That cleared the next bit of the ascent, and Heimdall and the death god scrambled up to claim the space before more hounds could fill it in again. That finally, finally brought them through the opening at the top of the stairs and onto the dark elf's refuge. The Asgardian fighter didn't look back but heard the enchantress and Kamorr ascend behind him.

The aerie was larger than the platform at the bottom of the flights of stairs or the landings Heimdall and his companions had negotiated on the way up. It was about as spacious as the All-Father's throne room. The intruders had come up at one end, and Malekith stood at the other, with more growling, baying hounds between. At least, Heimdall thought grimly, he could now see there was a finite number of the creatures. While fighting up the stairs, a person might have imagined magic was producing an unlimited supply.

A hound sprang at Pluto. He slammed his shield into the beast and, with a clang, hurled it across the platform as a white-and gray-furred sack of shattered bones. As he did, a second beast circled to take him from behind. Fortunately, flying above the melee, Amora spotted it and stabbed her hands at it. Her witchcraft turned it into a gaunt, mangy, rheumy-eyed thing without the strength to stand, then a carcass, then bare bones.

Kamorr lunged out from behind the shelter provided by the Asgardian warrior and the stranger deity as though eager to join in the combat at last. Dodging a hound's bite, he grabbed its foreleg, twisted the limb, and snapped it. The creature fell. Kamorr finished it with a stamp kick to the head and whirled to confront another.

Meanwhile, bathed in sweat, his mail shredded and the flesh beneath bleeding where hounds had momentarily gotten hold of him, Heimdall continued his share of the slaughter. Unfortunately, there were still a couple dozen creatures left, and it was little use killing them if he and his comrades couldn't do so fast enough to prevent Bifrost from finishing its work.

Or, he thought, maybe it was. Malekith ought to realize how the battle was going, ought to foresee the moment when the last of his wolf-like defenders would perish and the slayers would have him cornered. Ought to fear that if he'd completed the destruction of two Realms, his foes would exact retribution.

Though slashing at the lunging, slavering hounds currently menacing him, Heimdall nonetheless managed to shout, "Stop Bifrost, Malekith! If you don't, we'll kill you!"

When Heimdall encountered the dark elf with the divided face and multi-colored tunic in the depths of Tartarus, Malekith had been cool and calculating, but the present confrontation had stripped away his composure. Maybe he misjudged the situation and imagined the hounds could still win. Or he was so angry that, in spite of every cunning ruse and seemingly insurmountable obstacle, his enemies had gotten this far, he was willing to conclude the annihilation of two worlds despite the consequences for himself. In any case, his only response was a sneer, and the rounds of representations of the World Tree drew even closer together. They were so close now that only a person gifted with the eyesight of Mimir could have seen any distance left between them.

Despite what his senses and judgment told him, Heimdall refused to accept the inevitability of failure. He swung his sword again, and then a stripe of green radiance rose to become a vertical sheet along the platform. The sheet separated lengthwise into two, which as they moved apart swept hounds before them. The result was a cleared path running from his location to Malekith's.

"Get him!" cried Amora from somewhere overhead. "We'll keep the beasts off your back!"

Heimdall charged down the corridor. Recoiling, Malekith looked startled but wasn't too startled to take defensive action. A broadsword appeared in his hand, and a violet haze – the same shielding enchantment that had stopped his assailant's borrowed blade in Tartarus, presumably – seethed into being around him.

The Asgardian made an overhand cut to the shoulder. As he'd hoped it would, Hofund swept through the violet aura as if it were no more substantial than cobwebs. Malekith only evaded the potentially maiming stroke by hopping backward.

Heimdall immediately advanced to take up the distance. He didn't want to give Malekith the chance to come on the offensive, and, in fact, prevented it. As the next few ringing exchanges of cuts and parries demonstrated, the dark elf was a proficient swordsman, but he was better.

Hoping Malekith realized the same thing, the Asgardian said, "I'll give you one last chance! Surrender!"

Instead, his adversary mouthed a word of power, and the glaring eyes in his blue and black face flashed. Whereupon Heimdall went blind.

Now, of a surety, Malekith had the chance to attack and would make the most of it. Heimdall reflexively sharpened his hearing to the utmost and detected the dark elf's broadsword swishing through the air. He parried repeatedly, and his foe cried out in frustration that he still couldn't penetrate his guard.

After several heartbeats, Heimdall's sight returned, first as a blur and then with clarity. At this point, he thought, after assessing Malekith's style of swordsmanship, that he knew how to bring the fight to a conclusion. He'd catch the dark elf's weapon in a bind, disarm him, and hope that afterwards, with Hofund's point at his throat, Malekith would think better of his defiance.

He spun Hofund, and the two-handed sword trapped Malekith's blade just as he'd envisioned. He tore his opponent's weapon from his grasp to tumble through the air and fall clattering several strides away. He shifted Hofund back to threaten the now-defenseless sorcerer.

Malekith gasped and pitched forward. Heimdall barely jerked his point out of line in time to avoid spitting him. The Lord of the Wild Hunt fell facedown, exposing the deep, copiously bleeding wound in his back.

After another moment, a battle-axe appeared buried in the gash. So did the hand grasping the handle and the rest of Pluto's body. The Hounds of the Hunter had bloodied the stranger god, too, just as their fangs had scored and dented his breastplate and shield, but he was leering with satisfaction. Heimdall realized the deity must have used his helm of invisibility to make his approach undetected.

"Got you!" Pluto said to the fallen sorcerer.

"Idiot!" Heimdall cried. "We needed him to stop the magic!" He waved Hofund to indicate their surroundings and demonstrate his point.

Across the aerie lay the carcasses of hounds. A few survivors crawled or whined, clinging to life but too incapacitated to continue fighting. Somehow, though an arm and a leg were bleeding, Kamorr was still on his feet, and Amora in the air, the latter looking no more injured than immediately after the tentacles from the void had seized her. And at that moment, none of it seemed to matter, because the phantom World Trees were still shining and the ovals representing Asgard and Midgard were still in juxtaposition.

Amora swooped down to hover beside her fellow Asgardian

and the death god. "He's right," she said to Pluto. "The convergence is still happening."

"Can't you stop it now?" Heimdall asked. "With Malekith fallen?"

The enchantress spread her hands. "If I'd had a proper chance to study his perversion of Ulbrecht's original design… As it is, we can only wait out the destruction here and travel to one of the surviving Realms afterward."

"That's not good enough!" Heimdall rolled Malekith over onto his back.

He could still hear the dark elf's heart beating and breath whispering in and out of his lungs. "Stop the magic!" he said. "Or tell us how to do it! We'll tend your wound and save your life!"

It was no use. Malekith was clinging to life, but he was unconscious.

For want of a better idea, Heimdall scrutinized his foe. Malekith's red and black tunic with its starburst emblem was intact in the front. The cloth was in no wise filmy or flimsy, and blood stained portions of the garment from when the dark elf had been lying face down in a spreading pool of his own vital fluid. Still, with the sight of Mimir, the Asgardian discerned a faint glimmer leaking through the weave. He ripped the tunic apart to expose the source.

Malekith wore a pendant around his neck. At first glance, someone might have taken it for a simplified version of the starburst emblem. The silver medallion, however, had only seven points, each set with a tiny gemstone of a different type: a ruby, a piece of amber, a topaz, an emerald, a sapphire, an amethyst, and a bit of lapis lazuli.

The seven stones were red, orange, yellow, green, blue, violet, and indigo respectively, which was to say, the colors of Bifrost, and the shimmering revealed the pendant was a talisman of some sort. It still seemed a puny thing to be an essential component in the destruction of two Realms, but Heimdall judged he'd run out of time to search for anything else. Nor was there time to ask Amora to make a study of the thing and quell its magic properly.

He ripped the medallion from around Malekith's neck, breaking the chain in the process, dashed it to the floor, and stamped it under his boot. The tiny gems crunched, and their setting deformed, but it was only after the third stamp that he could tell the ovals corresponding to Midgard and Asgard on the various representations of Yggdrasil were moving apart. A heartbeat after that, the structures of glowing lines vanished, and without them, the aerie and the surrounding emptiness went from twilight to the darkness of a moonless, starless night.

With a snap of her fingers, Amora produced a floating, shining golden orb to serve as a lamp. She gave Heimdall a nod. "Well done." She looked beyond him. "It's up to you if you want to do something about that. Personally, I don't mind."

Heimdall turned. Pluto had raised his axe and stood poised to strike off Malekith's head. "Don't!" the Asgardian snapped.

The death god glowered. "Why not?"

Why not, indeed? Heimdall had felt an immediate disinclination to see any helpless warrior, even Malekith, dispatched in summary fashion, but now reason caught up with his instincts.

"Given his rank and the magnitude of his crimes, it's for my king and maybe yours to judge him."

Pluto grinned. "Maybe he died fighting. I won't tell if you won't."

"We also need him alive because our work isn't done." Given all that Heimdall and his companions had already endured and accomplished, it seemed unfair that was so, but it was. "We left a battle back at the camp, remember? We can use Malekith to end it."

"All right," Pluto sighed. "Hephaestus is a bore, but I suppose my brother would miss him. The dark elf can live if he's able. But I'm not carrying him."

"No one had better carry him until I stop the bleeding," Amora said. "Otherwise, we'll lose him on the way." She murmured a charm and twirled her hand in a casual-looking mystic pass. "That's better."

"All right, let's move." Heimdall sheathed his two-handed sword, picked up the still-insensible Malekith, and slung him over his shoulder. He then turned back to the enchantress. "Can you take us back to Midgard from here, or do we have to run back down those wretched stairs?"

"With Malekith hovering on the brink of death, the enchantments he wove into his refuge are weaker. In other words, I should be able to work the magic from here. Let's see."

She started the incantation that inscribed red runes on the empty air. Kamorr came hobbling up when she was partway through, and shortly after that, the lines of glowing symbols became a door-sized white rectangle.

Heimdall realized he was afraid to step through. Afraid that, despite everything, he hadn't destroyed Malekith's talisman in time, and he'd find only devastation or, worse, nothing at all on the other side of the portal.

But his companions, even Pluto, were looking to him to go through first, and a leader owed his followers a facade of confidence when he couldn't muster the genuine article. He took a breath, shifted the unconscious Malekith folded over his shoulder, and strode through the magical door.

He emerged in the dark elf's tent. It was as he and his companions had left it, which gave reason to hope the rest of Midgard still existed as well. Pushing aside the flap, he rushed out of the pavilion, and indeed, the Realm endured. The surrounding mountains weren't flowing from one shape to another anymore, and the gorgeous terror that had been Bifrost no longer curved across the heavens.

But it didn't take the gifts of Mimir to hear the battle still crashing and howling close at hand. Heimdall told himself that was better than if he, Kamorr, and the others had returned to find the Asgardian and Blackhammer warriors butchered and the dark elves in control of the camp. When he hurried through the rows of tents for a better view, however, it was clear defeat remained a possibility.

For the moment, the defenders' shield wall still held, everyone fighting furiously to keep it intact. But the attackers had more warriors, and, with Amora and Pluto absent and Ailpein, Gulbrand, and Bergljot gone to the secondary fights at the rune excavations, more mages, too. Altogether, it appeared to be an advantage that even Hephaestus, his cyclopes, and iron weapons couldn't offset.

The enchantress, the death god, and Kamorr hurried up behind Heimdall, looked over the conflict unfolding before them, and then, without the need for words, spread out, each moving toward the spot where he or she expected to be most useful. Heimdall raised the Gjallarhorn and blew to summon his steed.

Just a few moments after the sound and its echoes died away, Golden Mane trotted out from among the rows of tents. Though it felt like an eternity since Heimdall had ridden the winged stallion across the face of Midgard as hard as ever in his life, it actually hadn't been long at all, and in consequence, Golden Mane must have still been exhausted. Yet the horse snorted and tossed his head as if to reproach Heimdall. As if to say there was a battle underway and he didn't like being left riderless and apart from the action.

"Sorry," Heimdall said. "But here's your chance." He heaved Malekith onto the horse's back and climbed up himself.

Golden Mane started forward, accelerated to a gallop, beat his wings, and took flight. He soared upward, and Heimdall turned the steed toward the enemy. He sounded the Gjallarhorn again to make sure the dark elves saw him coming.

That could have worked too well. Sheltered behind the enemy shield wall, a sorceress with a left hand made of glass or crystal glared up at him and raised the artificial extremity to cast a spell. Before she could finish it, however, green light danced on the gleaming hand. It shattered, and the dark elf collapsed, dead or at least incapacitated. Heimdall inferred that despite the warriors jammed together and blocking her sightline, Amora must have somehow discerned what the other witch was attempting and acted to counter it.

He decided he needed to get on with what he had in mind before someone else tried to bring down him and Golden Mane. "It's over!" he bellowed to the dark elves below. "Amora the Enchantress has joined the battle! So has the god of death!

And here's your master!" He lifted Malekith and held him out in midair to afford his subjects a better view.

The Lord of the Wild Hunt was currently a limp, flopping, bloody scarecrow quite unlike the arrogant, mocking figure he ordinarily cut. Even so, the divided face, multi-colored tunic, and starburst emblem should be recognizable.

Once upon a time, Heimdall had menaced the vanquished King Skrymir to compel him to order his frost giant army to surrender. Malekith was incapable of giving a comparable command, nor did the dark elves lay down their arms in response to any implied threat to their sovereign. They might have believed him dead already.

But they faltered to see their mighty overlord humbled. The defenders roared and surged forward. The dark elf shield wall buckled in two places, Asgardians breaching it at one point and Blackhammers at another.

Suddenly knowing his side was going to win, Heimdall smiled. And did so again when the few surviving foes turned and ran shortly thereafter.

TWENTY-THREE

ASGARD:
THE DAY OF ASCENSION

Agnar the Fierce and Gotron the Agile both had white-blond hair and were formidable warriors, but the resemblance ended there. Agnar in his blue armor was a hulking, shaggy-bearded bear of a man who bellowed every time he swung his sword. Skinny Gotron in his purple trappings looked more like a weasel and certainly moved like one as he ducked and dodged Agnar's cuts and stabbed at the other warrior with his spear.

Clad in a handsome azure tunic and crimson trousers, his brown beard neatly trimmed, Heimdall stood in the holding area with Kamorr and Uschi and studied the contest as it unfolded. "Note how Gotron uses the spear like a fighting staff when he has a mind to," the Blackhammer said. "To strike with the butt end and block sword cuts when necessary."

"But Gotron trusts in his speed too much," Uschi said. Around her neck gleamed the golden torc Odin had bestowed on her for her role in saving the Realm Eternal. Heimdall had one too, but didn't wear it if combat was at hand even when the fights were merely sport. "He mostly relies on simple attacks when some feints might serve him better."

Neither the dwarf nor the Valkyrie was bothering to comment on Agnar's fighting style, and that only made sense. Heimdall had already defeated him in a previous match. He had yet to face Gotron.

The exhibition of martial prowess was in celebration of Asgard's recent victory over a company of storm giants who'd come up the new Bifrost. Heimdall had been all in favor of the creation of a second Rainbow Bridge as per Ulbrecht's original design, in part because, he'd been given to understand, it would occupy a special position in the cosmic scheme of things, and while it endured, no realms-destroying abomination like Malekith's version could ever exist again. Yet a skilled enemy warlock could still put himself and his companions on the new span as the recent foray demonstrated.

Standing in the waiting area with a blunt two-handed practice sword held casually, the rounded "point" resting on the ground, Heimdall knew he should be watching the current bout as keenly as were his friends in order to make useful observations of his own. But now that his thoughts had turned to Malekith, he couldn't help regretting that the All-Father had seen fit to return the sorcerer to his people upon payment of a hefty ransom.

He was glad, however, that Malekith hadn't gone home a king. Apparently, nobody thought the Rabid Wolf Tribe had been any great loss. The royal guard, however, numbered the younger sons and daughters of many a noble family among its warriors, and when it came out that Malekith had been ready to sacrifice all their lives to attain his goal – and then failed to achieve it – the parents hadn't liked it. While the sorcerer lay delirious in an Asgardian tower slowly recovering from his axe wound, a cabal of dark elf nobles crowned a new monarch in his place, one who'd been eager to render judgment on her predecessor. It just went to show, Heimdall supposed, that even the wiliest blackguard couldn't betray absolutely everybody all the time without suffering for it eventually.

He would still have preferred that Odin had sent Malekith to the block or left him buried in a dungeon for all eternity. Unlikely as it seemed, he couldn't quite shake the suspicion that the dark elf sorcerer might rise to threaten Asgard again someday. But if it ever happened at all, it would be a long time coming, and meanwhile, Malekith's existence was unlikely to be pleasant.

He hoped the same was true of Pluto's. Hoped that upon returning to his own system of worlds, Hephaestus had made it clear to the king of their pantheon that the death god had been Malekith's accomplice, and that the sovereign had taken appropriate action. Like freeing the spirit of Orien to dwell happily in the white houses of the underworld and chaining Pluto in Tartarus in the cyclops's place.

Still, Heimdall thought, maybe Pluto didn't deserve *quite* as severe a punishment as Malekith did. He *had* turned against the king of Svartalfheim at the end, and his companions never would have fought their way through the Hounds of the Hunter without him. Besides, torturing him too much would grieve Queen Persephone, although the Asgardian still couldn't understand what she found to love in her blustering, ill-tempered bully of a husband.

A musical soprano voice roused him from his musings. "Hello, Heimdall. I came to wish you luck."

He looked around. Resilient as any Asgardian, Amora had long since shed the marks of the mauling the tentacles had given her. She was once again as Heimdall had known her when Odin first sent her to aid in the building of Bifrost.

Or perhaps not quite. Though she'd done her best to mask it behind her customary attitude of insouciant superiority, at certain moments, the distrust and dislike of which she was so often the focus had seemed to wear and grind at her a little. Her manner was more genuinely carefree now that, in light of her role in the salvation of Midgard and the Realm Eternal, everyone had forgiven her previous transgressions.

Or nearly everyone. "What do you want?" Uschi growled.

Amora arched an eyebrow. "I already said. To wish Heimdall luck. We're all friends now, aren't we, and besides, I made a wager with Loki that Heimdall would best everyone he faced today." She turned back to him. "I know you won't let me down." She kissed her fingertips, touched them to his cheek, and walked away.

As he watched her depart, Uschi said, "Fancy her, do you?"

"No," Heimdall said.

"Liar! You may have the gifts of Mimir, but where some things are concerned, you're as blind as any man. By which I mean, she *hasn't* changed. The next treason will be along in due course."

Heimdall smiled. "She and I aren't together. I have no reason to believe we ever will be. But if we are and it all goes wrong,

I'm glad I have a comrade I can depend on to save me from the consequences of my folly."

Uschi grunted. "Somebody has to." For just a moment, she smiled back.

Still peering out into the fighting area, Kamorr called, "It's over!"

Indeed, it was. Agnar sprawled on his back in the grass. Gotron stood over him with the rounded point of his spear poised in front of his opponent's face, where the Fierce One's azure helmet didn't cover him. The luminaries in the tiers of seats cheered and applauded.

A massive figure, imposing as a mountain, Odin lounged on a throne in the midst of the spectators with Queen Frigga seated beside him, the ravens Hugin and Munin perched on the high back of his chair, and the wolves Freki and Geri lying at his feet. He held a silver goblet in one hand, his Uru scepter Thrudstok in the other, and when he raised the latter, the crowd fell silent.

"I declare Gotron the victor," the All-Father said. Gotron reached to pull the other combatant to his feet, and, though frowning at his defeat, Agnar wasn't so lacking in grace as to spurn the help. "Would you like a moment to rest before the final match?"

"There's no need," Gotron said. Either he was too vain to acknowledge he was fatigued or else he truly wasn't. Heimdall suspected the latter. Gotron was of the Aesir with the Aesir's hardiness. "If it suits Your Majesty, let's get on with it."

"It suits me," the All-Father replied. "Heimdall, come forth!"

"Remember what we told you," Kamorr said.

"I will," Heimdall answered. He hefted his sword and walked

out of the waiting area onto the field of battle. As he did, he spotted Amora, who'd returned to her seat, along with his sister Sif smiling encouragement, and Frey with his pointed beard and long curling mustache. Heimdall had once bested the Vanir deity when Frey was in thrall to the Lurking Unknown, and he wondered momentarily if the god was holding a grudge and hoping he'd lose the present contest.

Save for pride, it really didn't matter very much. Odin had proclaimed that the winner would receive a thus far unidentified but considerable prize, but Heimdall didn't particularly covet it. He was content with Golden Mane, the Gjallarhorn, Hofund, and the other treasures that had already come his way. He was only fighting on this sunny afternoon because the All-Father had suggested it in a way that implied what he said was actually mandatory. Still, since he was here, he meant to do his best.

He and Gotron stepped to their starting positions facing one another. They assumed their fighting stances, and then Odin boomed, "Begin!"

Gotron sprang into striking distance immediately. In a blur of motion, he thrust the spear at Heimdall's midsection.

Fast as the action was, however, it was a direct attack, and Heimdall parried it without difficulty. He riposted with a cut to Gotron's arm. If it scored, Odin might rule the spearman had to fight one-handed from now on even if the blow didn't incapacitate the limb in truth. Even wielding practice weapons, warriors occasionally broke bones in these competitions. They'd even inadvertently killed one another a time or two.

The riposte didn't land. Gotron was quick enough to retreat

and make it fall short. The combat then continued as it began, with neither man quite able to drive home an attack.

Gotron hadn't slowed down even a jot, but his continued preference for simple actions made it easier to block his jabs. So did the eyesight of Mimir, which enabled Heimdall to see even the tiniest preliminary movement and predict what the other warrior would try next.

For his part, he did make compound attacks, and some of the feints fooled Gotron, tricking him into shifting the spear out of line or twisting in the wrong direction. Gotron was so nimble, however, that he kept evading the true cuts, albeit sometimes only by a hair.

After one protracted exchange, the pair stepped back at the same time and, for a moment, studied one another. Heimdall read determination in Gotron's expression, and, behind that, enjoyment that came from facing a worthy opponent. No surprises there. Now that the bout was underway, Heimdall was feeling the same things himself.

When Gotron advanced again, he alternated ordinary spear thrusts with the spins of his weapon that Kamorr had warned of. Sometimes he whirled it low in an effort to slam it into an ankle, send Heimdall stumbling off balance, or, better still, knock him off his feet altogether.

Heimdall blocked the first of those sweeping attacks easily enough, but before Gotron tried the action again, it occurred to him that he didn't have to make defense *look* easy. When the warrior in purple bashed at his leg a second time, he leaped back further than was necessary, far enough that striking with even a two-handed sword was impossible. He tried to assume an expression of consternation as fighters sometimes did when an opponent found a weakness in their game.

Encouraged, Gotron pursued and every couple of heartbeats attempted the same strike to the ankles. Heimdall kept taking big retreats in what he hoped was a fair simulation of desperation. Well-wishers in the stands groaned to see him, as they imagined, completely on the defensive. Not Sif, though. His sister laughed, he was sure, because she saw through the deception.

Eventually Gotron grew impatient with the series of near misses and resolved to bring the duel to an end. He lunged and struck with every iota of his speed and strength. Heimdall wouldn't be able to jump back out of range this time!

In fact, Heimdall didn't try. Knowing what was coming, he sprang straight up into the air, and the spear strike whizzed harmlessly by beneath him. While still in mid-leap, he cut at Gotron's neck, and for once, overcommitted to his own action, the other warrior wasn't fast enough to duck or dodge. Heimdall stopped his attack with the greatsword nearly touching his opponent's neck.

For a moment, Gotron goggled in surprise. Then he laughed and let the spear fall from his hands in acknowledgment of defeat. When Odin declared Heimdall the victor, it was again only a formality.

Afterward, the All-Father summoned the three combatants to stand before his throne. "You all fought well today," the god of wisdom said, his remaining blue eye gazing down at them. The patch covering the socket where the other had once reposed was white, conceivably to match his snowy beard. "Given the valor you displayed battling the storm giants, I expected no less. But one of you defeated each of the other two, and that one will receive the prize."

Though Heimdall hadn't especially wanted the mysterious *prize* hitherto, now that it was his to claim, he was curious as to what it might be. He stood up straight and put together words of thanks in his mind.

Odin, however, then appeared to stray from the subject at hand. "Our new Bifrost doesn't pose a threat to the very existence of Asgard as the first one did. But the incursion of the storm giants proves it can still be a point of vulnerability. As it's far too useful and wondrous a creation to destroy, I've decided to choose a sentry to guard the span, watch for threats, and turn back travelers we deem unwelcome."

Heimdall agreed that was a prudent decision about a matter of potential importance. But he still didn't know why the All-Father had seen fit to announce it at this particular moment.

"The object of today's competition," Odin continued, "was to choose the warrior best suited to assume this duty. In other words, the prize is the watchman's role, and you, Heimdall, will take it on. You'll stand at the head of the bridge for all eternity and protect the rest of us."

Heimdall felt a jolt of dread such as rarely came to him even when facing his most formidable foes. He loved his life of traveling and exploring the Nine Realms as an agent of the Crown. By the Tree, *any* normal life would be preferable to simply standing in one spot until the end of time! That seemed scarcely less unbearable than an eternity chained in Tartarus. "Sire, surely there's someone better!"

"There isn't," Odin replied. "You won today. Also, you have your keen sight and hearing to aid you in keeping watch and the Gjallarhorn to sound if some major threat appears. You're perfect for the task. And I have to say, this affair with Malekith and his perversion of Bifrost isn't the first time you've ignored your orders and gone haring off. It's the third. I'm happy to find you a role where such temptations won't arise."

Now, Heimdall thought, he understood. Odin had expected him to defeat Agnar and Gotron and had accordingly chosen a *prize* that was really a punishment. It didn't even matter that each time he'd disobeyed, he and his comrades had saved the Realm Eternal from a calamity. The All-Father was nonetheless out of patience with an underling's continued flouting of his commands.

It wasn't remotely fair, and that burned away the trace of awe Heimdall usually felt in Odin's presence. From the ashes rose defiance. "Every time I've disobeyed the letter of your edicts," he gritted out, "it's been because I learned something that made it stupid to adhere to them. I've always abided by the essence of the oath I swore when I long ago entered your service, which was to protect Asgard as best I could from any threat, and I won't stand like a statue forevermore for the crime of having a brain."

Odin didn't answer back immediately. Maybe Heimdall's declaration had left him too angry to speak. Or, conceivably, it had kindled a spark of shame. Perhaps the two emotions were fighting for dominance inside him.

Queen Frigga, with her white hair piled high and framed by the wings of her golden crown, had long been Heimdall's champion, and she took advantage of the silence to speak. "Noble thane," she said to him, "*of course*, when the All-Father said *for all eternity*, he meant *regularly*. When circumstances warrant, we'll still send you on errands, and you'll have time away from Bifrost to enjoy your normal pursuits." She turned to Odin and smiled. "Isn't that so, husband?"

Heimdall didn't believe it had been before, but apparently the prospect of Frigga's disapproval combined with that of the muttering, discomfited onlookers and perhaps his own second thoughts, prompted Odin to relent. "Naturally," he grumbled, "that's what I meant, and so, captain, your little outburst was nonsensical. I forgive you, though, and still offer the reward I promised. Do you accept?"

Heimdall still didn't want the task, but he suspected the modified version of it the queen had suggested was the best outcome he was likely to achieve, and it would be reckless to spurn the *prize* a second time. "Yes, Your Majesty," he said.

"Then kneel," the All-Father said.

Heimdall did, whereupon Odin rose and extended Thrudstok. The mace-like scepter glowed and then hurled a flare of brilliant light. When the blaze engulfed Heimdall, he cried out at the most intense sensation he'd ever known. Before his mind could sort out whether it was ecstasy, agony, or something stranger he'd never felt before, everything, including his awareness of himself, went away.

Regaining his senses was like waking from deep, dreamless sleep. At some point before the beam of magic left him, he'd pitched forward and caught himself with his hands, which were still planted on the ground.

Standing back up was a revelation. He'd always been strong and hale even for an Asgardian, but even so, the ease and quickness with which he rose revealed an even deeper well of vitality. He sensed that, in time, altogether new abilities might reveal themselves.

In short, he suspected that to prepare him to be the guardian of Bifrost, Odin had raised him up to be a true god of Asgard.

TWENTY-FOUR

ASGARD:
THE FOLLOWING DAY

A feast had followed the exhibition of fighting prowess. Odin's guests dined on roast venison and pork; a stew of beef, onions, leeks, and peas; salmon; cheese; buttered sourdough bread; strawberries; and an abundance of other dishes. People ate heartily and drank beer, ale, and subtle wines and fiery liquors distilled by the light elves of Alfheim.

The drinking fueled enthusiasm for the entertainments. Skalds chanted tales of Asgardian triumphs, including a newly concocted and largely inaccurate one about the recent victory over the storm giants. People wrestled and threw a leather ball across the hall, the object being to strike someone else without being struck oneself. Dancers danced to the music of a pan flute, hornpipe, rebec, and harp, the musicians somehow making themselves heard despite the general uproar.

Even for hardy Asgardians, overeating and copious drinking eventually took a toll. In the last hours before dawn, people stumbled off to bed or lay snoring on or beneath the benches until only Heimdall sat still conscious in the hall.

Which was odd. Though he didn't feel much like celebrating, he was more or less a guest of honor at the feast, and to avoid looking churlish, he'd gorged and imbibed like everyone else. Yet he was still wide awake. It came to him that maybe he would never sleep again, that this was the first of the changes Thrudstok's magic had produced. With a twinge of bitterness, he reckoned it was a useful attribute for the sentry he was now condemned to be.

Such being the case, he might as well get to it. Later in the day, there would be an investiture where Odin would formally install him in his new role, but he was of a mind to discover exactly what he was in for without a crowd of onlookers expecting him to show gratitude for the All-Father's supposed largess.

As he made his way out of the hall, the hearing of Mimir revealed a heartbeat thumping beyond the door. He found Kamorr lounging against the wall on the other side.

Heimdall smiled. "I thought you'd passed out like everybody else."

Kamorr grinned. "You Aesir and Vanir only think you can drink. We dwarves could show you a thing or two."

"So why are you out here alone propping up the wall?"

"Well," the Blackhammer said, "I did take a little walk to clear my head. Then, when I came back, you looked like you were mulling things over in that way you have. So, I thought that instead of disturbing you, I'd catch you on the way out."

Apparently Kamorr had something on his mind. "I'm about to take a walk of my own," Heimdall said. "To look out over Bifrost. Come with me if you like."

The dwarf did so. Evidently, though, he was in no hurry to say what he wanted to say or was uncertain how to begin. Their footsteps echoing, but otherwise walking in silence, the pair left the All-Father's sleeping palace, crossed a courtyard, and passed through a gate in the wall of the great fortress of which Odin's residence was the hub. They headed on across the city.

Eventually, lamenting his own situation though he was, Heimdall's curiosity got the better of him. "If you're thinking how to bid me farewell," he said, "it needn't be some drawn-out maudlin affair, because it's not forever. Odin and Frigga will still send me on missions from time to time, and surely some of those errands will take me to Nidavellir. You can also, if you've a mind to, return to Asgard to visit me. The new Bifrost will make it easy."

Kamorr snorted. "Don't flatter yourself. You're a good comrade, but I'm not moping over the prospect of going a while without your company. Not exactly."

"Then what?" Heimdall asked, the Gjallarhorn swinging at his hip. "You surely aren't worried that the other Blackhammers will look down on you as they once did." Kamorr's fine new clothes and the silver rings gleaming on his arms seemed proof that the dwarf had nothing to worry about.

"No," Kamorr said. "They honor me. But having honors isn't the same thing as having a place. I still don't have a knack for mining, forging, or fighting weighed down with mail and shield like the usual run of dwarf warrior. I could spend my days in honored idleness, but that would bore me quickly. I'd rather be useful."

Heimdall thought he now knew where the conversation was headed, and despite his glum mood, it wrung another smile out of him. "Useful to me, you mean?"

"If you're willing," Kamorr said. "I hear you've acquired some lands and such over the course of your service to Odin. Someone needs to oversee them now that you'll be tied up watching the bridge. And maybe I could go with you sometimes when you fly off on those missions. We did all right watching one another's backs in Tartarus."

"We did at that," Heimdall said, "and of course you can stay on in Asgard as my lieutenant. Steward. Whatever. We'll figure it out as we go."

They passed through another gate, this one like a tunnel piercing the massive walls surrounding the royal city as a whole. Heimdall recalled when there had been a substantial patch of countryside between the cluster of houses folk had built outside the battlements and the edge of Asgard beyond. Now the head of Bifrost and the cosmic void lay not far ahead. As he understood it, no one had lost his or her farm, orchard, or home because Odin had decided to make the Rainbow Bridge maximally convenient for his household. Rather, he'd shifted lands to the sides, geography itself bowing to the force of the god of wisdom's magic.

At the top of Bifrost stood a domelike structure called Himinbjorg, the observatory where, evidently, Odin intended his sentinel to stand. At least, Heimdall thought, the roof would keep off the rain. With Kamorr trailing along beside him, he took up a position in the middle of the floor.

An endless abyss yawned before him, the darkness more profound than that of the starry night sky covering the lands stretched out behind. Even with the gifts of Mimir, he couldn't see Yggdrasil. That was as expected. Part of the reason for the Rainbow Bridge was to allow travelers to cross between worlds without having to endure that magnificent but mind-eroding vista.

He assumed Bifrost presently linked Asgard and Midgard. It generally would, to facilitate the Valkyries' collection of the valorous dead. He sought to peer far, far down the span of brilliant colors lying side by side to determine if he could look all the way into the world of mortals.

For a moment, he couldn't. Even his extraordinary eyesight wasn't enough. Then he felt a kind of painless burst in his head, and after that, he could. He was looking at the forest-clad mountains where Blackhammers had excavated new runes to replace Malekith's tainted ones and collapsed and concealed the entrances to the diggings when they finished.

Heimdall decided he wanted to see something else, and, in accordance with his will, his perspective swung to the west. It passed over a benighted human farm with goats and pigs in pens outside the longhouse and then revealed a ship in the open restless sea beyond the fjord. When he tried, he heard the rowers chanting as they pulled their oars and the crashing of the vessel through the waves.

Heimdall realized there must be a synergy between the gifts of Mimir and the Rainbow Bridge, another product, perhaps, of the transformation Odin had induced. It would seemingly allow him to see and hear anything to which he directed his attention.

In Midgard, anyway, where the far end of Bifrost currently

descended. Heimdall wondered if the bridge would shift termini in response to the will of its guardian and if his powers of perception would work as well when examining another Realm. "Show me Jotunheim," he murmured.

An instant later, he was looking through a howling blizzard with Skrymir's city barely visible in the distance. He rolled his perspective beyond the storm and found a pack of enormous, white-furred wolves padding through the snow.

Demons built a tower among the perpetual fires, lava flows, and volcanic eruptions of Muspelheim. The yellow bricks themselves looked like they were made out of some sort of petrified flame. The dead in Niffleheim bowed down to green-masked, jagged-crowned Queen Hela as she rode along the Shore of Corpses on a pale horse.

It was when gazing into Alfheim, however, that Heimdall beheld the most noteworthy sight of all, though it didn't seem so momentous when it initially snagged his attention. A light elf gardener was simply planting a sapling. She had it in the ground and was shoveling additional dirt around the roots.

Then, however, the gardener vanished. At the same time, the tree's trunk swelled, and it loomed taller. The branches flickered, bare and topped with snow, then leafy, then bare again with what Heimdall assumed to be the procession of the seasons. When the vision stopped a few moments later, the tree was an ancient giant taller than a watchtower.

Astonished, Heimdall realized he'd been looking into the past. He suspected it was going to take patience to understand and master this new ability, but once he did, he might be able to peer to the ends of time as well as space.

He smiled. For a fellow ever eager to learn, as he knew himself to be, standing watch as the sentinel of Bifrost might not turn out to be as onerous a duty as he'd feared. It might not be bad at all.

EPILOGUE

It took a while to relate the tale, but Trygve listened all the way through with wide eyes and without fidgeting. Meanwhile, Fandral was enjoying himself and his manifestly effective use of the tricks that made for good storytelling, like putting on different voices for the different characters and employing exclamations like *bang!* and *crash!* at the appropriate moments. He always liked being the center of attention, even if it was only the attention of a single boy.

Indeed, Fandral was enjoying himself so much that he nearly finished with the question skalds often asked at the end of a story: *would you know more?* But just in time, he remembered he'd been telling the tale to make a point, and it was time to see if he had, not to seek encouragement to launch into another yarn altogether. Even though the adventures of the Warriors Three afforded a wealth of good ones. Like the time...

With an effort, he stifled the urge to continue. "So," he said, "what's the lesson we take from the tale?"

Trygve blinked. From his momentarily surprised expression, he'd gotten too wrapped up in the wonders and battles of the story to remember it was supposed to be teaching him something. "Uh… today's foes can become tomorrow's allies," he said, "like the enchantress and Pluto did for Heimdall? So maybe we shouldn't just kill them when we have them at our mercy?"

Fandral paused to consider the suggestion. That particular moral hadn't occurred to him, but it fit.

After a moment, he chuckled. "Fair enough. I guess a story can teach more than one lesson depending on who's listening and what that hearer needs to learn. We might also glean that just because you meet a person in humble circumstances – like Kamorr, when Heimdall first took note of him – you shouldn't assume that's someone of little worth. But what did *you* need to learn, Trygve? What did I tell you at the beginning?"

The youth's face fell. Perhaps he'd imagined he might make his escape without any further allusions, even indirect ones, to his own recent transgressions. "The truth matters," he mumbled. "In the short run, it would have been easier for Heimdall to let Kamorr take the blame for poisoning the cyclops, but that's not what he did."

"As it would have been easy for Uschi to condemn Lady Amora without proof, but, sorely tempted though she was, that's not what she did either."

"I understand, and I truly am sorry for not speaking up before."

Fandral could tell the lad was sincere. "Then we'll say no more about it," he replied. "Run along home, and I'll see you when training resumes tomorrow."

ACKNOWLEDGMENTS

Thanks to Charlotte Llewelyn-Wells, Gwendolyn Nix, Marc Gascoigne, Anjuli Smith, Vanessa Jack, and everyone at Aconyte Books and Marvel who helped with this novel and its two predecessors. Also, thanks to Stan Lee, Jack Kirby, and all the other comics greats who worked to create the Asgardian corner of the Marvel Universe.

AUTHOR'S NOTE

The Prisoner of Tartarus concludes the trilogy that began with *The Head of Mimir* and continued in *The Rebels of Vanaheim*. We've followed Heimdall's rise from callow young warrior to the All-Seer of Bifrost we know from Marvel Comics and watched him acquire his unique abilities, the Gjallarhorn, the sword Hofund, his steed Golden Mane, and his sometime sidekick Kamorr along the way.

Heimdall goes on to have more adventures, some thus far unchronicled, and possibly we'll explore those in due course. For now, though, at least we have his origin complete.

The Prisoner of Tartarus combines Asgardian characters and lore with Marvel's take on Greco-Roman mythology. The stories where Thor encounters Hercules and his relatives include some of his more memorable exploits, and I hope this novel is a worthy successor.

There are, of course, many cool aspects of Marvel's version of classical mythology the current story doesn't even touch on. Maybe someday we'll have some *Marvel Legends of Olympus* novels, too.

About the Author

RICHARD LEE BYERS is the author of fifty horror and fantasy books including *This Sword for Hire* and *Blind God's Bluff*, novels for *Marvel Legends of Asgard, Forgotten Realms*, and the Impostor series. He's also written scores of short stories, some collected in *The Things That Crawl* and *The Hep Cats of Ulthar*, scripted a graphic novel, and contributed content on tabletop and electronic games. A resident of the Tampa Bay area, he's an RPG enthusiast and a frequent program participant at Florida conventions, Dragon Con, and Gen Con.

twitter.com/rleebyers

LEGENDARY WARRIORS
EPIC BATTLES

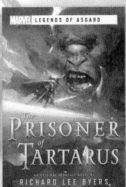

MIGHTY HEROES
NOTORIOUS VILLAINS

MARVEL UNTOLD

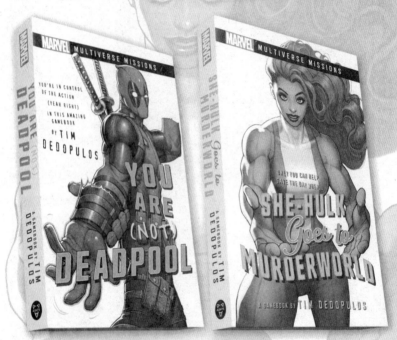